The Grey I

For Cathy, Tom, Luke and Paul for your help and encouragement over the years.
My thanks to Alexa Padou at Luna Imprints for her outstanding skill as an author and editor.
All rights reserved. No part of this publication may be reproduced, distributed, or transmitted in any form or by any means, including photography, recording, or other electronic or mechanical methods, without the prior written permission of the author, except in the case of brief quotations embodied in critical reviews and certain other commercial uses permitted by copyright law.
This is a work of fiction. Any resemblance to actual events or people is entirely coincidental.
Copyright 2020 Mike Skidmore.

PROLOGUE

GREY estimated ten hours to the crossing. Time enough for what lay ahead. Travelling on solid ground would be faster, but he chose to navigate the shoreline instead. The cliffs gave better cover from the soldiers hell-bent on vengeance.

His pursuers were on horseback, unable to navigate the wet boulders and slick seaweed covering the beach. Their only option was shooting from above, a near impossibility. Overhangs, deep fissures and loose rocks made leaning over the cliff edge treacherous.

Soon, there would be a conclusion, though not in the way these men expected. They believed they were hunting Grey. A dangerous mistake because he hunted them. What happened to the refugees demanded payback.

The previous night, he had spotted a fire spearing into the night sky a mile from the slaughter. Grey moved at a crouch to a ring of boulders and listened to four soldiers laughing about their conquest. One of them decided to take a walk in the dark and paid a high price.

Since then, the group had followed the obvious trail Grey left.

Once the men reached a place he'd chosen for an ambush, he would strike. First, though, he needed a rest to gather strength.

A swathe of stones, worn smooth by pounding waves, parted underfoot, throwing him shoulder-first onto the hard surface. He lay still for a long moment, breathing hard and cursing his clumsiness.

Ahead, a jagged rock headland sloped down into the ocean like a monolithic crocodile watching for prey. Grey spotted an overhang for shelter and made his way over, wary of tripping again.

For some reason, a round white pebble caught his eye. Rolling it in his hand, he thought about the far side of the crossing.

Whatever waited wouldn't be good news—it never was. Adversity followed like a bloodhound, and innocent people suffered.

This would be the last journey searching for his elusive father. Failure might see the end of a bitter man.

Grey's grip tightened, causing a wince from sand grating against a cut on his palm. When the sting brought a surge of anger, he threw the pebble arcing into the distance.

Soon after, a horse whinnied above. Standing up, he rotated his arm and stretched aching back muscles, feeling the satisfying pop, pop, pop of vertebrae.

'Get it done,' he hissed.

ARRIVAL

JEN dropped the can, water glugging out onto the floor. 'Dim'ead!' she shouted at herself. 'Stop filling the stupid thing so full.'

Her hand shot over her mouth, realising the noise might bring unwanted attention. Normally, she was good at sneaking in darkness, but the silvery moon lit up the streets, making it easier to spot a figure darting between hiding places.

Leaving it so late to fetch water from the underground pipes was stupid. Once again, Jen's bravado could have consequences because Scabs prowled the streets at night.

A glance showed an alleyway close by. Jen left the can, sprinted to a doorway and pushed her small body against the wall.

'Seen a kid over there,' someone shouted.

Scabs, must be. Guarders from the Station will be long gone, Jen decided.

Why the Council's soldiers followed her during the day, she didn't know. It wasn't as if scavengers like her posed a threat. Sometimes, being spied on was spooky; other times, it offered reassurance. Not that she knew for certain Guarders would come to her aid at any sign of trouble. It just helped to believe they might.

When a foot crunched debris in the main street, Jen knew the pursuers were closing in. Indecision paralysed her, trying to think whether to run or hide someplace else.

She ran, not daring to look back for fear of falling.

Loose bricks tumbled to the ground when her hand grasped the edge of a wall. A Scab slipped on rubble somewhere behind and cursed. Moments later, his footsteps faded away. They wouldn't give up this easily, though. Most likely, they'd try to head her off.

For a moment, Jen hesitated, thinking about where to go. There was a secret place, but if the Scabs found a way inside, it wouldn't be safe anymore.

She took the risk.

*

Grey surveyed the debris from shattered buildings. Roads lined with weeds, cracks spidering across the tarmac and rubble said it all; whatever caused the destruction had been very powerful.

A flickering flame from a broken window haloed an interior. He crept towards it, wary of displacing bricks. Peeping from behind a crumbling wall revealed three women and one child hunched over a fire. Ragged clothing and thin frames meant life was tough in the city.

For a moment, Grey considered going over to get information about what had happened and where to find food. He dismissed the idea. The group would likely be terrified, thinking their meagre supply was about to be stolen. Or worse.

Instead, he made his way back to the road. Not that he had any idea where he was going. That would come once he'd orientated himself.

Grey sensed someone watching, perhaps stalking in the hope he carried something useful. To avoid confrontation, he turned into a side street and ducked behind a gap between walls. Tuned to the slightest vibration, he sensed no movement. Whoever it was, they'd gone.

Nothing about him drew attention—from a distance, at least. Six foot tall, he had an average build, though it was difficult to tell through layers of clothing. Close up was a different matter. His face portrayed little emotion, and his eyes were dull, the spark extinguished from time spent around the worst of society. Surviving day to day, he travelled from beginning to end, preferring to be alone.

Grey wore a long leather coat scarred by years of service. A canvas bag hung over one shoulder, carrying a collection of possessions—his knife, spare clothing and supplies to last a few days.

As usual, the arrival had taken a toll, even though the crossing healed a wound sustained from fighting the soldiers. Finding somewhere to rest now took priority.

The remains of a large structure, its imposing apex still visible in the jigsaw of rubble, looked like a municipal building. He ignored the tinge of curiosity. Survivors wouldn't care about this place. Why should he?

Nowhere seemed safe enough for sleeping, so Grey moved on. Noticing a traffic light lying flat on the ground, he followed the direction it pointed. At one time, the decision would have brought a smile, but humour was a distant memory.

Outlines of tall offices, now only pitiful monuments to a former life, lay ahead. Steel girders wrenched from housings cluttered the ground like branches after a storm.

Grey hunkered down inside two jagged concrete slabs and considered what to do next. Food would soon become a problem, but there was no sign of what survivors ate. The people at the fire appeared undernourished, and the buildings were no doubt stripped bare. Cultivation would also be problematic in this environment, and livestock susceptible to raiders. Where supplies came from was a mystery yet to be solved.

Awakening from a meagre hour or two of sleep, he fingered his short brown hair and massaged life into his numb legs. Time to get going.

The sky darkened as he wove through empty streets with large buildings eventually giving way to smaller shops and houses. Uniform terraces spewed abstract mounds of dark brick across the road, slowing progress.

High-pitched shouting sounded from several blocks away. A girl's voice, maybe? Difficult to be sure from this distance.

None of your business, he decided and continued.

The route took him parallel to the noise—a stream of belligerent curses growing more frantic by the minute. Then, male voices. Angry voices.

Leave it.

Heading into a deserted street, Grey sensed someone behind a wall, though it lasted only a moment. It was enough to make him stop.

After a few moments, loose debris grated underfoot. He tensed for an attack, but the footsteps faded away, seemingly towards the confrontation.
Keep going.
Grey halted.
Damn it. What if it was a girl shouting?
Peering into an alleyway, the scene unfolded.

A small girl stood on a mound of debris, hurling rocks and raining obscenities down on three men. Scanning the area for signs of the watcher creeping up on him, Grey sensed nothing. Indecision gripped when the compulsion to leave fought against compassion. He shook his head, sighed, and stepped out of the shadows.

It took a few seconds for one man to spot the silhouette, causing him to lurch back in shock. 'What the...?' he exclaimed, pointing at the apparition.

One of the others spun around, trying to make sense of the stranger.

The last man's head moved in every direction, checking if the figure before them was alone.

'Who the hell are you?' Growled the biggest man in the group. 'Anyone else with you? Some other dick hiding out there, eh?'

It was a stupid question, betraying his idiocy. No one would give an affirmative answer in this situation.

Grey remained silent, chilling the atmosphere and building more tension in the men like he wanted. He wondered whether they would fight or run. It didn't take long to find out. The large man plucked up the courage to advance, then slowed when the stranger disappeared back into the gloom.

The thug gripped a wood bar of some sort, swinging it from side to side. Nearing the place where Grey had been, he cursed and lifted the weapon, ready to strike the stranger when he materialised out of the darkness. Before contact could be made, a vicious punch lashed out, hitting him in the throat and sending him crashing to the ground, gasping for air.

The others looked at their companion, then at each other. Decision made, they bolted for the exit, their boots echoing into the distance.

Grey turned to the young girl who had watched the exchange impassively. Her head tilted to one side when he took a step as if amused by the spectacle.

'We need to go.'

'Piss off.'

'It's not safe.'

'Don't pretend. You want the same as those shits. Well, I'm not gonna. So fuck off, weirdo and find some other *girl.*'

'Choice vocabulary.'

'What the hell does vocaboucrap mean?'

He didn't answer.

Voices sounded behind, causing her to glance over his shoulder. 'Knew they'd come back with more men,' she said with a self-satisfied grin. 'Now you're screwed.'

Before he could do anything, the girl disappeared. Grey remained in place, trying to decide whether to follow or run.

'This way, weirdo.' she called from the far side of the mound.

Grey picked up the downed man's weapon, a long axe handle by the look of it.

Then he turned and climbed the slope of bricks towards her voice, ignoring the cascade of rubble. The far side sank into impenetrable darkness.

'Here!' The girl shouted from below.

Scrabbling to the base he hit a solid wall. His hands found a hole barely large enough to accommodate his size. Tumbling into the dark, he crashed into something hard.

A snigger came from up ahead. 'Bet that hurt.'

He crouched in a tunnel that smelled like an old sewer, rancid mud sucking at his boots. One hand resting on a wall of slime, Grey trudged through.

Several times, invisible objects buried in the mud caused a stumble until a sliver of light highlighted a dead end of fallen stones. A ladder, rusted by age, protruded from the opening above. He kicked the third rung, expecting the worst, but it felt stable.

At the top, a large room appeared, dimly lit by moonlight filtering through an exposed roof. The floor was carpeted in bricks and old machinery parts.

'Pull the grill over the hole and push that lump of stone on top. It'll stop the Scabs—if they make it this far,' the girl said.

'Scabs?'

She didn't answer.

Fallen masonry led to a bank of rubble with an opening at the top. Wary of the watcher from earlier, Grey listened, heard nothing, and entered the gap.

'Over here, weirdo,' she called, followed by a 'G'bye.'

A corner in the wall felt clear enough to rest and wait for daylight before leaving. Grey dozed rather than slept with his back to the wall, senses tuned to any noise. His wet coat stank, but there was no other option to keep warm.

Dawn edged its way into the gloom. Soft spears of pale orange light captured disturbed dust when Grey stood and stretched the tightness from sore muscles.

Graffiti etched into the walls showed a name, insults and obscenities directed at Scabs.

Some things never change, he thought.

Daylight beckoned above a stone lintel lying on top of a pile of debris. He picked his way up it, disturbing as few fragments of brick and concrete as possible.

In all directions, buildings were torn apart. Fires had raged, judging by the blackened walls. It was a depressing sight, and he'd seen enough of the place.

Grey knew the Scabs, whoever they were, might still be around looking for the girl or the stranger who'd taken out their man. But there was no sign of movement. The three thugs he encountered had shown little regard for subtleties, and he doubted they were skilled in concealment. Even so, caution was better than complacency.

With that, he descended into the street below, stopping again and listening for the tell-tale sound of displaced detritus. Neither his senses nor peripheral vision picked anything up. It felt like he was the last man alive.

THE CAT GETS THE MOUSE

AFTER walking for some time, the sound of a dislodged brick confirmed someone was following. For sure, they were incompetent.

Taking a few more steps, seemingly oblivious to any pursuit, Grey poked his foot into the rubble as if searching for something.

He could feel them watching.

Rounding a corner, he pushed himself flat to the wall, dropped his bag and grasped the axe handle. The scrape of a foot warned him to be ready. A head peered around the brick —the girl from the previous night.

'That's a good way to get yourself killed,' he hissed, grabbing her hair and throwing her to the ground. 'Before you say it, fuck you, too. And no, I don't want what the Scabs were after.'

The girl sat up and glared at him, her long, matted hair and skin stained with grime. Dirty clothes hung loosely over a small frame.

Mid-teens at most, he thought. She held a wrench, of all things.

'What d'you want, weirdo?'

'Why are you following me?'

Fixing him with a defiant stare, she said nothing.

He pulled her up by the arm and kicked the makeshift weapon away. 'Let's go somewhere safe.'

'There's nowhere safe.'

Ignoring the comment, Grey dragged her across the street to the remains of an old shop frontage. Inside, she sat on the floor, arms wrapped around thin legs, her eyes darting from side to side, checking for an escape route. She wore soiled black jeans and a frayed dark blue roll-neck jumper too large for her body. Scuffed brown boots completed her wardrobe.

'Want some food?' Grey asked.

'What kind of food?'

He ignored her, took some from his bag and tossed it across.

'What's that?'

'Dried meat.'

'Won't eat anything I don't recognise. Don't want the shits. It could be human, for all I know. Heard about people eating them.'

'It's venison.'

'What?'

'Animal. All you need to know.'

She looked at the meat, then at him, smelled it and took a tentative bite.

'It doesn't taste like a human.'

Grey narrowed his eyes. 'You've tried them?'

'No way,' she answered with a disgusted look. 'Just heard they taste like 'og, and this doesn't. I'd have to be starving before I eat a person.'

The girl appeared close to starvation now.

'Where did you get 'og from?'

'Mind your own, weirdo.'

'Stop calling me weirdo.'

'So, what's your name?'

'What's yours?'

'Get lost,' she retorted.

He gave a resigned sigh. 'Grey.'

'Grey's a colour, not a name.'

'Only name I've ever had.'

She weighed him up for a moment. Then, as if betraying a secret, she mumbled, 'Jen.'

'Thought so.'

Her head snapped up. 'How the hell d'you know that?'

'Written on the wall back where you took me. Big statement.'

'What's a statement? You always talk long-word crap?'

'Yup.'

'How old are you?' Jen asked.

'Thirty-eight. And you?'

'Almost sixteen.'

Silence passed between them as she gnawed on the meat, turning it in her fingers between each bite, still unsure.

'Where do you get water?'

'Pipes.'

'Where?'

Jen raised her eyebrows to say, 'As if I'm going to tell you.'

'Where do you live?'

Her eyes skewered him. 'Why?'

'Just curious.'

'Fucking nosy, you mean. Get yourself killed by asking questions like that. You never tell anyone about your Dig.'

'What's a Dig?'

'Like digging a hole. Everyone knows that unless you're dim'ead stupid.'

When he gave no response, Jen went quiet, considering his question, until a bell rang in the distance.

'What's that?'

'It's a bell.'

'I know that.' Try as he might, Grey was running out of patience.

'Work time.' A sigh reserved for foolish questions followed. 'There'll be people heading to the Station. And Guarders.'

'Guarders?'

'They protect them from Scabs.'

'Are you going to tell me?'

'Tell you what?'

'Where you live?'

No answer, so Grey changed the subject. 'Why were you following me?'

'Wasn't.'

'You were,' he said, his tone emphatic.

Jen thought for a moment. 'Because you helped me last night. People don't do that around here—unless they want something.'

'I've already told you I don't want *that*.'

16

She glared, then relented and nodded vaguely over her shoulder.

'So, what do you want from me?' Grey asked.

'Nothing.'

'You do.'

After thinking for a minute, she said, 'The Scabs are after me.'

'Why?'

'Obvious, isn't it? Anyway, you owe me because I helped you.'

'I helped you, so we're even. Why do you think I could help? If I wanted to. Which I don't.'

'You beat up that man.'

'So?'

'Doesn't matter—you already said you're not willing.'

'Indulge me.'

'What's that supposed to mean?'

'Never mind.'

'Can I go now?' Jen asked flippantly.

Grey nodded at the exit.

When he reached the entrance, the girl was nowhere in sight. A flash of movement caught his eye.

Probably her.

He reconsidered. Jen had dark clothing. Whoever this was wore khaki.

Do I care?

Grey shook his head and followed. He rounded a corner and saw the ruins of a large building constructed from granite blocks. A fallen lintel lay across the entrance, with the word 'Library' chiselled in Roman script along its length.

Edging inside, he saw movement.

It wasn't Jen.

A man crouched behind a fallen block, making no move to draw his bow.

The camo trousers marked him as a soldier of some type. Most likely a Guarder.

Creeping over, Grey took the man in a firm headlock—one arm around the chin, the other holding the head. 'Move, and I'll snap your neck.'

The Guarder dropped his bow without being asked.

Grey lowered him to the ground and pushed the side of his head into the floor. The man winced when stones bit into his cheek.

'Why were you following her?'

When he said nothing, Grey ground his head into the debris.

'Screw you.'

He forced the man's face even harder into the dirt and twisted it. The Guarder spat dust and fragments from the corner of his mouth. 'Don't want to hurt the girl, just keeping an eye on her.'

'Why?'

'Orders.'

'From who?'

No response.

'One more chance.'

Jen emerged out of the gloom. 'Don't hurt him. Guarders only watch me. They don't mean any harm.'

Grey punched the man's jaw, knocking him out.

'Let's go.'

'Where?' Jen asked.

'Your Dig.'

She went silent for a few seconds, looked over her shoulder and shrugged. 'Okay.'

Grey followed Jen along a street of derelict shops. She stayed ahead, glancing back now and then. They climbed a mound of rubble and stopped at two concrete slabs. She lifted loose chunks of masonry off a corrugated metal sheet to reveal an opening.

At the bottom was an old underground station, still displaying some white tiles on the walls and a handrail beside a long flight of steps.

Fresh air coursed through the tunnel.

More than one exit. Good choice.

'Hold the rope,' Jen said. 'It'll show you the way.'

They stopped at what Grey assumed was their destination. A door moved inwards when she pushed with her shoulder.

'Wait here.'

After the rasp of a striking match, a candle flickered to life.

Grey wondered where they came from.

The flame hinted at a compact room, difficult to make out until two more were lit. An open green metal box stencilled 'ARMY' sat in one corner, candles and matches inside. Which seemed odd in a ravaged city.

Tin plates and mugs lay beside two mattresses with a pile of sacking on top for blankets. Next to the wall were dirty clothes and a rusty can, still displaying print. Washing wasn't high on her list of priorities, so it had to be drinking water.

As if reading his mind, Jen said, 'That's my spare can. I lost the other last night when the Scabs came. Not much in there, though.'

Nothing personal was apparent except for scattered books on the floor. Grey assumed she'd found them in the library.

Jen noticed his frown. 'Got to go on a scavenge soon.'

She sat cross-legged, watching Grey leaning against a wall on the other side of the room. Sensing her unease, he tossed his bag across.

'My knife's in there. Keep it if it makes you feel safer.'

Her shoulders relaxed. 'So, who the fuck are you?'

Instead of answering the question, Grey said, 'Can you do me a favour?' Immediately, he regretted his choice of words.

Jen tensed. 'Fuck off. I told you I'm not interested in that kind of thing.'

'Not what I meant. Can you stop using that word? I don't like hearing it from a girl's mouth.'

'What word? And I'm not a *girl*,' she snapped.

He ignored the last comment, knowing it was pointless to contradict her.

'You know fine well which word I mean.'

Jen shrugged indifferently.

Grey looked away, trying to find a way to explain. 'It makes me—angry.'

'Why should I care what you don't like?'

'Because I care. And because you hope I will help you.'

Jen straightened, her eyes widening. 'Will you?'

'Still thinking about it.'

'But?'

'Still thinking about it,' he repeated slowly to emphasise the point.

She thought for a moment, then relented. 'Okay, I'll try not to swear. But only for tonight, weirdo.' she added with a smirk.

QUESTIONS AND ANSWERS

'WHAT happened here?' Grey asked, circling his finger.
 Jen considered the question. 'My mum said it was rocks from the sky. Big ones.'
 'Meteorites.'
 'What the fu...' She stopped herself and continued, 'What's a meteothingy?'
 'Big rock from the sky.'
 'Ha ha.'
 'Where is your mother?'
 Jen answered quietly, looking at the floor. 'Scabs took her when she made me run away. She said they were coming to get me because I was nearly old enough for...you know.'

He ignored her reasoning.

'They take all the younger ones from mothers who do it for them in exchange for food and other stuff. That's why I don't know who my father is. Could be any of those dirty shits. She told me to come here because she knew someone who'd look after me. Made me promise never to go back to our old Dig.'

Her voice quivered, but Grey said nothing. Showing concern would make the girl think he cared. Information, food, and water were all he wanted before moving on. After that, her life was her problem.

A moment later, Jen composed herself. 'Didn't come here straight away, though. Stayed in the place I took you after you beat up that Scab. That's when I wrote the words, the ones on the wall. I sneaked back to the Dig after two days, but my mother wasn't there. I didn't think she would be. They always kill people who cross them.'

Jen rubbed the floor with her fingers as if wiping away the memory.

She glanced at Grey, took a deep breath, and returned to the story. 'When I went back to the place I'd stayed, a woman was waiting for me. Never said how she knew I'd be there. I asked a few times, but she said it was luck. Don't believe that, though.'

'Who was she?'

'Called herself Plain Jane—a saying from the old days. I just called her Jane. She was kind. Fed me, taught me some reading and showed me how to survive. Sometimes, she went out alone and came back with candles and matches after the electricity went out in here. I asked Jane why, but she said it was a secret. She showed me where to scavenge, though, just in case something happened to her. Made me talk better, too, so I don't sound like a Scab.'

Grey raised his eyebrows. 'And the swearing?'

Jen gave him a wicked smirk. 'Sometimes, she got some cooked 'og. That's how I know what it tastes like. No idea where it came from.'

'What happened to her?'

'Didn't come back about a month ago.' Jen shrugged, feigning indifference. 'Been on my own ever since. Fucking Scabs got her like my mother, I reckon.'

She glanced up, aware of the slip.

'Sometimes that is the right word to use.'

Grey changed the subject. 'Do you want something to eat?'

Feeling around the bag, Jen pulled out meat and threw a piece over. The knife remained untouched. Neither said anything whilst they chewed, not that Jen could, given the amount crammed in her mouth.

'Will you show me where to scavenge and get more water?'

She fought to swallow a mouthful. 'You going to help me if I do, then?'

'Maybe.' Although he still wasn't sure he would.

Jen gave a 'please yourself' shrug, pretending not to care. 'Up to you.'

'Do you still think I'm a weirdo?'

'Not so much. But you look strange.' She pointed at the spiral tattoo circling one side of his neck. 'Why have you got that?'

'It's a mark. Sort of like a label—shows who I am.' Grey almost said, 'What I am.'

'Why haven't you joined up with other scavengers?'

Jen sighed as if the answer was obvious. 'Not enough food to go round. Especially of late. Anyway, everyone keeps to themselves because the Scabs don't like us mixing. I'm not sure why.'

Tired of talking, she picked at a broken fingernail, then moved to her bed, wrestling with the sacking. 'Got to sleep for a while. It'll be a late one tonight.'

Grey nodded, wrapped himself in his coat, and rested against the wall. Within moments, he fell asleep, more at ease than he'd been for some time.

*

After dark, they traversed the edge of a crater. Ragged shards of concrete and protruding steel supports thrust upwards like jagged teeth around a gaping maw. Waves of undulating rubble stretched as far as Grey could make out in the darkening sky.

Weaving in and out of the grotesque sculptures, he scanned the area for movement whilst keeping a watchful eye on Jen.

'I know how to creep, dim'ead,' she hissed when he pulled her back into the shadows for the third time. 'Been doing it long en...'

'Quiet.'

Some way ahead, a flash of light reflected off damp concrete.

He pointed.

'Already seen it, shit-for-brains.' She didn't notice his raised eyebrow.

'It's a tote. There'll be a Scab on the other end of it—smoking.'

'Stay here. I'm going over for a word,' Grey said.

'What?'

'Not a friendly word. More a persuasive one if there aren't too many.'

'I want t...'

'Stay.'

A tut and mumbled expletive followed.

Grey made his way over uneven ground, keeping low and carefully placing one foot in front of the other. He heard the murmur of voices, then a laugh.

Four men leaned casually against the side of a slab. Only three appeared to be holding a weapon; the other had probably laid his down, out of sight. One smoked, the acrid odour tainting the air. It occurred to him that tobacco, like matches, was a strange thing to find in the city.

Grey crouched in a shadow and listened. After several minutes, their conversation switched to him and Jen.

'Jez took one to the throat.'

'Clumsy idiot,' muttered the man with the tote before hawking a gob of phlegm and spitting onto the floor. 'Never 'ad any brains, thought he was invincible. Never liked 'im since I first set eyes on 'im.'

Another man chuckled. 'Notice you never said that to his face.'

'Piss off. They were after the little bitch we been told to watch out for. Shame they didn't get her. Would have liked a piece of that.'

'Me, too.'

Three of them laughed.

Despite his intention to avoid any sense of responsibility for Jen, Grey felt his anger rising. Some things couldn't be ignored, and this was one of them.

The third man, younger than the rest, stared at the floor, shifting his weight from one foot to the other, uncomfortable with the conversation. He was the kind of obese made for cruel jokes.

Grey hadn't come to kill; he just wanted answers, although he knew they were unlikely to be forthcoming without some level of coercion. Having heard the conversation changed his intentions.

'Need a piss,' Tote Man said, walking away and disappearing behind a mound of concrete. Unfortunately for him, it was where Grey hid.

The Scab slumped in his urine.

Grey approached the remaining men fast and low, the axe handle arching in a ferocious swipe. The nearest Scab took a blow to the head, sending him crashing into a fallen slab. In one fluid motion, Grey turned to face the other two. Except there was only one. The boy had made a run for it—or so he thought.

The charge against his back threw him to the ground, taking the bulldozer with him.

Rolling just in time, Grey avoided the entire body weight by inches. An iron rod caught his shoulder when he stood, sending him staggering sideways.

Regaining his balance, he turned to face the last man standing. A tall, thin Scab with a weasel-like face stood waiting. Black hair, glued to his head with grease, ended in a ponytail. He crouched, swaying from side to side with his weapon held in both hands.

Grey looked at the ground, pointing the handle down. 'Doesn't need to go any further,' he said, nodding at the other man's weapon. 'I just want to ask a few questions.'

He waited for Ponytail's response. It took a few seconds because Grey's stance confused him as he knew it would.

Then, the man charged. He was fast on his feet, but not fast enough. At the last moment, Grey stepped to the side, his leg delivering a heel-kick to the Scab's knee. Instantly, he brought his handle down onto the back of Ponytail's head.

The boy was halfway to his feet when Grey snapped, 'Stay down,' then looked at the two felled men.

Ponytail's chest wasn't rising. The other slumped against angled concrete, head tilted at an acute angle.

When stones crunched behind, he spun. Jen came out of the shadows. She glanced at the dead men and gave a 'tough shit' shrug.

Stomping over to the kneeling boy, she kicked him in the nuts.

The young Scab rolled around like a barrel, clutching his groin, and vomited.

When Jen looked at Grey's face, she took a step back. He knew what she saw. His eyes had taken on the cold, hard look of a killer, and his face was white with barely controlled fury. The Rage had taken over.

SCAVENGE

THE boy leaned back against some concrete blocks, looking terrified.

'Relax,' Grey said. 'Give me answers, and I'll let you go.'

Frenetic nodding followed.

His piggy eyes darted about, and sweat ran down his face despite the cold.

Jen sat on a rock a few yards away, staring at him, then Grey, and back again, her face unreadable.

Grey pointed to the outline of a wall.

'Wait over there.'

He focused on the boy when she was out of earshot.

*

Grey found Jen later. She sat with her back to him and didn't look over when he approached. Part of him hoped she had gone after witnessing the Rage.

'I need to lie down and rest for a while,' he said.

Jen didn't reply.

Reaching into his bag, he pulled out a leather flask and sipped the bitter liquid. It increased the Rage if taken before a fight and eased pain afterwards. He closed his eyes and relaxed his muscles.

Grey jerked awake when someone shook his leg. Jen stepped back in fear, moonlight reflected in her blue eyes.

'What was that, back there?'

He paused, thinking of the best way to put it. 'It's how I was trained. A way to deal with violence. I only use it when there is no other choice.'

'You were—a Guarder, then?' Jen asked hesitantly.

'Of a sort, yes.'

She watched him briefly, her expression sceptical.

'Going to be tricky to scavenge if we wait until daylight. Guarders leave the Station early to collect workers. Scabs will be looking about, too, when they find the bodies.'

Grey stood and rotated his shoulder. It was painful but usable. He took another small sip of Juice.

'What's that?'

'Energy,' he replied curtly, not wanting to get into a long explanation.

He considered what the boy had told him. He knew the layout of the Station where workers lived, and that Guarders manned the perimeter. They carried bows and guns; the latter used less of late, which was interesting. There were also sheds for growing vegetables and raising 'ens 'n 'ogs. And the Council ran the show.

Grey had also questioned him about Jen and her mother.

'Do you know the girl?'

'Never seen her before, but I knew we was looking for her. Know nothing 'bout her mother. They'd have killed her, though, if she narked 'em—don't take well to people who do that.'

The boy had little else to offer, and Grey hadn't been sure he cared about any of it.

He only let him go because he didn't join the discussion about Jen.

*

Grey and Jen headed towards the Station through a maze of derelict buildings until they reached a rusted razor-wire fence. Beyond this, dwellings had been repaired to provide adequate shelter for workers.

On the way, they passed a multi-storey car park which had collapsed in on itself, the occasional concrete pillar poking through jumbles of rubble. Buckled remains of rusty cars told Grey no one had the means for smelting on a large scale—a depot with single and double-deckers scattered like dominos across the ground confirmed it.

This answered another question. There were no buses and very few cars anywhere on the streets—not enough for a typical day in a metropolis. Meteorites had struck in the early hours with little warning. The government must have played down the danger, knowing catastrophe was inevitable.

Jen led him to a department store where windows had once paraded goods. One side of the first story remained intact, with bricks reaching the top.

A gap of about thirty feet separated the store and razor wire fence. No Guarders were visible on the other side, which was an odd lapse in security.

At the top of the debris, they lay flat to look around.

Grey was intrigued when Jen had told him she came here on scavenging runs, assuming supplies would be closer to the Dig. It didn't surprise him to learn it wasn't the source of her water. Lugging a heavy can would be impossible from this distance.

The lady who rescued Jen had shown where and how to tap a pipe carrying water into the city, closer to her Dig.

Somewhere a reservoir still functioned, Grey decided, although she said the water sometimes gave her the shits.

He was looking forward to that trip to wash himself and remove the stench on his clothing. Asking Jen to do the same would no doubt fall on deaf ears.

Grey thought about what the boy had told him regarding the Station, which he now realised was only a generic title. Nothing visible in the dim light resembled a railway station, which he had assumed gave the area its name.

He could make out silhouettes of the sheds and the occasional orange dot from a tote. Only one building appeared to have illumination. Where the power came from wasn't evident, but Grey thought there might be a small hydroelectric generator somewhere.

Jen told him to wait while she went in for some stuff. When he heard her call, he should go down to the department store entrance.

'We'll hide there until it's safe to head back.'

Grey protested, but she was insistent. The route inside meant crawling along a narrow pipe into the compound and squeezing through a gap in the shed wall. He was too big to get through.

It was only once Jen left that a question arose; she had nothing to carry supplies in?

After a long and uncomfortable hour, Grey heard her below.

'Give me a hand, will you? This is bloody heavy.'

Supplies bulged inside a sack, which also served for bedding.

The pain made him wince when he lifted the haul. Juice would help, but it was running low. Nor was it likely the plant it came from would grow in this place.

'We've got to hide until the workers go in,' Jen said, whilst taking two misshapen carrots out of the sack.

They each ate one, wiping them first with a sleeve to remove dirt. Grey tried not to think about pig manure used as fertiliser.

He peeled his, then offered the knife to Jen. She shook her head, looking disgusted at his waste of food.

The carrot tasted good after living off dried meat for some time.

A gap between bricks provided a reasonable view into the street. Easy to see out, hard to see in. Groups of Guarders headed towards the living areas before the bell sounded.

Soon after, huddles of people appeared. The sight wasn't as dismal as Grey expected. Ages ranged from children to adults; the oldest appeared to be around forty. Life expectancy was low, which wasn't a surprise.

What he didn't notice were any girls of Jen's age.

Many workers chatted as they walked along, nodding now and again at a Guarder. They appeared well-fed, and although their clothing was worn in places, it looked clean.

Whoever ran the Council had earned the workers trust.

Estimating about seventy people, Grey asked Jen if that was the sum total.

'Some what? You're talking in fu—puzzles again.

'I meant, is that everyone, or do others come from a different direction?'

'That's it, as far as I know.'

Not much of a workforce. Too few for a thriving community, Grey thought.

*

No Scabs, Guarders, or scavengers appeared on the way back to the Dig.

Jen tipped carrots, potatoes and brassica leaves onto the floor. She gathered them together whilst glancing at Grey, still wary after the crater.

Pouring water from the container over a handful of vegetables, Jen wiped them with her arm. 'Only clean what you want to eat,' she said, 'or it rots them. We'll go for water after a rest.'

'What's it like inside the sheds?'

'The one I go to is just storage for piles of veg. Candles and matches sometimes.'

Grey thought for a moment. Why would the Council place stores so close to the fence?

'They keep 'ens and 'ogs down the far end,' Jen continued. 'Never seen any, but you can hear them. And smell them when the wind blows.'

'You don't find meat?'

'Not since Jane disappeared.'

She handed over a crowbar. When he reached for the can, she pulled it back, 'Don't need your help now. You can carry it back.'

*

Jen didn't look over her shoulder when traversing the underground tunnel, seemingly unconcerned whether Grey kept up.

His shoulder still throbbed. Lugging the water back would be painful without Juice.

Jen explained she'd never seen Scabs in the area during the day. 'They probably get water someplace else. I bet it's cleaner than the stuff I drink. Other scavengers know about this place, so we need to be careful. I've only been chased a few times—lost another container once, and it took a while to find a new one.'

'No one will chase us today. I'll make sure of that,' Grey said firmly.

They needed water—period.

Now and then, he thought he sensed someone following. Maybe just debris shifting in the breeze or perhaps the slip of a foot. He remained alert, just in case.

Jen stopped at the corner of a wall and whispered, 'See that grate? We've got to lift it and go down. That's the easy bit; getting the can up is hard. There's no one down there now, though, or the grate wouldn't be over the hole. Too risky trying to open it from below. It'll be dark inside, and a candle is useless because the breeze blows the flame out.'

Grey used the crowbar to lift the grate as quietly as possible before climbing a metal ladder into a tunnel. Inside, the walls were greasy, and the floor covered in foul-smelling mud.

'Are there rats down here?'

'Not many. Other scavengers take them.'

Thirty yards in, the tunnel veered off to the left, revealing a small room. Steps led up to a steel platform, cleared of debris.

The space was dimly lit by patches of light creeping from a grate above. Several large pipes spanned the walls, disappearing into each side. In the centre, a large circular tap poked out of the brickwork. Grey assumed it was a valve of some sort. Layers of flaking rust suggested it hadn't worked for some time.

A well-used conventional tap sprouted from an adjoining pipe.

Jen used two hands to turn it on, grunting and muttering from the effort. 'Some stupid dim'ead tightened it too hard.'

Brown, sludgy water trickled out. She waited for it to clear before pushing the can underneath. It still didn't look appealing, and a faint sulphur smell permeated the air.

'It's got worse of late,' Jen said.

Grey had to carry the can with his good shoulder hanging down, his other palm flat to the slick walls for stability. Given the container's weight, leaving the axe handle hidden outside was a good decision.

Once in the open, he crouched to regain his breath and windmill his arm a few times before closing the grill.

Jen watched, tapping a foot.

As they crossed the street, something whistled and cracked against a wall ahead. A dull clang sounded from the can when it hit the floor.

Grey grabbed Jen and pushed her behind the wall. He risked a quick look around the corner. Catching sight of a bowman, he ducked back when another arrow bounced off the brick.

'Next one won't miss,' came a voice somewhere behind. 'Come out, peaceful like. We won't hurt you unless we have to.'

Grey said nothing.

He looked towards Jen. She wasn't there.

Cursing, he picked up his handle, ready to follow, when a shout came from the left.

'Got the girl.'

Sounds of a struggle, Jen swearing, and a yelp came from behind.

The bowman shouted from the street. 'Hold on to her, you idiot.'

'If you hurt the girl, I'll kill every one of you,' Grey yelled.

Someone laughed.

He knew there would be at least three men—Jen's captor, the bowman in the street and another trying to sight him from a higher vantage point.

Footsteps pinpointed someone approaching. Timing the move perfectly, Grey dived to the floor, turned, and kicked out, forcing the assailant to topple over him. His knife pricked the man's throat. 'Struggle, and you die. Now reach to your left and grab the bow.'

The man complied.

Pushing with his feet, Grey edged them back to the wall, using the captive as a shield. In the shadows, he rolled the man over and rendered him unconscious with a jaw punch.

A man on the rooftop called out, 'He's got Pe...'

Grey's arrow cut him off. Screaming, the second bowman tumbled from the roof, hitting the floor with a thud.

Suddenly, a shotgun blasted brick from the side wall.

'Don't even think about trying that again.' It was a new voice. Deeper. Authoritative. 'Your little friend has a gun to her head. My man's finger is itching to pull the trigger.'

With no other choice, Grey came out, hands in the air. Six Guarders circled him. One man wore bloody teeth marks on his hand. Grey smiled at him. In return, he received a hard punch to the gut.

The blow forced a wheeze, but he kept his eyes on the man and grinned. Teethmarks cursed and threatened castration.

With a smirk, the man with the shotgun appraised Grey, then nodded at two Guarders who peeled away to retrieve their fallen comrades.

'Leave it,' he said to Teethmarks who shrugged off the two holding him and mouthed, 'Dead man.'

Grey's wrists were bound tight. Jen's weren't. She stood a few paces away, her arm held by a woman. The Guarders wanted something otherwise, he'd be dead. But what?

Patience. You'll find out soon enough.

'Follow us and keep quiet,' the gunman, who was clearly the leader, commanded.

'Do as he says,' Grey snapped at Jen when she opened her mouth to curse.

The woman beside her stood out. Her hair was shiny, clean and tied back in a long ponytail. She wore it better than the Scab at the crater, that was for sure.

The leader had a barrel chest and an unkempt ginger beard suited to his sizeable frame. Thick arms bulged beneath a rough woven jumper stretched tight around an ample stomach. A long bone-handled knife poked out of a worn leather belt. The shotgun completed his armoury.

He led from the front, setting the pace. Every so often, his meaty hand halted the Guarders. After a glance around to check the surroundings, he moved on.

Twice, Grey spotted movement from scouts farther up a street until the group rounded a corner, and everyone stopped. A man waited with a team of horses.

Two newcomers appeared from opposite sides of the road, armed with bows and handguns. They spoke with the leader, who then inclined his head, and the men melted back into the buildings.

'You ride?' He barked at Grey, who nodded once, eyeing the man.

'Not the girl, eh?'

It didn't need an answer.

The group made their way through a residential district with row upon row of red brick, terraced houses shattered into mounds of hubris. The labyrinth of streets forced Grey to abandon referencing landmarks for future use.

Jen held his coat as if her life depended upon it.

She had cursed and fought like a demon when a man had tried to lift her onto Grey's mount. Not even the leader's threatening shout for silence had calmed her down.

Jen only complied when the woman took her to one side, squeezed an arm, and whispered something in her ear. She yanked herself free and allowed the Guarder to lift her.

The mounts had no saddles and only a rope for reins, which wasn't a problem. Grey had ridden this way before. Jen kept her back straight, struggling to match the horse's rhythm. He attempted to put her at ease by leaning back and calling encouragement.

The response was predictable. 'Fuck you!'

When the horses kicked up plumes of dust, she coughed. Too theatrically, Grey decided and ignored her, focusing on their surroundings.

They eventually reached the razor-wire fence east of where Jen scavenged. Grey took in the Guarder, who emerged from a small hut to let the party through. He also noted where the horses were led.

Thirty-six oblong buildings were spread along two parallel rows, some constructed from mismatched brickwork, others from concrete blocks. Panels of clear corrugated plastic formed some roofs whilst others had rusted metal sheets. Large paving slabs, free of weeds in between, formed a path separating the structures. The entire place looked utilitarian.

Murmurs, shuffling footsteps, and items scraping across the floor filtered through open doors. Two women appeared, transporting seedlings from one shed to another.

Stacks of pallets, tools, wheelbarrows, and scraps of wood and metal leaned against one storage shed. The obnoxious smell of pig manure carried by gusts of wind came from a barn some distance away.

To the right, Grey noticed several army vehicles. Flat tires said they were no longer used, no doubt because there was no fuel left.

He wondered if the Council had sufficient Guarders to protect herds beyond the compound. The numbers and accommodation said it was unlikely. Calculating the size of the fence, he decided it stretched at least four hundred yards. Lines of green suggested mature crops at the far end.

Grey thought he detected the faint hum of what could be a generator coming from somewhere he couldn't see.

Dominating the concourse, a flat-topped square building looked in good repair. A hundred yards on each side, maybe more. The plain façade, punctuated by identical windows, glowed white in the sun. Grass edged the brickwork, and manicured scrubs bordered a pathway to imposing wood doors.

The leader barred the way once they reached the building's entrance. He skewered Grey as if deciding whether he was worthy of access.

After a few moments, he spoke abruptly. 'The name's Ben.' Raising his eyebrows to emphasise the question, he asked, 'Yours?'

No answer.

Ben waited a moment, shrugged, and brought out his knife. Grey tensed, ready to fight regardless of the consequences.

'Whoa, now.' The leader held a palm up in a show of good faith. 'Just want to cut the ropes.'

Grey relaxed a little, keeping his eyes on the ape-like hands moving towards the binding. The rope dropped away, leaving red welts around his wrists.

'You're not prisoners here,' Ben said.

The two men cupping holstered revolvers suggested otherwise.

'Just want to chat.'

The amicable tone didn't fool Grey. 'Why are we here?'

'All in good time. Maybe let you both get a wash and eat before we talk. Your name first, though? We know hers. Jen, isn't it?'

Jen's mouth opened in surprise, her tiny fists clenched, and she stomped her foot. 'How the hell d'you know my name?'

'I knew the woman who looked after you. She was one of us. Before the Scabs took her.' Under his breath, Ben muttered, 'Scum.'

Jen gave him a hard stare before looking down and kicking a stone.

Ben faced Grey. 'Well?'

'Well, what?'

The man's jaw tightened. 'Your name?'

Grey made him wait, the message clear. All in due time—my time, not yours. After a long moment, he gave his name.

Ben frowned.

'Grey, like the colour. Okay?' Jen snapped.

They were both led through large double doors into a hallway. Another set opened in front, and Guarders filed out. Ben exchanged nods with them.

Seconds later, the bell sounded home time for the workers.

A wide corridor ran down the length of the building. Doors lined each wall, interspersed by more corridors. The

Guarders from the city peeled off to the right. Teethmarks looked over his shoulder to deliver Grey another 'dead man' look.

Ahead, an entrance opened, and a woman wearing blue jeans and a cream jumper came out. Two armed men flanked her.

She spread her arms. 'Welcome.'

Ben nodded in Grey's direction. 'That's Grey—like the colour.'

Jen rolled her eyes.

The woman was striking for her age: late sixties, maybe early seventies. Cropped white hair framed a long face with prominent cheekbones. Her delicate skin appeared almost transparent, complimented rather than betrayed by fine lines. She could be mistaken for a kindly matriarch except for the diamond-hard blue eyes. Judgmental. Cold.

'I'm Bella,' she said, then turned to Ben. 'Take a break, you must be tired after your journey.'

He was about to protest, but she narrowed her eyes on him.

'No doubt you have many questions, as do I. We will talk after you have rested a while.'

It all added to Grey's sense of unease about the whole situation. Whatever was going on here wasn't good. And he thought he now understood more about what it might be.

Bella focused on Jen, frowned, and said, 'Maybe give your hair a cut, do you think?'

'Like fuck!' Jen protested.

The woman snapped, 'We don't like that kind of talk around here, especially from a...'

Grey cut her off before she could say, 'girl.'

'Jen, we both smell bad, and your hair looks like a home for mice.'

His attempt at humour backfired. She stomped through the door, Bella indicated, a female guard behind.

'You take the second door, Grey. Wash your clothes in the same water. We don't have a lot to spare. Someone will bring something clean to wear whilst yours dry. We'll eat afterwards.'

'Word of advice. Don't call Jen a girl. She's kind of sensitive about that.'

Bella gave him a tight smile and left.

Two men waited inside the bathroom for Grey, each armed with batons.

He was a little disappointed they didn't attempt to use them.

HAIRCUT

A plain stone bath waited at the far side of a cold, featureless room. Twelve inches of lukewarm water wallowed beneath an ingrained scum line. To the side lay a chunk of well-used soap, a long hair adhered to the surface.

The Guarders watched Grey wash himself, then his clothes as best he could. A man walked into the room holding a collarless shirt and trousers with ties on the waist. They were old and stained but clean enough to wear without discomfort.

The men escorted him to a compact, windowless room lit by a dim bulb. Coated with flaking green paint, two iron-framed beds sat on opposite walls.

'Please enjoy your accommodation, sir.' One of the Guarders sneered. The other sniggered.

When they locked the door, no footsteps echoed along the corridor.

'You're not prisoners,' Ben had said.

Grey lay back on the uncomfortable bed. When Jen walked in he was taken aback.

Her hair, a mousy blonde, had been cropped short with no attempt at styling. It gave her a boyish look but couldn't hide the pretty features. 'Girl' was the right word; she didn't look at all womanly. Her skin, pink in places from scrubbing, had a fresh appearance only someone young could own.

'What are you looking at, dim'ead? Never seen someone have their hair cut before?'

Grey had to turn his head away to suppress a laugh.

Jen couldn't contain herself. 'Fuck you.'

It tempted him to bait her with, 'It brings out the girl in you,' but he decided against it. She was pissed off enough.

'At least I can see what you look like now.'

'Yeah, well, I can see what you look like. Weirdo, with a stupid drawing on your neck.'

'Still got my hair though.'

Jen turned to stomp out of the room, remembered the locked door, then threw herself onto the bed facing the wall. Within minutes, she was asleep, exhausted from the day's events.

Grey lay back smiling, then brought himself up short. He slapped the wall, angry at relating to her.

Hours later, a Guarder awoke them, rapping loudly on the door.

'You're both wanted. Now!'

Grey's stern gaze challenged the man to make him move. The Guarder's eyes betrayed a flicker of uncertainty, no doubt warned about his capacity for violence.

They entered a large room. Four identical fold-up tables on spindly legs had been pushed together to make one uneven surface. Two old wood benches lay on opposite sides. On one sat Ben, Bella, and a new man.

Ben's introduction was brief. 'Irvine.'

The newcomer made to stand, noticed the bear's frown, and sat back down.

'Not too steady on my feet these days,' he said, though Grey suspected it was an attempt to cover his embarrassment.

Irvine appeared to be around Bella's age. Tall and thin, he had unkempt white hair and veiny hands. His pale eyes studied Grey from behind round glasses in need of a clean.

He was too intellectual for a worker, too old and gaunt for a Guarder, Grey decided.

'I'm the resident plant man,' Irvine said, a smile on his thin lips. 'Agronomist is the fancy term. Not a great one for labels. Not much need here.'

Grey noticed Jen's slight smile. It looked sincere—she liked him.

They sat opposite Ben, Bella, and Irvine whilst the Guarders took positions on each side of the entrance. After a light tap on the door, a woman came in with a metal tray, holding slices of cold meat and potatoes on tin plates.

Jen reached across to grab some meat, but Bella grasped her wrist. 'When I say, and not before. We expect manners around here.'

'Bitch,' Jen muttered under her breath, receiving a glare in return.

Ben stood to fetch a jug of water and white enamel mugs from a table on the other side of the room. He handed one to each of them, then poured a clear liquid into each mug. Jen looked at it as if he'd performed a magic trick.

'Filtered.' Irvine said, a note of pride in his voice.

Bella nodded permission at Jen, who grabbed a slice of fatty meat. She shoved it into her mouth and asked, through bloated cheeks, 'Is this 'og?'

'Human,' Grey said.

Jen stopped chewing and tried to say, 'Dick,' but it came out as 'Duck.'

The others turned to look at him, alarm on their faces.

Interesting response.

Whilst they ate, Grey stole glances in Jen's direction.

Her teeth weren't in good shape, discoloured and chipped in places, but the occasional smile made up for it. Her hazel eyes would have hypnotised boys in a different life. In this world, they were bereft of a young girl's innocence, replaced by mistrust, anger—and hurt.

At first, she'd been irritating, like a persistent mosquito, and he'd had little sympathy for her. Now, he felt responsible for her safety. Temporarily, at least, which didn't sit well.

Consequences, Grey. Consequences.

*

'We have an offer for you,' Bella said. 'However, before we get into that, I'm sure we both have questions for each other.'

Grey sat back, stony-faced.

'No doubt you're aware it was a hail of meteorites which caused the devastation we see today. I thought you might like to know all the facts.

Bella raised her eyebrows. Grey nodded. Information was always valuable.

'Before the strike, a comet neared Earth. Its distance caused some concern, but no immediate threat was expected. However, unlike other heavenly bodies, comets are known to be erratic and unpredictable. No one foresaw the collision with a colossal asteroid. The impact sent hundreds of thousands of fragments to the planet. A meteorite fifty yards across can create a one-mile crater, give or take. The energy generated on hitting the atmosphere would be over five hundred kilotons of Trinitrotoluene—TNT—scorching large areas. Which is where the heat and fires came from. To put it into perspective, the worldwide destruction exceeded the capability of every nuclear weapon we had.'

Grey knew what Jen was thinking from her frown—what the hell was the woman talking about?

'There was little point in warning the population,' Bella went on, 'because the devastation was unavoidable. As you know, few people survived, and society descended into a dog-eat-dog mentality.'

She paused, looking Grey straight in the eye.

'This brings me to the reason for our conversation. As an outsider not aligned with any group, you have survived better than most. Given what we know, you are skilled at dealing with other *dogs*. Your physical condition suggests you have avoided the illnesses many people suffered. We are curious how you managed this?'

Ben's eyes narrowed. 'I'll cut to the chase—who the hell are you?'

'Who the hell are you?'

Grey didn't react when the big man lurched upright, his face contorted with anger.

'We can do this the easy way or the hard way. I'm happy with either.'

The Guarders moved to stand behind Grey, ready to deliver whatever punishment Ben ordered. Irvine looked away, seemingly uncomfortable with the aggressive display.

'Enough,' Bella snapped.

The bear thumped his hands on the table and sat, breathing in short bursts. Grey matched his stare, showing no sign of fear.

'You need to understand the anger directed at you, Bella said. 'Two of our people have suffered injuries at your hands. The man you shot with the arrow died about an hour ago. Ben has only just been told.'

'They asked for it.'

When the big man struggled to contain himself, Bella held up a hand in his direction.

She continued in a calm, measured voice. 'I will do you the service of answering your questions first, after which I must insist you answer ours.'

Grey remained silent, forcing Bella to continue her explanation.

'Prior to the strike, me, Irvine, and other experts were brought here. Ben's father, a major general in the army, and a platoon of soldiers provided security. We're the remaining leaders of that group. My area was genetics. You already know Irvine's. Our mission was to rebuild society. However, contact with other groups like us ceased. Attacks, in-fighting, illness—that type of thing incapacitated them.'

Irvine looked down at the table, appearing to be troubled by her words.

'We survived because of Ben's father. He ensured unity and the protection we needed to prosper. He is no longer with us, and Ben took over. From a military standpoint, that is. Below ground, there is a very large bunker—built in the event of a nuclear war—where we stayed initially. It still holds a lot of stores.'

Bella inclined her head and looked expectantly at Grey. 'And you?'

He took his time to answer.

'Not much to say. Travelled around, kept to myself, survived.'

'That tells us nothing,' Ben growled.

Grey shrugged. 'Tells you all you need to know—name, rank, and serial number. Standard practice for a prisoner, eh?'

Before the bear could react, Bella rapped her fingernails on the table. 'You're not prisoners here.'

'Then why the interrogation and guards?'

She ignored the question and hardened her expression. 'Tell us how you survived and why you came here. We'll leave it there for now.'

He let the silence hang, emphasising once more that compliance was his choice alone.

Irvine cleaned his glasses, replaced them and stared at Grey. It was difficult to tell whether the man was concerned or intrigued. His distasteful glance at Ben, however, spoke volumes.

'Please, just answer Bella's questions.' Irvine asked, clearly trying to diffuse the tension.

Jen gave him a friendly smile.

Grey appraised the agronomist. 'As you've asked—politely. I have basic military training and know how to look after myself. Staying clear of people was a sensible precaution. I lived in a farmhouse and ate from the land. Over time, supplies became difficult to find, and raiding parties increased. The city seemed worth a look. That's it.'

Bella nodded in satisfaction. Her eyes said otherwise.

Grey directed his stare at Ben. 'Is it my turn now?'

'Your turn to what?'

'Ask questions.'

'This is not a negotiation.'

Bella cut him off before he could say more. 'We'll answer what we think appropriate. Carry on.'

'Why is the city divided? You on one side, the Scabs on the other. It makes no sense. They have no obvious source of food that I can see, and you have supplies. Why haven't they mobilised against you?'

'They've tried.' Ben's tone oozed arrogance. 'We have weapons and well-trained men.'

'Not so easy now, though.'

'Why?'

'You're running low on ammunition.'

'Bollocks.'

'Really? One man I talked to at the crater—I assume you know about that—said guns are fired less these days. If you've regularly used live ammo in the past, the Scabs would reach the same conclusion as me. Supplementing bullets with arrows says it all. I assume the government's allocation of stocks proved insufficient.'

Grey knew he'd struck home by Bella's pursed lips and Ben's reddening face. Irvine gave an almost imperceptible nod.

Bella stiffened, attempting to reassert control. 'We provided food, shelter, and security for survivors by creating a safe zone and compound for the farm. Scabs—an apt name the other survivors use—were tribal and chose ghettos over civilised behaviour. Gang wars regulated numbers, and newcomers were harshly dealt with. They're also not as bright as you have suggested.'

'Still doesn't tally.' Grey said. 'It all sounds too convenient.'

Bella weighed him up for several seconds before speaking.

'We trade,' she said sharply. 'It doesn't matter how. Just accept it as a fact.'

Grey wouldn't. 'You give them food and other supplies like tobacco in return for what?'

No one answered.

He changed tack. 'What about scavengers like Jen? They're neither Scabs nor your people. They have nothing to trade.' He narrowed his eyes. 'And yet you allow Jen to steal supplies. Why?'

Jen tugged his shirt. Ignoring the others, Grey leaned closer and whispered, 'It was too easy to access the storage shed. Let me finish.'

'You're a clever man,' Bella said, 'but I won't answer your question.'

'I'll answer it for you, then. My guess is your numbers have declined because of one major reason: the gene pool. Low birth numbers, high mortality rate and related illnesses. You would know all about the specifics, wouldn't you?'

Jen struggled to follow the conversation. 'What the hell's a jean pool'?'

No one responded.

Grey continued outlining his theory, ignoring Bella's tapping and icy stare.

'You need Scabs to generate new genes by breeding outside of your people. They provide girls of a 'certain age'— mostly taken from scavengers they've impregnated—in exchange for supplies. You monitored Jen for that purpose and ensured she was looked after when her mother disappeared. But you didn't count on Jane's demise. Making sense so far?'

Bella's cheeks flushed. Ben's fists tightened. Irvine looked away. Jen gasped and made to stand, her small fists clenched. Grey grasped her arm and squeezed lightly. 'Let it go, for now.'

She pulled, and he held firm. 'It won't help. Just let me finish.'

Her muscles relaxed a little then she dropped her head. 'Okay.'

'You were going to bring Jen in until I turned up—an unknown quantity. For some reason, I'm useful. Otherwise, you'd have tried to kill me.'

Ben growled. 'If I wanted you dead, you'd be dead.'

Grey smiled. The man's knuckles turned white. Bella put a hand on his arm, gripping the table with the other. Blue veins pushed through her paper skin.

'Like me to continue?' he asked, a hint of amusement in his tone.

The woman's eyes lanced through him when she nodded.

'You have a problem with the water supply.'

Irvine sat upright and looked at Bella. She flicked her head to one side as a 'go ahead.'

'Can I ask how you have come to this conclusion?'

'Jen told me the water has given her...'

'The shits,' Jen interrupted.

'The water was dirty, pressure almost non-existent. You're no longer able to control quality or quantity. Big problem, with people, livestock and crops to look after.'

Irvine blew out his cheeks at Grey's deduction.

'My guess is there's a reservoir that was used to generate hydroelectricity before the strike. However, it would be impossible to operate now without a lot of expertise. So, you have a small unit constructed by the government. And it no longer functions because there isn't enough water. Also, Jen's Dig had electricity until recently. My guess is that it was one of only a few places supplied, given your capacity. Most likely, the other Digs were used by people like Jane to protect your— investments.'

Grey didn't wait for a reaction. 'The vehicles outside aren't used anymore because there is no fuel. Yet you have a generator. I figure that is driven by methane from pig and hen manure.'

'It's crude,' Irvine confirmed. 'And we also have some solar panels, but there are still—err—a few problems without Jackson, our engineer. He...'

'We don't need to talk about that,' Bella cut in, then squinted at Grey. 'Anything else to add?' The sarcasm in her tone implied her patience was at an end.

'Actually, there is. When Jen asked if the meat was 'og and I said, 'human,' you all went quiet. Which begs the question—how do you provide nutrition for the livestock?'

It turned out to be the last straw. Bella slapped her hands on the table and shot up. 'Ben! Take them back to their room.'

'With pleasure.'

*

'Calm yourself,' Grey kept repeating to himself on the way to their cell. But once they reached the open door to their room, a Guarder pushed Jen hard through the opening—big mistake.

Grey slammed his head into the corner of the wall, breaking his nose with a loud crack. The other Guarder reacted slowly but managed a glancing blow with a baton on his injured shoulder. Grabbing the man's shoulders, he smashed his forehead into the surprised face, crumpling the Guarder to the ground. When he picked up the discarded weapon, ready to finish what he'd started, Jen grabbed his arm. 'No!'

Grey thought for a moment, then dropped the weapon. She was right. Killing the man would only make the reprisals worse. And there would be reprisals.

He joined Jen inside their room and closed the door. There was no point trying to escape. Other Guarders stationed inside the complex would only force them back.

Jen sat in silence, wringing her hands. She waited until he'd calmed, then quietly asked, 'Were they going to do that to me?'

There was no way for Grey to avoid the truth. 'Yes.'

'Why? I did them no harm. And Jane, why didn't she tell me?'

'She wasn't the woman you thought she was.'

He watched when tears dribbled down Jen's face but made no move to offer comfort.

Keep your distance.

Moments later, she sniffed and wiped a hand across her wet cheeks. 'They're animals, worse than the Scabs, and they deserve to die.'

'Yes, they do.'

*

The Guarders came soon after and bound Grey's hands.

One man held Jen down when she screamed to leave him alone. He had a hard time of it. She kicked and flailed whilst trying to sink her teeth into his arm. Curses and thumps to the door sounded behind when Grey was pushed down the corridor.

Three Guarders set about him with punches. Fighting back would be pointless, so he rolled to the floor and curled into a foetal position, waiting for it to end. He made no sound to show suffering, infuriating his attackers.

Ben's voice halted the onslaught. 'Leave him. He's had enough—for now.'

Grey sat up.

'Not so tough, eh?' The bear said.

'I've had worse. You didn't have the balls to try it alone, did you?'

He watched impassively when the man took a step, shaking with fury. Ben wanted to beat him senseless but couldn't because they needed him. Grey smiled inwardly, enjoying the psychological victory.

Red-faced, Ben turned away, thudded to the door and grasped the handle before turning back to look at his victim.

'You're a dead man.'

'Check the mirror if you want to see a dead man,' Grey retorted.

'Take him back to the room.' Ben growled to the Guarders.

When they threw him inside, Jen jumped up to help.

'It's okay. Looks worse than it is.'

Grey was taken by surprise when she tried to hug him. He held his hands up, rejecting the display of affection and eased her away.

'Why?' she asked, crestfallen.

He didn't know how to answer.

Jen thumped onto the bed. Part of him wanted to console her, but he ignored it. Showing concern would have unacceptable repercussions.

'Screw you,' She spat, then turned her back to him.

Grey assessed his injuries: right eye slightly swollen, cut on the head, bruises and minor abrasions. His ribs hurt, but a few pokes confirmed they were intact.

He dozed for a while, eventually rolling to face Jen, who stared across, her head resting on an arm. 'You didn't tell them the truth about who you are, did you?'

'They didn't ask. Just wanted a bit of payback. It's nothing I can't deal with.'

'You gonna tell me?'

'Tell you what?'

'Who you are.'

'No.'

'Didn't think so.'

Thirty minutes later, one Guarder held a pistol whilst another brought a tray of food and their cleaned old clothes into the room. Both of them turned away to dress.

They ate a meagre bowl of bland stew, lacking salt.

The door opened, and the same man entered. 'Push the tray towards the door.' When Grey reached for it, he barked, 'The girl, not you.'

'I'm not a girl, you dim'ead shit!'

*

In the morning, Jen yelled for a piss. Grey took the same opportunity to look for any potential escape routes. Nothing came to mind. Six identical locked rooms stretched down a long corridor, closed by two substantial doors. No ducting or windows offered a way out.

Overpowering the guards might be possible, but what then? Hostages? Grey had little faith Ben would care enough about his men to exchange. It didn't look good.

Early evening, after he and Jen had eaten, Guarders ushered him outside.

Bound and at gunpoint, they took him to an unfamiliar room. It was small, square, and furnished with a table and three chairs. Only Bella and Ben came in, clearly not a meeting suited to Irvine's demeanour.

The woman began. 'I decided to hear you out at our last meeting for two reasons: first, we wanted your cooperation, and second, it allowed me to understand who you were. Today, we get down to serious business. Though, our original intent has changed.'

Grey shrugged, feigning indifference.

'We had a specific offer. Join the Guarders and help with our gene pool. However, that is now impossible. For reasons I'm sure you understand.'

She paused and offered a self-satisfied smile. Ben winked at him.

Grey's clasped hands tightened.

Smug bastards.

'The next option is not as appealing for you as it is for Ben.'

Bella observed Grey.

'Get on with it,' he said.

'Yes, sir,' The bear answered with a mock salute.

'The Scabs abducted our engineer two months ago,' Bella continued. 'How is irrelevant.'

Grey glanced up at the ceiling, tired of the games. 'He looked after the water supply, and they persuaded him to divert the flow.'

'Correct. A message was delivered offering to exchange our engineer for some specific supplies. We were giving this due consideration because we would like him back. Now, we have an extra bargaining chip—you. One group of Scabs is larger and better organised than the others. We know they are recruiting new members, and your actions have humiliated them. A new message arrived last night. They want you rather badly. Probably as a trophy to re-establish their credibility.'

She paused, waiting for a reaction, but Grey bid his time.

'We would have ignored this before our meeting yesterday and focussed on their initial demands. However...' Bella shrugged and left the sentence unfinished.

'And what happens to Jen?'

'Oh, she will breed. But with just one partner.' Bella looked at Ben, the meaning clear.

Grey fought against the Rage for Jen's sake. Protecting her was his responsibility. For now, at least.

Not trusting himself to speak, he nodded.

Ben smirked.

'Good,' Bella said. 'It will take a few days to make the arrangements. You can stay with the girl. I suggest you keep our discussion to yourself.'

*

'What happened? What did they say?' Jen asked when the lock clicked shut.

'Nothing much,' Grey lied.

'Bullshit. I'm not dim'ead stupid. Tell me.'

'Like I said, nothing much.'

Jen jumped to her feet and started kicking the bed in frustration. 'You treat me like I'm some idiot kid.' Fists clenched, her head came forward like a snake preparing to strike. 'TELL ME!'

Knuckles rapped on the door. 'Quiet!'

'Fuck off!' Jen yelled back.

She maintained a death stare on Grey until he relented.

'Okay, I'll tell you what I know; just sit down and be quiet.'

He explained what they wanted him for, leaving out Bella's specific intentions for her.

Afterwards, Jen curled up on the bed and sobbed.

IRVINE

THE female Guarder who had coaxed Jen onto the horse brought uncooked vegetables and water for breakfast. She mouthed, 'Look,' when lowering the tray.

A short note from Irvine lay under a bowl.

It explained that he and the female Guarder, Annie, would help Grey and Jen escape and accompany them. He promised to reveal all once they were safe and detailed how it would happen.

Jen read the note carefully, reread it and asked the obvious question. 'Can we trust them?'

'What do you think?'

'Irvine seemed—sort of—okay.'

'My thoughts, too.'
'What about her?'
'No idea.'
'Do we have any choice?'
'No.'

*

They spent a frustrating day waiting for the evening.

After what seemed like an eternity, the light went out, plunging the room into darkness.

Grey listened at the door for the change of guards. He heard a muffled exchange between a woman and a man, then footsteps fading down the corridor. A thud from the remaining guard vibrated against the wall, followed by a key inserted into the lock.

Annie stood at the entrance. She indicated to follow, putting a finger to her lips for silence. The corridor was deserted except for a Guarder slumped on the floor, blood running from a deep gash on his head.

Grey shook his head when Annie offered a gun. She frowned before moving on.

At the fourth opening down, the woman ushered them into a room, closing the door gently. The window in front provided a glimmer of moonlight.

Annie took a quick look outside before gesturing to Grey. He could see the shape of a sentry standing close to the main entrance. No doubt another stood on the far side. Jen tried to elbow her way to the window, but he pushed her back.

'Fu...' She began to say until Grey hissed at her to stay quiet.

Annie reached into a corner and pulled out two bows, quivers and his handle. He raised an eyebrow.

'From the armoury,' she whispered.

The woman offered Grey a bow, then signalled to wait. He shook his head, pointing at himself. Annie looked at him momentarily, then agreed, holding out his handle and knife. He refused both.

Grey pushed the window open for a clearer view. Jen remained silent.

Annie tugged at his sleeve and mimicked a tote.

It took a while for the sentry to light up, at which point Grey slipped outside. He lay on the grass, embracing the building. The sentry stood next to the shrub border, his face alternating between darkness and an orange glow.

Grey snaked in shadow until he reached the shrub. As expected, another man stood on the far side.

He felt around and grasped a small stone, throwing it beyond the second Guarder. Both sentries froze and gripped their holstered handguns. The farthest indicated his eyes with two fingers and walked away.

Rising like a dark spectre, Grey grasped the remaining man's mouth, jerked his head and lowered the body.

The investigating sentry, focused on his task, heard nothing.

With a lunge, Grey grabbed him around the throat and held tight until his body sagged.

Annie brought his handle, and Jen followed behind. She led them to the generator shed a distance away, where Irvine waited inside.

'Over here,' he whispered, pointing to a flight of iron steps. He handed Grey his coat and canvas bag, then gave Jen an oversized black zip-up jacket.

Grey left his handle hidden by the generator. He would be coming back—alone.

Irvine flicked a switch at the bottom of the stairway to turn on flickering lights down a tunnel. At the end, an unlit pipe, some six feet in diameter, curved to the right. Irvine explained it led to the reservoir, half a mile away to the north.

Jen hadn't said a word since their departure. Grey sensed she was working up to something. 'You okay?'

She spoke without meeting his eyes, 'You're going back, aren't you?'

'Yes. Once you're safe.'

Irvine looked over in alarm.

'Something to deal with.'

The agronomist was about to protest when Annie put her hand on his. 'I'd be going with him, but I need to protect you and Jen whilst he's gone—or doesn't come back.'

'You better come back.' Jen hissed.

Despite the anger, Grey could tell she was trying to hold back tears.

Irvine looked from her to him, back again, and sighed. 'I suppose I should have expected this.'

Jen strode into the opening without a word.

Eventually, the agronomist brought them to a halt. 'We're getting close to the pump room. Need to be as quiet as possible. Scabs will guard the place. They'll need to be—err—dealt with.'

A hundred paces later, he held up his hand.

Grey drew an arrow and edged around a corner.

At the end was a dimly lit dome of steel. From the centre a small pipe curved to the floor, releasing a stream of water. Barely enough to maintain the flow to the city.

Attached to a gantry, a rusty ladder disappeared into a circular opening above. One Scab sat on a chair next to it, snoozing.

Grey sent an arrow into his neck to stop him screaming.

Irvine retched at the sight.

Looking up the ladder, a faint circle of light appeared far above. Grey breathed a sigh of relief when he realised the dying man's groans were unlikely to travel that far up.

He climbed, the bow and quiver around his body, knife between his teeth. At the top, he stopped below the exit, then risked a quick look over the edge.

Two men, forty paces away, talked animatedly. One leaned against the wall. The other faced a wall of pipes, circular wheels and dials.

Grey signalled Annie ten feet below with his fingers to show distance.

The Scab next to the door began searching his pockets for something. Grey took the distraction and slid out of the hole, moving behind a lip in the wall.

His only option was to notch the arrow and fire whilst running. The first Scab took a shot through the shoulder. The second bolted, Annie, sprinting after him.

Grey wasted valuable seconds dispatching the Scab he'd downed before chasing after her.

Annie dived and grasped the man's ankle. A moment later, she straddled him, her knife pressed against his throat.

'One chance,' she hissed.

The Scab didn't need further prompting.

'Two more—sleeping—down there.' His wide eyes signalled the direction.

Annie thumped the knife's pommel into the man's temple.

At the passageway's end, Grey sneaked around the corner to two adjacent doors lining one wall. He crept to the first, opened it carefully and listened—no sound of breathing.

Stereo snoring and snuffles came from the second, which was slightly ajar.

He whispered instructions to Annie.

She shot her nominated target through the side. Grey wasn't interested in leniency when he fired an arrow.

Annie took deep breaths to regain her composure, then looked at Grey and stepped back. The Rage was frightening for anyone to witness—cold-blooded, emotionless efficiency without compromise.

He knew she would be asking herself who the hell he was? What he was?

Irvine looked ashen from the carnage, unable to control his trembling hands. Jen calmed him without looking at Grey.

They exited through a bolted iron door set beneath a small hillock.

Annie pointed to a rowboat further along the shore. Irvine appeared worried at the prospect.

'What's on the far side?' Grey asked.

'Small building. Pipework inside.'

'Occupied?'

'Never seen anyone before.'

'Wait for me there. If I'm not back by dawn, make your own decisions. Look after Jen—and Irvine,' he added as an afterthought.

When Grey put a hand on Jen's shoulder, she shrugged it off.

'See you soon,' he whispered.

*

Annie had explained where Bella and Ben slept. Grey figured there was enough time to reach the compound and find them before the sentries changed. Taking the pair out in bed didn't have the same appeal as a confrontation—especially with the big man. But there was no other option. A noisy fight would alert Guarders.

Grey reached the top of the stairway to the generator shed and waited for his eyes to acclimatise in the darkness. A gun clicked to his right.

'Stay where you are, dead man,' said Teethmarks.

A light flickered on, revealing three other Guarders holding batons. Bella and Ben stood to one side.

'Well, well,' the bear said, 'Look who we have here—thought you might return to the party. Didn't realise the sentries change in the early hours, eh? The man gave a self-congratulatory grin.

Bella glared with pure hatred in her eyes.

Grey smiled. He'd got his wish for a fight, after all.

The odds were against an ordinary man facing this number of adversaries. But he was no ordinary man. It was time to let them see his other self.

He savoured the heat coursing through his veins as the Rage built inside. His cold eyes focussed on Ben whilst his mind processed the Guarders' positions. Slow, deep breaths relaxed his tight muscles in preparation for action. Only extreme violence would satisfy the fury he felt towards these bastards.

One Guarder walked past Teethmarks and delivered a baton blow to the back of Grey's legs. He fell, using his hands to stave off kissing the floor. A second thump took him across the back, the quiver absorbing some of the blow.

Ben waved the henchmen back to stand beside him and gave a cruel laugh, cut short when Grey pushed himself upright. Two of the men glanced at each other. No one should have been able to stand after blows like that.

When Grey smirked, Ben lost control and surged, aiming a meaty fist. He didn't connect; his arm was deflected, followed by a straight punch to the solar plexus.

Before Ben could double up, Grey grabbed him by the shoulder and spun him around to face the others. Teethmarks couldn't get a line of sight, his pistol wavering from side to side.

Bella screamed, 'Kill him!'

With all his strength, Grey launched Ben at Teethmarks, who took the bear's weight head-on. His hands lifted in an involuntary response when Grey followed the momentum. At the last second, he twisted to the side, wrenching the henchman's arm back to dislocate the shoulder. The gun skittered across the floor towards the stairwell.

He pushed the writhing Teethmarks onto the floor, dived for the generator and grabbed his handle. Holding it at his side, he turned and faced the other three Guarders, who stood motionless in shock.

Bella crept towards where the pistol lay.

'Don't,' Grey hissed, 'If you want to live.'

Ben got to his feet, breathing hard, and undid the strap on a sheath to lift the bone-handled knife. Then he and his three henchmen spread out into a wide semi-circle whilst Bella backed away.

Grey feigned an attack on the man to his right, who stepped back a pace, then swerved to another on his left. An audible crack came when the handle landed.

Before the others could take the initiative, Grey ran for the stairway, shouldering Bella to send her to the floor. He spun, lunged at the approaching Guarders, twisted to the left and struck one across his thighs.

The last henchman halted mid-stride, looking ready to run, but Ben grabbed him by the arm and catapulted him at Grey, who sidestepped, grabbed the man's shoulders and hurled him into the generator. A heavy thump, then silence followed.

'Just me and you now, Ben. Not what you expected—eh?'

The bear gripped his knife.

Grey threw his handle to the side. 'Let's make this easier for you.'

This time, Ben kept his control and began circling. He faked a few swipes and then launched an attack, swishing his blade. Grey grabbed his thick wrist and sent an elbow crashing into his exposed nose. The knife and Ben dropped to the floor.

Knealing on his chest, Grey used one hand to grip the throat, and plunged the knife deep into the bear's groin. Ben bucked and thrashed, red in the face, until the frenzy subsided.

'That's for the girls.'

Meanwhile, Teethmarks was trying to drag himself to the exit. Grey walked over and placed his foot at the base of the man's neck. With both hands, he grabbed the head, and jerked it back.

When he turned to Bella, she held the gun in shaking hands.

'You—you—bastard,' she hissed, then pulled the trigger.

The bullet took Grey in the side, spinning his body to the floor. He peered down at the wound, then at Bella, pushed himself to his feet, and staggered towards her. She fired once more, but panic sent the bullet wide.

The woman had no time to shoot again. Grey clamped his hand over hers, still holding the gun, and pushed it to her head.

His cold eyes bore into Bella's.

'Here's my offer. Either I deliver you to the Scabs, who I know will enjoy your company, or...' He jerked his chin at the gun.

'No, please.'

'Yes, please.'

'But...'

'No buts. A promise is a promise.'

Bella closed her eyes and fingered the trigger. Grey exherted pressure to complete his demand.

He gripped the stairway's rail to steady himself. Shouts sounded from farther down the compound. Heading down the tunnel was out of the question. They would catch him once the Rage subsided and the pain took over.

After a long moment, Grey searched a Guarder's pocket and found a box of matches.

He unscrewed a cap on the generator, tore a long strip of fabric from one man's shirt and inserted it. Once it flamed, he made for the shed door.

The livestock pens seemed a good place to go while the men tackled the fire which would soon be visible. Gritting his teeth, Grey pressed onto his wound and moved cautiously.

He stopped at one of the pen's corner posts, breathing hard. Hiding inside with the pigs was too dangerous because they'd smell his blood and attack. The hens would panic and squawk if he went near them, so that, too, wasn't an option. He'd have to go straight for the horses.

The stables would have at least one sentry nearby for security. Grey had a plan for that.

Near the building, he sat against a stack of pallets. His wound still bled and hurt like hell. If it wasn't tightly bound soon, he might pass out. He needed to reassert the Rage to survive. He thought about Jen and Bella's intentions for her. He thought about the Scabs supplying young girls. He thought about the scavengers desperate for food. His anger grew.

Grey screwed his eyes, clamped his jaw and pressed hard on the wound. The agony was followed by a surge of heat when the Rage took over.

Only one Guarder waited at the stables. Fixated on the glow in the distance, he heard nothing until it was too late. A tap on the shoulder turned his head, exposing his neck on one side. The man's eyes shot open when he saw the flash of a blade.

Soon after, Grey wore the Guarder's khaki shirt and trousers over his own clothes.

At the gates, a sentry peered into the gloom at the sound of hooves.

'Been told to bring the horses here,' a shadowy figure said.

'Why only four?'

'No idea. Ben's orders. You know what he's like when he's questioned.'

The sentry fingered his gun, unsure about what he'd heard. 'What's going on over there,' he asked, pointing at the glow.

'Hay caught alight near the generator shed. Probably some idiot smoking nearby.'

Grey closed the gap. He chuckled. 'Talking of fire, you got a tote?'

For a moment, the man squinted at him, then shrugged. He rummaged in his trousers, took out a tin and flicked the lid open. 'Here.'

When he struck a match and lit the tote in Grey's mouth, he frowned. 'Not seen you before. Hold on a minute, you're the pri…'

Before the Guarder could finish, the tote jabbed into his eye. He lurched back, holding his hands to his face. A knife in the ribs sent his body to the ground.

Grey cut a length of the dead man's shirt and bound his wound, grimacing when it tightened.

Outside the gates, he struggled to mount a horse. When he finally pulled himself up, he leaned his head on the mane, trying to summon more strength. If he didn't get to the reservoir soon, it was game over.

GOODBYE

ANNIE scanned the surroundings, trying to determine which direction the sounds came from.

'We need to run,' she said, 'They'll be here soon.'

Irvine's head turned from side to side, frantically trying to decide on a route. Jen stood motionless, staring into the distance.

'No,' she said. 'We don't.'

Moments later, a wraith-like form on a horse emerged out of the dark with three others tethered alongside.

Jen reached Grey just as his body tumbled to the ground.

*

When he awoke, his side wound had been properly bound. Annie and Jen were nowhere in sight, but Irvine sat close by. He handed Grey a flask of water, which he gulped, ignoring the rivulets down his chin.

'Where are the other two?'

'Annie's gone to the far side of the reservoir to check for signs of pursuit. Wants to get moving as soon as possible. Jen's having a walkabout. I told her not to stray far, though.'

'How long have I been out?' Grey asked.

'Not long. Annie cauterised the wound and stitched you up. Fortunately, the bullet went straight through. How you're not in agony is beyond me.'

Grey knew why. Jen must have given him Juice.

Running feet sounded behind. His sharp intake of breath made her let go when she threw her arms around him.

'Sorry,' Jen said, then paused. 'If you do anything like that again, I'll cut your balls off.'

She smiled. Grey smiled back, though inside, he wasn't happy. The girl had become too dependent on him. It needed to stop.

Annie returned soon after, a little out of breath. 'Couldn't make out any sign of movement overland.'

'They'll be busy deciding who should fill the vacancies,' Grey said.

Jen's eyes lit up, wanting to hear all the details. When he refused to reveal anything, she sulked.

'There's a small storage facility two hour's ride from here,' Annie explained. 'It's where we—they—kept basic supplies for emergencies on scouting trips. We can camp nearby. The cover's not ideal, so someone will need to keep watch. Plans can wait until we get there.'

'Sounds good,' Grey agreed.

They arrived at the facility an hour later.

It wasn't a building, just a small underground bunker accessed by a metal grate.

Annie passed a few bulging sacks and an army-stamped metal box to a breathless Irvine. The sacks contained blankets, the box held dried meat and water.

They secured the horses, unrolled blankets, and ate. Grey lay on his back whilst the others sat around.

No one spoke for a while until Jen demanded Irvine tell all.

He nodded and adjusted his glasses. 'I was a Council member along with Bella, Ben, and Jackson, the engineer. There were others at the beginning, but they died of one thing or another. Everything progressed well until about three years ago when several things happened. First, there was a typhoid outbreak. We didn't have enough antibiotics left, so many people died.'

Jen cut in. 'What's typhoid and antishit?'

'Illness and medicine,' Grey said, shaking his head when she nodded sagely.

'Ahem.' Irvine cleared his throat loudly, a little impatient. 'As I was saying. Second, population numbers were declining for the reasons Grey identified. The problem increased after the typhoid. Around the same time, Scab numbers began to grow.

'So, you made a deal with them.'

'Exactly. Some joined the workforce, which was problematic, while others remained outside the Station. We gave them food and other supplies as a reward for keeping newcomers out. Saved Ben the trouble.'

'There weren't enough of us,' Annie corrected.

'Quite. The last part of the arrangement was the breeding program. I'd prefer not to dwell on that.'

'Jeans,' Jen chipped in. 'Like Grey said—the jean pool thing.'

'Well—yes.' Irvine seemed uncomfortable that she'd understood. 'Contrary to what Bella and Ben said, there was a leadership of sorts within the Scabs, so it was relatively straightforward to strike a deal. Until recently, that is.' He turned to look at Annie.

She nodded and picked up the explanation. 'Guarders took out key people from time to time whenever Ben felt they were growing too powerful. We made it look like the work of another Scab group to avoid repercussions. Of late, there was intel—Guarder speak for information, Jen—about an unknown force attempting to merge the Scabs. It was easier because they were becoming disillusioned with the deal. Particularly since the amount of food had declined.'

'A lean year with the crops,' Irvine interrupted.

'They abducted Jackson, the engineer,' Annie said, 'and forced him to divert the water flow to force the Council back to the negotiating table. We tried to take back the facility through the tunnel, but it proved impossible with so many Scabs waiting for us. Guarders were slaughtered in the confined space. Ben saw it as a move towards a takeover. He assured us he had a plan. I wasn't convinced.'

'That why you decide to leave?' Grey asked.

Annie played with a stone, and mumbled, 'Not just that.'

Irvine took over, leaving the woman to her thoughts. 'I'd had enough of it all. Bella and Ben made decisions irrespective of my opinion. Jackson was too weak to stand up to them.'

He went quiet, adjusted his glasses, then sighed, 'I suppose I was just as guilty. Scared of them, you see. The final straw came a year ago when they began feeding the dead to the pigs. Scabs supplied most of the bodies. Some people protested whilst others took a fatalistic view. Everyone seemed to accept it in the end. Maybe there was a bit of persuasion from Ben's closest men. Who knows? I was against it, of course.'

Grey picked up his worry that they would think badly of him. Before he could reassure the man, Jen interjected.

'Shit! I ate some of them 'ogs. Must have eaten humans, too. I'm gonna puke.'

Irvine smiled at her comment. 'I wanted to get away. Didn't know how—or how to survive beyond the city. But then Annie and I got together and started making plans.'

He turned, hoping she would take up the story. She shook her head. Irvine fidgeted, seemingly uncomfortable about what came next.

'Ben had a—err—insatiable appetite for women. Are you sure this is okay, Annie?'

'Carry on. I can handle it.'

'Okay.' After a pause, Irvine continued, 'Those that didn't agree to his demands were—encouraged.' Annie avoided his attention until recently. It was worse for her because...'

She took up the story to save Irvine's obvious embarrassment. 'I prefer the opposite sex.'.

'What?' Jen asked, wide-eyed.

'Leave it,' Grey said sharply.

'But—'

'Leave it!'

Irvine cleared his throat. 'I found Annie in tears one evening. She'd had a bad ...' He trailed off and looked at her with open hands, desperate for help.

'The ugly bastard tried to force the issue, but fortunately, I held him off. After that, Irvine and I decided we wanted to leave.'

'Why include me and Jen?' Grey asked.

'Oh, that was easy,' Irvine replied perkily. 'It wasn't hard to see your animosity towards Bella and Ben, and I knew you would never let that man, you know...' His meaningful glance at Jen finished the sentence.

She glared at Grey. 'So that's why you told me shit all.'

He nodded.

Grey asked Irvine about other facilities like the Station and why they hadn't joined forces.

'Ah. Now that's another story. Initially, there were forty secret bunkers across the country—food, stores and arms in case there was a nuclear war, as Bella said. The plan was to bring everyone together over time and restore society. Most people didn't survive for reasons you know. They also had to contend with groups of outsiders, just like us. But we had Ben's father, and he was a good man. Strong, fair and damned clever. Maybe Ben could have been like that if Bella hadn't got her claws into him.'

'No way.' Annie snapped.

'Anyway. Telecoms degraded. Occasionally, messengers travelled between sites, but most disappeared without a trace. The Council—Bella and Ben—cut all contact with other facilities. To avoid, as she put it, 'being seen on the radar.' Although I have wondered whether she was protecting her little empire.'

Irvine raised both arms in the air for dramatic effect. 'So, there's your story, Jen.'

'And your plans now?' Grey asked.

'Good. I'm glad you asked that. We're heading to the last facility we had contact with—on the coast, west of here. Their prospects will be good if they've survived because of the fishing. With food so plentiful, they may have avoided the likes of Scabs. Bound to find decent people around. That's right, isn't it, Annie?'

'Probably,' she answered noncommittally.

'Getting there will be a bit of a trek. But with your help, it will be easier.'

Irvine smiled at Grey and nodded expectantly. His optimistic expression slipped when nothing came back. At a loss, the agronomist turned to Annie for help. She gave him a 'don't look at me' shrug.

'Well, maybe we should sleep on it first. I appreciate that you might need time to think about it.'

Grey nodded.

*

The following day, Jen awoke and peered around to see what the others were doing. Irvine and Annie stood together, gazing into the distance.

'Where's Grey?'

Annie turned and said softly, 'Sorry, he's gone.'

Jen glanced from her to Irvine, hoping it might be a joke. Their expressions told her it wasn't.

'No!' She jumped up and scanned the horizon. Seeing nothing, she sprinted, arms pumping until her breath gave out.

After a few moments, Jen ran in a different direction, her head swivelling, frantically searching for signs of Grey.

Then the yelling started. Every swear word she knew came out in a torrent of abuse.

Spent, she dropped to her knees and sobbed.

Annie came over. 'Come on, we've got to go.'

Jen shrugged off the arm around her shoulders and ran back to the camp.

When she started berating Irvine, the former Guarder restrained her. Jen kicked and twisted against the arms grasped around her chest. Annie held on until she slumped in submission.

Irvine tried distraction. He took a tattered piece of paper from his pocket and spoke in a cheerful tone. 'Here, Jen, look, I've got a map, and this is where we're going.'

'Fuck off.'

*

Grey sat against a pile of boulders too far away from the others for Jen to spot him. He knew leaving was the right decision for them both. She would be better off around people who didn't have Rage inside them. But guilt disagreed.

'You're a worthless piece of shit. Always were, always will be,' he said to himself.

PURSUIT

AFTER a small sip of Juice, Grey mounted up.

Two hours into the ride, the outline of hills on the horizon caught his attention. Shelter from the wind, maybe decent grass and water for the horse.

Mid-afternoon, his mount stumbled on its right leg. Rubbing from the fetlock to the knee revealed nothing, but soon after, the horse began limping. Not enough for serious concern, but too much for a canter. Which wasn't a bad thing in itself because his wound throbbed from jolting.

At the hills, he led the horse along a narrow path, winding up through loose shale. The limp hadn't worsened, but the animal was exhausted, and he wasn't far behind.

Ragged cliffs curtained the edge of one rise, providing a good vantage point and somewhere to rest.

He tethered his horse to a thin tree stump surrounded by sparse grass and sat close by, watching the horizon. In the far distance, what looked like a tiny dust cloud materialised. Guarders were heading this way, and they'd be at the hills before sunset.

Riding wasn't an option, nor was a direct fight if there were a number of riders. What to do?

*

Guarders had spotted the horses' trails near the storage bunker.

'Gottya!' The leader growled.

One set of hoof prints headed north, and three went west. Grey had to be the lone rider, trying to lead them away from the others.

No one ever used the leader's real name. They knew him as Chance on account of his 'to hell with it' reputation. Fearless and violent in the extreme, Ben had put the man in charge of scouting.

Chance looked like a pit bull. Squat, muscled, and bald, with black eyes and a crooked nose broken more than once.

He had surveyed the carnage back in the burned-out shed, a smile on his thin lips. Chance by name, Chance by nature. An opportunity to take over as Council leader. Like Ben, he was a scary SOB, and no one would have the guts to challenge him.

The first task was to restore order; the second to capture the dick who caused chaos. He needed Grey as a token to cement his position.

Chance scratched his head, thinking about his quarry's options. There were two landmarks: a line of hills and a river a long way beyond. High ground would be a good place to rest after a gruelling chase. The river wouldn't be visible from the hills, but if Grey got there, he'd follow it, hoping there might be a settlement somewhere farther along. Whether he chose to go up or downriver was anyone's guess. They had to catch him before that.

Chance decided to make straight for the hills, assuming Grey would rest there. Of course, he'd see them coming, but one man against so many couldn't stand for long. The shit could decide to make a run for it in the dark, though. In which case, several men needed to make a detour and get behind him.

'You three,' Chance said, go wide, then wait on the far side of the hills in case Grey tries to escape in the dark. The rest of us will ride slower to give them time to get ahead.'

The Pit Bull brought the Guarders to a halt at the bottom of two interlocking hills where the remains of a worn pathway snaked in between. He looked around for a place to camp, deciding on a flat area near a line of mossy rocks.

'Reckon he's on the ridge watching us?' One man asked.

'Got to be. If he makes a break for it tonight, our men over the hills will stop him. If not, we'll catch him in the morning. You four take the first watch. Sal, get a fire and food going. Woman's work, eh?'

'Up yours,' she retorted.

*

Grey lay on his stomach and watched between two rocks. Fifteen Guarders plus the leader. He looked like a mean bastard by his stature alone. When he stood by four men and pointed, they each took sentry positions around the camp. A woman set about making a fire whilst the rest cleared sleeping areas and laid out bedrolls. No slacking or back-chat. The stumpy, muscled leader clearly wasn't a man to be messed about.

He was smart, too, making camp for the night. An idiot would try to get the fugitive in the dark with no guarantee of success—and lose men in the process. Which meant Grey had the advantage of time for the the moment.

Two choices presented themselves. First, make a run for it, which would be problematic for his horse until it was rested. And he didn't know what lay beyond the hills. Second, take out some of the men to lessen the force against him. He decided on the latter.

He waited until nightfall and crawled to the first sentry a distance away from the camp. The man was sitting on a large boulder when the handle crossed his throat, pulled him onto the rock and cut off his air supply.

It was too risky to circle the camp for the other sentries, so Grey decided on a sleeping Guarder. A knife in the back caused him to thrash and yell.

The commotion brought everyone to their feet, shouting, cursing, and running about in confusion. As expected, the Guarders didn't sleep for the rest of the night. Tired and edgy men made mistakes.

Dawn crept over the ridge, bringing a boulder rolling down the slope. Displaced shale swished to the side, distracting Grey's pursuers.

Soon after, an arrow lanced into a Guarder. Another hit the man next to him.

Bullets pinged off rocks in the general direction of fire.

'Stop shooting you dickheads. You're wasting ammo,' the leader yelled.

Grey ran behind a line of toothed rocks and then stopped to see what happened next. The Guarders had come together to receive orders. Another smart move by the leader. He knew his quarry wouldn't be stupid enough to hang around. He'd have an escape route. Which Grey did.

A vertical seam up the cliffs lay half in shadow. Edging inside, he climbed. There were solid hand and foot holds, but reaching up sent waves of agony across his waist.

By the time he made the top, sweat ran down his face, and his arms trembled. He lay on his back to gulp air, then looked below. Most of the Guarders were readying themselves to ride.

Three men remained in place in case he turned back towards the reservoir. The rest split into two groups to find another route to climb on horseback.

There was no time to lose if Grey was to reach the far side of the hills and put distance between him and the Guarders. After that, he'd just have to hope there was somewhere farther on to lose them.

At the last rise, his senses picked something up. Men were waiting in ambush. The leader must have anticipated Grey's direction and sent Guarders wide. Yet again, the man had proved his worth. But every negative had a positive. In this case stealing a fresh horse with no impediment.

Grey slapped his mount's rump and sent it down the hill. As he thought, when it neared the base, two men emerged from beneath a ledge. They'd spend a while discussing whether the fugitive had been captured or killed on hills.

Only a few sips of Juice remained in the flask. The question was whether to take some now or wait. No, best to wait. Grey looked around for a way to get the Guarders. To the right, he spotted a V-shaped dip running to the bottom. He edged across, keeping out of sight, then slid down inside. Pain sent needles into his wound, leaving no choice but to change his mind about taking some Juice.

Once at the base, he crouched behind a rock, assessing how to reach three horses. Three? Where was the other man? Grey closed his eyes, trying to sense him. There. Farther to the left.

Killing the Guarder would be easy with an arrow. But if the shot wasn't accurate, the man could scream. It had to be the knife.

Grey lay on his stomach and wriggled towards his target. Regardless of the Juice, each movement brought a sharp intake of breath. Eventually, he reached a rock where the Guarder crouched on the other side. A flick of a pebble brought him around the side, gun in hand.

When his head poked over a ledge, Grey's knife came up under his chin. Now for the horses. It needed a touch-and-go sprint to get there before the remaining men had a chance to react. Fortunately, they were still talking. Unfortunately, one of them held a rifle.

Grey made it to the nearest horse and mounted with a gasp. Heeling one of the others startled the animal, which sent it running away, followed by the rest. He used them for cover when his mount took off.

Fifty yards on firing started. Bullets missed, sending puffs of dust from the ground. Then one from the rifle didn't, taking Grey in the thigh.

He slapped the reigns on the horse's shoulder, kicked with one leg, leaned his head over one side of the neck and galloped.

More shots followed, none reaching their target. They ceased when Grey was out of range. But it would only be temporary. The Guarders would eventually catch their mounts and give chase, soon to be joined by the rest of his pursuers.

An hour or so into the ride, the two men remained a distance behind. To their rear, a dust cloud said the leader and his group were close behind.

Some way ahead, trees spread in a line far into the distance, suggesting a riverbank. If Grey could get there, it might provide an opportunity to escape. Which he desperately needed because his mount was struggling.

When the bank drew near, he drew in the reins. There was no choice but to slip into the fast-flowing river to avoid more shots. Grey considered his weapons and cursed—taking them along would impede progress. For a moment, he reconsidered taking the bow, then decided against it after taking a second look at the turbulent flow swirling against old tree trunks.

He swam around obstacles, crashed into others, and fought through whorls.

After what seemed like forever, he grasped a fallen log and hauled himself to the far side. Thick roots, anchored to the bank, offered temporary shelter. A sip of Juice, deep breaths and long exhales allowed him to think his situation through.

Grey knew he wouldn't make it far on foot without being caught. His only opportunity meant stealing a horse if the group split up to search the river.

*

Chance brought the Guarders to the bank and scoured the ground. Blood on the ground said Grey had taken a shot.

The Pit Bull narrowed his eyes. 'He's around here somewhere. Spread out and search the water for signs. Ride nice and slow. Nowhere far the shit can go with a wound. And he doesn't have a bow. Find him.'

*

Grey lay hidden behind a fallen tree, watching a Guarder scanning the area. Spotting tracks in the mud, he stopped. A well-disciplined soldier would call for the others; a fool would dismount and follow on foot, looking for glory. Grey counted on the latter, and he was right. He took the last of the Juice.

The Guarder cocked his gun and jumped from the horse, then followed the prints, stopping every few paces to look around.

Grey slid from behind the trunk and waited for the man to halt. A solitary boot poked out of the mud, too compelling to ignore. When the fool crouched down to inspect it, he got a surprise.

The gun was whipped out of his hand, followed by an arm around his throat and a knife lancing into his side. A minute later, the Guarder's writhing stilled.

After pushing the body under an overhang, Grey wiped the blade and slid his foot into his wet boot. Taking the dead man's gun, he hid once more to await the next rider, who turned out to be a woman.

Grey pointed the gun. 'Drop your bow and get off the horse—slowly.' She complied, making no move to resist.

'What's your name?'

'Why?'

'Name.'

'Sal.'

'Lucky for you, Sal, I try not to kill women,' he said before rocketing a blow to her jaw.

Grey looked at the gun in his hand, deciding whether to keep it. He rejected the option for personal reasons, threw the weapon into the river, picked up the woman's bow and mounted her horse. He considered taking out more men but decided against it. Better to get as far away as possible before the others came after him. Which they would. This time, however, he'd be better prepared.

*

Two Guarders helped Sal to her feet. Chance strode over, his face a mask of fury, and punched her hard in the stomach.

'Useless bitch.'

He brought the group together once they reached the last man, waiting farther down the river. The missing Guarder was already history in Chance's mind.

'He'll likely head for the village given his tracks go in that direction. Only place around to hide.'

*

Grey spotted the village late evening. He avoided the main thoroughfare and came in from a side street, glad to see houses still standing. After easing down from the horse, he tied it to a lamppost. Riding had widened the leg wound, causing him to limp. Thankfully, the one in his side remained closed, though it still hurt like hell.

The only sign of life was an orange glow from one house. Grey waited for the watcher he sensed to show, counting on curiosity rather than malicious intent.

'I've got a gun,' a man said from the shadows.

Grey dropped his bow and put his arms in the air. 'Only want to talk.'

'Just go, and you won't get hurt.'

The tremor in the stranger's voice tipped Grey off to his bluff. 'You don't have a gun.'

'We've got nothing worth taking.' A woman's voice.

'I need help.'

'What kind of help?'

'Bullet wound.'

'I knew he'd bring trouble,' the man said, talking faster.

The woman appeared and gave Grey a once over, her eyes resting on his bloodied trousers.

'Follow me.'

Sat around a fire the couple introduced themselves as Ruth and Robert. Both were in their seventies. He looked like he'd snap in a strong wind, but she had the resilience of a younger woman.

Ruth set to work stitching the wound with a darning needle and thick cotton thread. Robert winced each time the point went in. Grey gritted his teeth until it was over.

'Thank you.'

The woman nodded in response.

'Robert. Bring some bowls and spoons.'

The man trudged into the kitchen without a word.

Grey thought about leaving straight away, then changed his mind. The Guarders would likely wait until morning to begin searching. Moving in the dark would be too risky now he had a bow.

Ruth ladled rabbit stew from a pot on the fire into the bowls. 'Only thing alive around here. Well, apart from us.' She smiled at her joke.

'Snares,' Robert added.

Grey took a sip. 'Tastes good.'

'We survive on our wits,' the old man said with pride.

His wife laughed. 'You mean like threatening someone with a gun you don't have? It's more likely to get you shot.'

'She's right,' Grey added.

Ruth explained they were the only people in town, although it was more of a large village, in her opinion. Everyone else had moved on in search of something better. She and Robert stayed behind, convinced a long journey would prove too arduous because they had no horse.

'Besides,' she said, 'We've lived here our whole married life, always intending this to be our final resting place. And aside from a group who pass by occasionally, we're on our own. We keep out of their way, and they leave us be.'

'Do the men look like soldiers?'

'Yes. It gives us a sense of security when they are in the area.'

Ruth frowned and met his eyes. Grey wasn't surprised; the woman was smart. It wouldn't be difficult for her to conclude his question meant something. But she said nothing and allowed her husband to ramble about his gardening prowess.

Grey waited for a lull in the conversation to explain about the men coming for him.

'What?' Robert exclaimed in alarm.

His wife placed a calming hand on his arm. 'Let's hear him out.'

'Do the soldiers know where you live?'

Robert shuffled. 'Maybe.'

When Ruth asked why the men were after him, Grey edited the story, leaving out the more disturbing aspects.

'You think they'll hurt us?' She asked.

'No. It's only me they are after.'

'Try to keep them away from this side of town.'

'I'll do my best. Put out the fire and stay inside so you don't draw attention. Whatever happens, it will be over soon.'

Grey departed, leaving Robert ashen, and Ruth sat stiffly.

It took five minutes to reach the far end of the town and five more to find a vantage point for the forthcoming fight.

*

Chance's group waited for sunrise before approaching the town. It had been almost too easy following Grey. Clear tracks and the occasional blood trail kept him on the scent.

He stopped at the edge of the street, raised a hand to halt, and then waited.

'Leave or die.' Grey shouted.

'Screw you.'

'Your choice.'

The voice came from high up, drawing Chance's eyes.

'Lower your gun, Stevie, you retard. He's not stupid enough to show. You two go to the far end of the village and work your way back on foot. Move slowly and keep out of sight. Grey will see you leave and know why, but it'll split his attention.'

An arrow whistled from a rooftop, throwing a Guarder to the ground. A second took another in the shoulder. The others dived behind their horses and glanced nervously around.

'Back off, out of range,' Chance ordered.

He scratched his chin in thought, then sent two more men arcing around Grey's position. 'He'll have no choice but to move. It will be cat and mouse, but he'll eventually slip up, and we'll nail him.

*

Grey had already considered his next move. Fighting at ground level would be suicide. Better to stay on the rooftops and pick off Guarders one by one. There were still risks, not least of which was traversing the precarious roofline. Men could get to him but detecting them with his senses would be easier.

First, though, he had to kill the men the leader had sent around his position. He didn't have to wait long.

One Guarder stood and took aim from behind a flat roof. An arrow hit him in the chest before he could fire. The second made it within twenty yards before Grey sensed him. He wormed to the left, crouched behind a chimney stack and scraped a tile against the brickwork. The noise sent the Guarder to his knees, waving his gun side to side. Now, it was a waiting game.

Sure enough, the man made his way closer to Grey's position. Seconds later, a sharp blade found his throat. A spontaneous shot reverberated across the roofs before the man's breathing subsided.

With no time to lose, Grey backed away and headed towards the town centre.

A shout came from the street below. 'Only a matter of time before you die.'

Answering was pointless.

When Grey regained a clear line of sight, the scene below twisted his gut.

Ruth and Robert stood beside the stocky leader, holding a gun at his side. The first men he'd sent had found them.

'Your move, Grey.'

Silence.

'Need some persuasion, eh?' A punch thumped into Robert's chest, knocking him to the floor, where he hunched up, wheezing.

'Don't hurt him anymore,' Ruth pleaded.

'You hear that?'

Grey was thinking fast and trying to decide how best to save the couple.

'Too late!'

A shot ended Robert's life.

Ruth screamed, pulled away from the Guarder, and fell at her husband's side. The leader's weapon tracked her head.

Common sense evaporated, and the Rage took over. Grey stood, prepared to let loose a volley of arrows, when Sal, the woman he'd knocked out, levelled a new bow.

Guarders froze.

'Drop the gun, Chance, and move away,' she said.

'You won't.'

'I will, you piece of shit.'

Everything happened at once. Grey saw Chance lower the gun and then run towards a building, dodging from side to side. Two Guarders followed close behind. Sal's arrow missed the leader's back by a fraction. Grey put one through another below. Sal swung her bow and hit a man in the thigh when he raised a gun. When he fell, she grabbed Ruth and hauled her to an open door.

A scrawny-looking man raised his arms in surrender. Grey shot him in the chest, turned and put a second arrow into the Guarder Sal had downed.

Everything went quiet. Only the hush of a breeze sounded, flicking the dead men's hair.

Grey rested for a moment to clear the image of Robert from his mind. He moved silently across the roof to where Chance hid, knowing a frontal assault from street level wouldn't work.

All three men spun around when the rafters erupted, and Grey crashed into the room amidst a cascade of debris and dust. One Guarder raised his arms to fend off falling wood before a knife swept across the side of his neck. A second swung his gun from side to side, trying to find a target in the swirling white particles. Grey came from below and took him in a headlock, intending to use him as a human shield.

The Guarder grabbed at his arms, trying to dislodge the grip whilst raking the floor with his feet. Grey's leg wound tore open, sending spears up the bleeding thigh. His muscles trembled as the man pushed against him. With a heave, the Guarder threw himself backwards, crashing them to the floor.

Grey held onto the man's neck, cutting off the air supply despite the sharp edges of broken bricks tearing into his back.

He realised too late the irrationality of an assault driven by fury when Chance walked over. The man raised his pistol and shot through them both.

Gasping for air and coughing dust from his mouth, Grey refused to give in. He pushed the body away and forced himself upright, ignoring the pain.

The leader backed off, dropped his gun, and sneered. 'Bare hands. I'm gonna enjoy this.'

He shoulder-charged Grey into the wall behind, lifted him onto his shoulder and slammed his body to the ground. Chance straddled him and squeezed his throat. With the last of his strength, Grey tried to lift it away, but a punch hammered into the side of his head.

Chance reached for the remains of a concrete block, smirking as he prepared for the final blow.

HAVEN

ANNIE led them towards the coastal community Irvine had identified. Jen made life as difficult as possible by sulking, refusing to speak, and stalling for time. She stormed off whenever a blazing row erupted, only to return when hunger called.

The journey had been hazardous. Not from hostiles but from the land they crossed. Countless strikes had devastated vast areas, gouging the ground and spewing rubble everywhere. The horses struggled, refusing to go near the edge of a crater. Annie had to grab Irvine and Jen's mounts a few times to steady them as they wove between gaps in the impact sites.

All three were close to exhaustion when riders appeared ahead.

Irvine and Jen turned to Annie, who remained silent, studying the approaching men.

'Follow us,' the leader said.

They traversed a worn path until a band of blue water cut the horizon. A low structure came into view. Sentries opened two tall gates topped with barbed wire. One carried a gun, the other a bow.

The building, constructed from rocks discoloured by seaweed, dominated the compound. Close to the fence, a single guard with binoculars stood on a wood lookout tower scanning the area.

A small, bespectacled man waved Annie, Irvine and Jen inside the building.

'Please, take a seat,' the stranger said, gesturing with a flat hand. 'First, in case you don't already know, the settlement where you are now is called Upper Haven. Farther up the coast, we have a smaller community at Little Haven and beyond that, the farm. I'm John, and it's my job to assess whether you may be suitable for us. Ewan, who runs things around here, will make the ultimate decision.'

Jen and Annie sat impassively. Alarm crossed Irvine's face.

'Don't worry, we'll provide supplies and let you go if that's what you want. We're not barbarians like some groups out there.'

A guard placed food and water on the table.

John nodded to the meal. Jen didn't take in what the food was in her haste—until she tasted something white and slimy. Disgust creased her face. 'What's this crap?'

Their host chuckled. 'Never had fish before?'

'No. I'll close my eyes and force it down, but never again.'

John chuckled. 'I'm sorry to say if you remain here, it's all we've got.'

He asked questions whilst they ate, writing answers in a small book.

'First names?'

Two of them answered. Jen glared at him for trying to poison her.

Irvine said he was an agronomist and started explaining the title. John held up his hand.

'I know what an agronomist is.'

Annie said she was a Guarder. He appeared to know the term.

Jen shrugged. 'I'm no one.'

John smiled. 'Everyone is someone around here—if they're prepared to work.'

He focused on Irvine. 'You sat on the Council with Bella, if I'm not mistaken. And you,' he continued to Annie, 'must have been one of Ben's people.'

Irvine pulled off his glasses and opened his eyes wide in shock.

'It's okay, we know all about the Station from couriers.'

John sat back in his chair and studied them. 'Easier if you stay here tonight. I'll introduce you to Ewan in the morning.'

Two men led them to a small room.

'Good sign,' Annie said. 'They haven't locked the door.'

*

Jen awoke with a start when Irvine shook her shoulder.

He was bouncing with enthusiasm. 'Come, come and see, it's incredible!'

Standing on a cliff, they looked out across the ocean. Jen took in a view she'd only seen in a book. A rising sun tinted the water orange on the horizon, and surf rolled lazily onto a sandy beach dotted with rock pools. Small rowboats leaned to the side, waiting to be launched.

Irvine pointed. 'See the buoys—round things—offshore. That's where the fishing boats are moored. Looks like they've made an early start.'

Below, people moved amongst stone cottages roofed with abstract patterns of driftwood. To the right, wood steps followed the cliff's contours before disappearing under an overhang. Directly ahead, a monolith of rock rose out of the sea. Arches underneath sucked in waves and threw them out in cascades of foam.

Jen tried not to look intrigued by the screeching seabirds diving from the rock and wheeling out to sea.

Irvine jumped when Annie appeared beside him. Jen rolled her eyes at his skittishness. She did it again when his knuckles turned white from grasping the wood rail on the steps down.

At the bottom, a curve of rocks surrounded a cave; the mouth bricked up except for a door in the centre.

Inside was a huge, impressive room with a flagstone floor and natural walls.

Ewan awaited them. He was tall, thin, and walked with a stoop. His white close-cropped hair circling a bald head betrayed a man in his seventies. Piercing blue eyes beneath unruly brows gave an air of authority.

'Welcome, welcome. Please. Sit.'

They perched around a large, polished table, with neatly stacked papers and pre-sharpened pencils sprouting from a pewter tankard. Ewan was clearly a man of order.

An anchor and serpent tattooed on his arm transfixed Jen. '

'Admiral. Navy. Had this done when I was a young petty officer.'

Jen looked confused.

'Ahh, don't know what that is? Think of me as a soldier—Guarder—patrolling the sea. Right then, let's get straight down to business. Don't have a lot of spare time. It takes a lot of organisation to run a place like this. First things first. You are welcome to stay. If you want to, that is?' He raised a questioning eyebrow.

Irvine nodded several times to show his enthusiasm.

'Good, good. Let me explain how it works around here. Everyone has a job, and we work regular hours. Families live in the cottages along the beach, singles in the dorms, except for a few exceptions. I run things, as you will have surmised. We have a democratically elected Council, though.'

Jen frowned. Irvine noticed.

'Democracy is where people vote on important decisions. Not like the Council at the Station. They're more of a dictatorship—where they told us what to do.'

'Quite, quite.' Ewan's impatient tone implied he wanted to move on. 'Shall we continue? There are many specific jobs—fishing, processing, maintenance, and farming. I'll come onto that in due course,' he said, raising his palm to head off a question from Irvine, whose mouth had shot open.

'We also have an excellent medical facility.' A note of pride in Ewan's voice. 'Real Doctor. We look after people well. I have very little trouble—just an occasional skirmish, but nothing serious. We deal with that sort of thing firmly. Rules are rules.'

Annie interrupted. 'What about protection?'

'Yes, yes. I was about to come to that. I'd like you to join the Rovers. Dealing with occasional raiders, lookout detail, scouting for supplies—we don't like the term scavenging. One of our Captains will tell you more about operations in due course. I trust that's acceptable?'

She nodded.

'Irvine,' he continued, 'you'll work on the farms. We've about fifty acres just north of here—more crops than you can shake a stick at. Pigs, hens, and sheep, too. We need a man of your credentials. Ambitious plans, you see. Ambitious plans.'

Irvine beamed.

'We trade for meat occasionally, but mostly we eat fish— cod, herring, mackerel, whatever's in season. Now then, that leaves something for the girl.'

'I'm not a girl,' Jen retorted, glaring at the man.

A flicker of anger crossed Ewan's face at her tone.

'Processing. I think.'

'What the fu—'

'Jen!' Annie snapped. 'That's enough.'

'Irvine,' Ewan said, 'I'd like to talk to you about what happened at the Station. Andy here will show you two to your quarters.'

'Digs,' Annie whispered to Jen.

COWBOYS

GREY tried to rub the sticky grit from his eyes, struggling to coordinate the movement. A hand lifted his arm and placed it back on the bed before dabbing at the glue with a wet cloth. He felt warm water trickle down a cheek and into the nape of his neck. His eyelids fluttered open, revealing the blurred silhouette of a woman. At least, he thought it was a woman.

'Where am I?' The sound came out in a mumble.

'Shush. You're safe, so rest a while longer.'

Grey lifted his head to bring her face into focus, but the pain was too much, and he slipped back into oblivion.

The next time he came to, it was evening. A flicker of firelight found its way into the room. Walls rippled and appeared to move in and out. Nausea threatened when he turned his head, trying to make sense of the surroundings.

Instinctively, he gripped the side of the bed and touched rough fabric. He was in a tent and had no idea how he'd come to be there.

Muffled voices sounded outside, but his calls were too weak to hear. Grey gave up and closed his eyes, attempting to remember anything useful. A girl speaking, no, cursing. Ben, who was he—and the white-haired woman beside him? A man holding a rock above his head. No matter how hard he tried, his mind refused to join the pieces.

The following day, Grey awoke more lucid. Sunlight pierced his eyes through a gap in the tent. Blinking away the misted vision, he lifted his head with effort and glanced down. Someone had wrapped bandages around his waist and thigh. Touching his head revealed yet another. Damn, did he hurt.

Grey now knew who he was. And what he was. The events since arriving in the city were still a little hazy. But they would come together in time. He remembered the girl, Jen, and felt a stab of sadness—and guilt. Was she safe with—Irvine—and the woman whose name he couldn't recall? He hoped so.

Flashbacks to the man holding the rock had haunted his dreams through the night. Death had been a certainty. Yet here he was.

Once again, voices came from outside, along with the sound of activity. Men grunted with heavy lifting, cursing as something thudded onto the ground. A woman shouted, and an argument broke out, cut short by bellowed instructions. Surrounding the noise, Grey heard—cattle.

The tent flap opened, and a man's head poked through.

'Brought some food. It's what passes as porridge around here. Personally, I hate the stuff.'

'How did I get here?'

'Time enough for that later, we're moving on. I need you on a wagon as soon as possible. I'll send some boys shortly to carry you.'

Three men came into the tent. Grey tried to get off the bed, but one of them gently pushed him down. 'Stay still. The legs fold under; it's a camp bed of sorts. Bloody uncomfortable, right?'

'Tell me about it,' another said.

Outside was chaos. People were packing boxes, dismantling tents, and loading wagons. Whooping children ran between adults, only to be chastised when they got in the way.

Men on horseback herded the cattle, shouting and whistling commands. Dogs barked in excitement as they circled the herd. Clouds of dust swirled through the camp, stinging Grey's already painful eyes when he was lifted into the back of a wagon and laid on a pile of blankets.

'Like the wild west, eh?' One man chuckled.

Grey lay in the wagon, unable to see anything but the sky. He tried to sleep, but the driver seemed determined to hit the deepest ruts possible, jolting his battered body.

After a few hours, the wagon lurched to a stop. The tailgate dropped, and a woman climbed on board. She wiped away sweat shimmering across his forehead before inspecting the bandages. Fresh blood had leaked into the fabric, and her fingers came away wet with a crimson residue.

'You'll survive. You're a tough bastard, Grey, that's for sure.'

He was about to ask how the woman knew his name when she jumped off the back, clicking the tailgate into place. Her face was familiar, and he began searching his memory for clues. Nothing came together.

The sky turned from blue to the pale orange of early evening before they stopped again. A cacophony of noise erupted when people jumped from wagons and began unloading heavy items. Pegs hammered into the ground, shouted orders and clanking utensils painted the scene. Somewhere in the distance, whistles and whooping brought the herd to a halt.

The same men lifted him from the wagon and lay him on the canvas bed. Grey saw the camp's full extent on the way to a tent. There were at least thirty similar shelters surrounding him. Maybe sixty to eighty people belonged to this nomadic community of cattle herders.

How the hell had he got there?

*

Sal leant over Grey to change the dressings. She sensed him watching, only looking away when she prodded the tender flesh.

'Still don't know who I am, right?'

'I know your face, but...'

'Sal. We kind of met at the river. Do you remember Chance?'

'No, who's he?'

'The shit who was about to bludgeon you to death with the rock.'

She saw him frown, the machinery of his mind clicking into place.

'You shot him?'

'Yup. And enjoyed it.'

'To save me? Why?'

'Don't get ahead of yourself, Grey. I killed him because I hated him and what he did to the old couple. You remember Ruth—and Robert?'

He thought for a moment. 'Yes. I do.'

'You are just a by-product. And I don't kill injured men,' she added. His lack of response told her he had no recollection of what he'd said before he knocked her out.

'You brought me here, though.'

'Only because Ruth asked me. I considered leaving you back there. We'll talk more later. Got some things to do first. I'll bring food when it's ready.'

*

Fires dotted the camp, and isolated groups talked in their own world. Men poked embers, showers of sparks made children jump, and laughter cut through the hum of voices. Sal and Grey leaned against a wagon wheel, taking in the environment without speaking.

He broke the silence, snapping her back to reality. 'Why did Ruth help me—after what happened?'

'Best you ask her. Not my place to explain. I just followed her lead. Easier on my conscience that way.'

'Where is she now?'

Sal pointed to a large fire. 'With one of the bigger families. They've adopted her. Or she's adopted them. Bit of both, maybe.'

'So how did you—we—end up here?'

'Long or short version?'

'Short.'

'We had to patch up your wounds in the building. Ruth didn't have the strength to help carry you far. The next day, we buried Robert. Ruth said a few words, cried a little, and then packed her grief away. She's a strong woman, not one for emotional discussion. That's her business as she sees it. The only time I saw a chink was when we went back for you. Her hands trembled a little, and she kept looking towards Robert's grave while tending your wounds. I guess she was trying to control the anger. When I told her I was moving on, Ruth didn't want to stay—too many memories. A farming community was a few days upriver, so we headed there. Passed it a few times out on patrol. We used a door to make a litter for you and left the next day. Neither of us expected you to survive.'

'So you joined these people instead?' Grey asked.

'Drovers. They call themselves Drovers. We came across them watering the herd at the river. They told us raiders had attacked a settlement several miles away, and it wasn't safe to be out alone.

'Where are they heading?'

'West. They have encountered too many raiders themselves in their regular area of late. Lost a few people and a lot of cows.'

Grey frowned. 'Why west?'

'They know about a fishing community and hope to trade.'

'You staying with them?'

'Maybe. Not sure if I'm the herding kind, though.

At that, a shadow crossed Grey.

'Time for me to go.' Sal made to stand.

'It's okay.' Ruth said. 'This will only take a minute.'

Grey tried to speak, but the old woman cut him short.

'I helped get you here because I'm not an animal like those soldiers—and you.' These Drovers are lovely people, Grey and they don't need your kind here. Once you're able, go!'

'I intend to.'

*

Grey's wounds improved as they travelled. After a few days, he could walk unaided and ride up front.

Sal thought a lot about the man along the way. He was dark, dangerous, and closed as tight as a rusted padlock. She asked about his past, where he was going, the tattoo on his neck—anything to get past the veneer. Nothing but clipped, evasive answers came back.

The less he said, the more she wanted to know. The saying about curiosity killing the cat came to mind. And he was more than capable of killing a cat. Yet Sal couldn't help being intrigued and chided herself for even considering him attractive.

A week later, Grey announced he would leave the next day. She tried to appear nonchalant but caught his eye and turned sharply away, angry at being found out.

Sal helped pack supplies on the horse. Grey seemed indifferent to her presence.

He refused a gun and took an axe handle she'd found for him.

After a brief goodbye, he mounted and rode away without glancing back.

Sal sighed, wondering if she would have gone if he'd asked.

Probably not

THE CAPTAIN

FISH guts and blood splattered Jen's hands and arms. Tiny scales glistened on the stone surface, sticking to her face when they sprayed from her scraping blade. She spat with disgust whenever some made it into her mouth.

Jen hated fish and hated this place.

'Salt!' Pete shouted, pointing towards the barrels at the back of the room.

She hated him, too. 'One day, I'll gut you,' she muttered.

After spreading fillets across the barrel, Jen scattered salt over the top, wincing from a finger cut. 'Fuck.'

Pete made a gesture with his tongue. 'Been waiting for you to ask.'

He was an arse through and through, relished giving orders, and constantly undressed her with his slitted eyes. Jen knew he would try something at some point.

A few days later, it happened.

Pete made the mistake of coming on to her when she returned to the dorms. He appeared out of the shadows and tried to grab her. It ended with a knee to the balls and a kick in the ribs for good measure.

'Screw you.' Jen said as she walked away, leaving him squirming on the ground.

Ewan summoned the pair the next day. Pete argued he was just being friendly. Jen had her say the only way she knew how. The consequence was a week confined to the dorm and a new job—deckhand.

On her first morning, Jen stomped across the sand, looking for a boat called 'The Violet.' It proved impossible to make out amongst other boats bobbing in the bay, only differentiated by coloured cabins.

Jen watched men shoving a rowboat to the water's edge. One of them waved her over. She took a step and then halted when a disturbing thought came. *I can't swim.*

Someone tapped her shoulder.

'You'll be the new girl then.'

A wisened old man wearing what Jen saw as a ridiculous white cap squinted at her.

'Call me Captain. Now join the other deckhands. There's rubber boots for you in the boat.'

'I'm not a girl. Got it?'

'Touchy. If that's the best you can do, keep your mouth shut and follow orders—to the letter.'

Jen hopped to pull up the boots. When one man chuckled, he received an icy glare. After wading through shallow water, she grabbed what the idiot called a 'gunnel' and cursed whilst trying to get a leg over the top. Fortunately for the crew, no one offered to help.

The Captain sat at the stern, telling two deckhands to put their back into rowing. Jen remained rigid at the prow, trying not to look fearful.

'Any of you touch my arse, and you're a dead man,' she snapped whilst scaling the wood ladder hung from The Violet's port side.

Sniggers came from the men.

On the first day, there was nothing to do but watch the goings on and retch over the side. Tied off to a buoy on their return, however, proved extremely annoying. Decks had to be scrubbed with a broom, fish scales and slime scraped off gunnels and knives cleaned.

Jen's new job was like being at the processing hut and feeling nauseous at the same time. Once back on dry land, wobbly legs took some managing on the way to the dorms.

Early mornings, late nights, and leftovers from the canteen were the routine. Sleep a luxury.

During the coming weeks, Jen reluctantly found herself intrigued by how nets were cast, ropes knotted, and sails trimmed to the Captain's orders. Despite tripping over things and getting soaked by hauls of fish, she gradually learned how to help. Not that being a fisherman had any interest. She needed knowledge. Any knowledge—as Grey once said—was helpful. It angered her whenever he came unbidden to her mind. She hated him.

When they first met, Jen didn't like the Captain with his stupid sailor's hat, leathery face, and too many wrinkles to count. His fiery temper pissed her off even more.

The crew called him Ahab out of earshot. Where that came from didn't matter. It was the insult she relished.

No one entered the Captain's cabin without invitation. He locked the door at night, so peering through a dirty window was the only way to get a closer look inside. The compass and charts piqued Jen's interest.

*

No sailor wanted a woman onboard, let alone a foolish girl, and the Captain was no exception. He was furious when the Council insisted she became a deckhand.

'Discipline and hard work are needed,' Ewan said. 'Make sure she gets it.'

Over time, once it was clear Jen would never give in, the Captain warmed to her. She worked hard, stood up to the men, and appeared to enjoy being on the boat. He'd catch her looking out over the waves and watching him in the cabin. Stubborn but not stupid, he decided.

His prejudice waned. Momentous because encouraging a female to learn the ways of sailing, especially on a working boat, was out of the ordinary.

'Want to steer?' he asked Jen one day.

'No.'

'Yes, you do.'

'Why?'

'Seen you watching. Come on, give it a go.'

Periodically, the Captain allowed her to pilot the boat, ignoring her refusal to interact. She pretended not to be interested, but her concentration said she was.

One day, he saw Jen walk over to a crew member who stepped back with his arms aloft. A little later, he asked about it.

'Called you a dirty old man. Won't do it again, though. People don't like a filleting knife pressed into their gut.'

The Captain chuckled. 'Good on you. Good on you.'

*

Jen warmed to the Captain, too. He cursed more than she did and added some fresh insults. Fishdick, especially, because it was rude and demeaning. Sure, the old man could be annoying, but he shared his knowledge, and Jen took it all in for good reason.

Upper Haven was a prison, but the sea brought a sense of freedom. And escape if she could one day steal a small sailboat.

Learning to swim proved a scary challenge. Jen watched youngsters diving into waves after work and on her day off. No way would she ask them for help. Instead, she walked far down the beach to practice after stealing a swimsuit.

On the first attempt, only Jen's thighs made it into the sea —the second her stomach and the third a quick duck. When a dive into the water almost resulted in drowning, defeat loomed.

Eventually, she started copying how kids swam and developed her own version of the crawl. Unexpectedly, she began to enjoy it.

BREAD AND BEER

IRVINE was in his element, being the only agronomist. Potatoes, carrots, onions, beetroot—they grew it all. There were even polytunnels housing tomatoes—bloody tomatoes. Astonishing.

He and Ewan spent a lot of time together discussing the farm. With Irvine's expertise, the man had said, they could grow wheat and barley.

'Bread and beer. Bread and beer. It makes my heart beat faster just thinking about it. You're the man for the job, Irvine. Man for the job.'

Ewan had an annoying habit of repeating a statement.

Annie scouted most of the time, but they met up when possible. Irvine was delighted she liked the community, especially with a new lover. Jen was another matter. It saddened him to see her so surly.

Though she was still hurting about Grey, Jen wouldn't admit it and hated the work she'd been given until recently. For some unfathomable reason, she took to fishing.

Jen's behaviour towards other people angered Ewan. The unseemly language was distasteful coming from a young girl. Irvine wished he wouldn't use that term because the response was predictable.

According to Ewan, the total population was precisely two hundred and forty-six people.

The infirmary had a qualified doctor, nurses, and a reasonable amount of equipment. A team of engineers maintained an array of solar panels, providing enough electricity for essentials. Construction, maintenance, and fish processing ran efficiently, as Ewan explained at their first meeting.

Twenty-three sailboats split between Havens, caught more than enough food to keep everyone full and healthy. And forty Rovers policed the area.

Ewan introduced Irvine to the Council soon after they arrived. It comprised seven people with decisions made collectively. They took votes on serious matters. Ewan was Chairman, although he sometimes called himself the CEO, as a humorous reference to the past.

They promised Irvine a seat on the Council in due course. All in all, he was a contented man.

*

Annie settled in well with the Rovers—Ewan refused to call them soldiers. They were well-organised, adequately equipped, and restrained.

'Fair, firm and disciplined.' The Captain told her. Mostly, they roamed a fifty square mile territory, with the occasional search broader afield for anything useful. Though nothing had turned up for some time.

Irvine and Sandy, her new partner, got on well. Jen all but disappeared off the radar. Annie had tried to get through the armour but tired of the girl's attitude and gave up.

One thing worried her. The Rovers had come under fire from a sizable group a few weeks before she joined. Three soldiers suffered injuries, one seriously, before the attack ended.

It remained a hot topic, with the unit speculating about who lay behind the confrontation. The Captain insisted they were just a bunch of opportunists, but several Rovers disagreed. They believed there was more to it.

On patrol one day, Annie's ears pricked up.

'It's him,' someone said, adding a woo-woo ghost impression for dramatic effect. A chuckle ran through the men.

'Who's that?' She asked.

One Rover explained, 'We took in some nutcase a while back who started talking about a big bastard called 'the Tzar.' The bloody Tzar—who the hell has a name like that?'

'Load of bollocks,' said another man, followed by more chuckles.

The Rover beside Annie leant in close and whispered, 'I'm not so sure.'

THE TZAR

FORMALLY known as JJ, the Tzar glared at the man. 'Why did you steal more than your share?' He asked.

'I needed food. My family, they...'

An enormous fist banged on the table. 'My food!'

The Tzar pushed himself upright, knowing precisely what his size did to people: six feet nine inches tall, shoulders a yard across and four hundred pounds of muscle and fat. Deep-set dark eyes, long black hair and a bird's nest beard completed the terrifying giant.

'Please,' the man before him begged.

'Please,' mimicked the Tzar, then turned to one of his men. 'Take him. Show them all what happens to thieves.'

They dragged the man from the room, his pleas echoing down the corridor.

*

JJ had been a prisoner when the strike hit. The authorities labelled him a high-security risk and a danger to society. Now, he owned society—in the north-east, at least. The rest of the country would follow in time—he hadn't chosen the title 'Tzar' on a whim.

'Big boned,' his mother had said.

'Pig ugly' was his father's description.

They were both right.

JJ's family had lived on a run-down estate. Weeds, broken washing machines and old bikes, mostly stolen, decorated the gardens. He was free to roam as he chose.

His local gang had terrorised the neighbourhood. Minor things, as he saw it, like breaking windows, shoplifting and the occasional mugging.

Given the teenager's size, it didn't take long before he established leadership over the group. The incumbent, two years his senior, received a vicious beating and relinquished control—albeit from a state of unconsciousness. It was time to make some real money.

The first burglary didn't go well, although it had some reward. One gang member dislodged a vase, which crashed and splintered across the floor. They had all run for the entry window, scrabbling to get through first. JJ was too slow and fat to leave before the homeowner grabbed his trousers—a big mistake. The man fell after a head-butt, like JJ had seen in the movies. He kept kicking the idiot in the ribs, enjoying every crack.

'Ace!'

The newspapers had run the article about a man found battered to death. JJ loved it and pinned the cutting to his bedroom wall. A later story stated the coppers were still looking for the killer. That also made its way to the wall, accompanied by a drawn policeman's head sprouting a dick. Over the next few years, he created a collage of the gang's unsolved crimes—until his luck ran out.

JJ had beaten a rival to death in broad daylight and went down for life. The thirst for vengeance after someone hammered a gang member senseless overcame common sense. More so when the perpetrator offered a challenge. JJ was incapable of letting anything he considered a personal insult go.

The judge had called him a callous individual with no remorse. Not that JJ gave a toss when the old prick pronounced the sentence. Escape was a foregone conclusion.

Prison had honed his skills: how to intimidate and extort, smuggle contraband, set up scams and deal with threats of violence.

He'd also become interested in books. At first, it was normal stuff like sci-fi, adventure, and cop stories, but over time, his attention shifted.

JJ devoured books on war. Especially the Second World War. And in particular, the Nazis. He loved the salute, precision marching and the red armbands of Hitler's SS.

Absolute obedience through fear.

The only serious problem came from a vicious beating. Four men had jumped him in the toilet block, one of them crashing a stolen metal bar onto his head, sending him thundering to the floor. Kicks thudded into his body for several minutes until the attackers stood back to admire their handiwork. JJ had forced himself upright to face the prison's hard man. Two hundred and eighty pounds of gym-hardened muscle stood before him.

'Screw you,' he had spat through broken teeth.

'No. You won't screw me or anyone else.' He kicked JJ with all his might in the groin, causing severe damage.

Whilst recovering in the hospital, he seethed. Visions of what he would do to the bastard consumed his mind. A month later, he returned to his cell. Soon after, his nemesis came out of solitary confinement, strutting like a cockerel in a crowded hen coop.

JJ had waited until the large man and two of his cronies entered the same toilet they'd used for the beating. He walked in while his main target was taking a shit in a cubicle.

The first attacker received a hammer blow to the face. Blood, bone and gristle exploded from his nose. Then, the second had plunged a shiv into JJ's thigh. He grabbed the man's hair and threw him across the room. The yelling ceased when a kick imploded his rib cage.

JJ turned his attention to the cubicle, seeing a shadow on the tiled floor. His nemesis was waiting, probably equipped with a prison-made weapon.

Not that it stopped anything. JJ had shoulder-charged the door, smashing it from the hinges. The ex-ruler of the prison lay against the toilet, only his head and neck poking above the door's edge.

JJ walked along the prone door, looking down at a purple face and bulging eyes, then jumped.

An extended sentence and indefinite solitary confinement followed.

The giant had stalked around his cell, struggling to devise an escape plan. A permanent limp compounded his frustration, the constant ache poking at aggression. Wall punching and bellowing provided the only release.

Then, the meteorite strike came.

The prison took a hit from a smaller projectile, levelling half of the buildings. Survivors had poured out of shattered walls, but JJ took his time, hunting any prison guard he could get his hands on. Once sated, he corralled some ex-cons and began his reign of terror.

JJ was ambitious, ruthless, and clever in a way that belied his non-existent school qualifications.

Two years later, he'd taken over a large town, exterminating the useless residents, and forced the rest into servitude. Then he'd jettisoned JJ in favour of the Tzar and designed his own armband. Black, with a red 'Z' to signify his title. It looked hellish and scary.

Eventually, he controlled two hundred square miles and established an infrastructure to support his growing territory. The north-east side of the country had come next. It took much longer than expected because of logistics, weaponry, recruitment, and many ambitious, well-armed thugs.

Now, it was time to rebuild the 'Empire' and take the rest of the country—particularly the west coast. His Troopers, as he named them, made forays across the area, testing defence capabilities and gathering info. Finally, he was ready to move; his first target—the Havens.

It tempted the Tzar to go for the Station before the coastal community because his men in the city described it as ripe for taking. However, he needed a reliable food supply, and fish was on the menu.

Securing the farm and Lower Haven would be easy, but surrounded by cliffs, Upper Haven needed a different approach.

The Tzar had a plan for that.

COURAGE

TWO Rovers returned to the polytunnels and a barn surrounded by a high wood fence. Irvine watched one man pointing frantically into the distance. The other fell from his horse, wounded by a bullet.

Guards ran for their positions whilst two men ushered the workers into the barn away from the gates. The doors were locked and barred once everyone was inside. Some workers became animated in panic, but most stood like statues, staring at the entrance.

Shots rang out, and bodies began thumping to the ground from the balustrade along the fence. Guards yelled orders, others screamed, and the smell of cordite filtered through the barn doors. Then, all went quiet except for the pitiful groans of wounded men.

Irvine placed an arm around a sobbing woman whilst trying to control his tremors.

A Guard shouted from the wall. The agronomist thought he heard a distant voice from beyond the gates. A scream followed another shot. Once again, silence came. Whoever was attacking must have delivered an ultimatum. Minutes later, the compound gates creaked open, and horses filed through.

Wood snapped at the back of the barn. Whispering and shuffling feet told Irvine that some people were leaving, but he was unsure whether to join them. His head whipped from side to side as if motion held the answer.

When sounds of rapid gunfire resonated in the compound, Irvine knew guards were being slaughtered by the men who had come through the gates.

The woman he'd hugged followed when he forced himself through the opening. Outside the barn, terrified workers ran, heading for ladders leaning against the balustrade. They bunched together, looking nervously behind whilst waiting to climb.

'Come on, come on!' Irvine shouted to no one in particular, his heart threatening to give out.

After an eternity of jostling, he reached a ladder and pushed the woman ahead. When she hesitated, he shoved harder. His eyes were wild as panic threatened to overwhelm him.

Soon after, the shooting petered out.

*

The Tzar looked over the remaining farm workers from the barn. His eyes eventually rested on one man. He was big, at least six feet five inches tall, with muscular arms and a thick neck. And he matched the giant's stare.

'Feeling brave, lad, eh?'

The man didn't respond, nor did he look away.

'Fancy your chances, do you?'

The Tzar walked over, and the others moved back.

'What's your name?'

Only a glare came in answer.

'Tell you what. Give me your name, and I'll let you have a go. Fair fight.'

After waiting to see who blinked first, the man said, 'Davey.'

'How old are you, Davey?'

'Twenty-four.'

'Step forwards, Davey Twenty-four.'

The man hesitated.

'Aw, come on now, not gone all chicken on me, eh?'

Suddenly, Davey charged. The Tzar, a seasoned street fighter, sidestepped and cuffed him on the back of the head, sending the man sprawling. When he rose, a sledgehammer punch cannoned into his jaw. Davey spun and hit the ground. A boot thumped into his ribs, rolling him over, his arms clasped around his side.

'Look at me, Davey Twenty-four,' the Tzar growled.

He did, and the giant's foot pressed hard onto the exposed throat. The man bucked, straining to lift the giant's leg. Soon after, all movement ceased.

'This—is—what—happens—to fools—who challenge me.' The Tzar bellowed.

He walked away, glaring at a Trooper and tilting his head at the workers. A maelstrom of bullets followed. Screams filled the compound until a shroud of silence descended.

*

Irvine looked uncertainly at the drop over the fence. The sudden eruption of gunfire ignited violent shakes through his old body.

'Keep control. Keep control,' he whispered to himself.

It was at least twenty feet to the ground. Many of those who tried limped away. Unsurprisingly, the older folk remained on the balustrade, not knowing what to do.

Irvine had never considered himself a strong man in any capacity. For the first time in his life, a steely control asserted itself. In the panic of herd mentality, he issued instructions. The answer to the predicament was rather obvious to his mind. No one had used the ladders leading up to the walkway because they wouldn't reach the ground on the far side. Lashing two together would.

Three men hauled one ladder, then a second from the compound. They hurriedly used clothing and belts to tie them together and then to the fence.

Irvine made the precarious descent first and helped the others.

Escapees fanned out in different directions, many supported by others, but he knew they wouldn't make it. The attackers would round them up—and shoot them.

The remaining people looked to Irvine for instructions.

'Err, let me think for a moment—got it!'

They skirted the fence and turned a corner towards a natural underground stream, accessed from a small grate fifty yards away.

'This way,' Irvine whispered, and his entourage obediently followed.

Once at the grate, they climbed down and walked at a stoop along a channel. At the far end, it opened into a cavern, dammed to create a storage pool. Everyone waited, entirely in the hands of lady luck.

Irvine didn't know where his courage came from, but as evening fell, he made for the entrance, intending to find out what had happened. Listening below the exit, he heard nothing.

At the fence, voices mumbled from the far side of the barn. It didn't sound like many remained—hopefully. Taking a deep breath, Irvine chanced the ladder, cursing when it wobbled.

Only silhouettes of buildings were visible when he climbed into the compound. Sneaking around the barn, he saw six men sitting by a fire. Each wore a black armband sporting a symbol of some sort.

Maybe he could lead his group away with so few remaining—or wait until the men departed. If they departed.

A cough and then footsteps sounded close by. Frantically looking around for somewhere to hide, Irvine decided on the barn. Retracing his steps, he squeezed through the gap in the wall. It was pitch dark inside. Then it wasn't. His eyes adjusted to reveal a mound of bodies in the centre.

The sight and smell of death had Irvine hunched in a corner, rocking back and forth, trying to stifle sobs. But he had no choice but to wait until the way was clear. The monsters had done their work. Surely, they would go soon.

By morning, the agronomist was so shaken and desperate to escape the carnage he considered giving himself up. The piled bodies changed his mind.

Shouting sounded like it came from beyond the fence. Had the sentries discovered the grate? Muffled gunshots confirmed his fears, and guilt tore at him for the lives snuffed out.

The doors rattled, and then a man entered. He circled the corpses poking some with a boot. Seemingly satisfied, he left.

Irvine pushed out from beneath bodies, unable to hold back vomit.

A minute later smoke drifted inside, then flames, then the roar of fire assaulting the barn doors. The agronomist pushed through the gap, an involuntary coughing spasm doubling him up. No one heard.

Blood rushed to his head from building fury.

The bastards had gone, so they didn't have to smell burning flesh.

On the far side of the fence, he considered options. Upper Haven was too far and exposed to walk. Besides, the savages might be there. Little Haven, however, could be deserted by now if they'd finished their work.

It took Irvine two hours to reach the outskirts, where smoke still spiralled upwards. When he stumbled into the first burnt-out house, he was desperate.

After an hour hunched on the floor, he forced himself upright and made for the seafront.

Two men watched the bay, waiting for something. Boats, he assumed. Which meant Upper Haven was being attacked from the sea.

Irvine edged closer and saw a line of bodies stretched far along the sand.

Never had he contemplated taking a life until this moment. Anger consumed him when the horror bubbled like searing lava to the surface.

He pushed over a wood lintel to create a crash, hoping to attract a lookout's attention. It worked. One of them came to investigate. The killer didn't look concerned, probably assuming it was just falling timbers from a burnt-out cottage. Irvine tried to stop the shaking throughout his tired body when the man neared.

A thick piece of charred wood whacked into the lookout when his head poked through a door. Irvine pounded him until exhaustion forced him to his knees.

'Ed!' the remaining man shouted. 'Ed, what the hell you up to? Aw crap,' he complained and went to find his comrade. 'Ed, come on, stop dicking ab...'

The man pitched forwards from a blow and Irvine kicked him—a mistake. His ankles were seized, and he toppled over, glasses flying skywards.

Both of them stood on shaky legs. Irvine panted, trying to focus whilst the lookout shook his head to clear the fog. He came forwards, brandishing a knife, but missed with the first thrust. The agronomist grabbed his wrist, trying to wrestle the blade away.

Still weakened by the first blow, the man fell to the floor, Irvine on top. The blade hit home, piercing the lookout's chest.

After staggering to his feet, Irvine spat on his victim and lurched for the door. He should have double-checked the man was dead.

A bullet tore through his lung, sending him to the floor, gasping for air.

Irvine's last thoughts were for Jen and how he'd failed her.

SMOKE

GREY headed north, paralleling the coast, before turning inland.

He intended to travel up the country's centre, skirting a spine of small mountains he knew. Shelter, fresh run off and lowland grass for the horse took priority. He considered making a detour to look at the ocean but decided against it. Why waste time? Besides, the sea was where Jen and the others had been heading, and he had no wish to make his guilt even worse.

A derelict cottage provided refuge to avoid the heavy clouds driven by an easterly wind.

The rain lashed down for two days, giving Grey too much time to think about Jen. And, surprisingly, Sal.

He had avoided explanations about himself and consequently knew very little about her. A small part of him regretted that. The woman had saved his life, and she was attractive.

Grey shook his head, angry at himself for acknowledging the last thought.

When the rain faltered, he continued the journey, welcoming the opportunity to leave introspection behind.

As evening fell, a small settlement came into view. From a hundred or so yards away, a rider-less horse grazed on sparse grass. Grey's senses detected movement amongst the ruins. Faint, but there.

A shot rang out, pinging the ground close by.

Jumping from his mount, Grey ran behind the remains of a dry-stone wall, bow drawn. Two choices. Double back to avoid confrontation or retaliate. There was always the chance whoever they were could track him in daylight, an irritation he could do without. Better to sort it now.

The wall was close enough to the building for a silent approach. Bow abandoned in favour of the handle, Grey crouched and moved slowly.

Moonlight glinted on metal, betraying the gun's position.

There were no give-away whispers or furtive movements. This person was alone—except for dead people, judging by the pungent odour.

His handle dropped over the shooter's head and pulled him backwards.

Grey hissed in his ear, 'Anyone else around?' The man rocked his head from side to side. 'Sure?' More rocking.

The handle tightened, cutting off the air supply until the man lapsed into unconsciousness.

At least twenty bodies lay scattered around the immediate area. One decapitated, the head taken for a badge of honour. Grey searched for supplies, then stopped when a woman moaned.

She lay face down, dry blood caking her back. And she was naked.

Grey rolled her over and looked down—at someone he knew.

'Annie. It's Grey.'

Her eyes flickered open, then closed. When she tried to speak, he moved close to her lips. All he could make out was, 'Jen. Irv...' before she died.

Fear for Jen gripped, then guilt. He had thought she was safe, but now she was in danger from the evil shits who'd done this to Annie. Colour drained from his face, and boiling anger took over.

The unconscious man groaned when Grey shook him. When his eyes settled on the terrifying apparition above, he screamed.

'Who—did—this?'

Grey took deep, slow breaths, trying to control the urge for violence. After a few moments, calm returned.

'What's your name?'

'J—J—Joey.'

'Okay, Joey, I'm not going to hurt you. Just tell me, what happened here?'

The story confirmed Grey's worst fears. Jen was in extreme danger.

A group of men had surprised and chased the Rovers. They had taken refuge to fight it out, but the attackers had a greater force and more ammo. Joey's Captain surrendered, only to be slaughtered along with the patrol.

Three Rovers had made a run for it and hidden for a time. One of them ordered Joey to return and help any survivors whilst he and the other man headed for the farm.

Grey learned as much as he needed about Upper Haven, Little Haven and the farm.

'Up,' he said firmly to the man. 'We're leaving.'

He figured Irvine would be at the farm, maybe Jen with him. Joey said he'd heard of the agronomist through Annie but knew nothing of the young girl's whereabouts.

After a hard day's riding, they found many tracks. This wasn't a band of raiders. It was an army.

Only the burnt-out shell of a barn remained at the farm to tell the tale. Charred bones inside added the last chapter.

Joey vomited violently. Grey remained stony-faced on the outside. Inside, his stomach churned. Was Jen amongst the dead? But if anyone could get out of this situation, she could. Her wiliness and stubborn streak might—might—have saved her.

They followed the tracks to a fork. One set headed for Upper Haven the other veered off towards the smaller settlement. Grey chose the latter because it was the closest. And the only option for Joey. His family lived there.

A mile away, trails of smoke curled into the sky. The ashen Rover galloped straight for his home. Grey let the Rage consume him, ready to exterminate anyone in his way.

The first cottage he came to was empty. The second wasn't.

Three men lay inside; one was Irvine, with a hole through his back. The other two wore black armbands. When Grey worked out what had happened, he bowed his head in respect.

'How the hell you did that, Irvine, I'll never know.'

Joey joined him ten minutes later and stepped back when he saw the white face and icy eyes.

'Did you find your family?'

'N—no. But there's a long line of bodies along the beach. Can't go there alone,' Joey uttered, shaking his head.

Sure enough, they found his family. The Rover dropped to his knees, wailing. Jen wasn't amongst the dead. She had to be at Upper Haven—had to be.

And that was exactly where Grey and the Rage were going.

First, though, Irvine and Joey's family had to be buried. There were too many other corpses to receive the same dignity.

Grey recognised the granite hardening Joey when they set off. Vengeance was a powerful antidote to grief. Temporarily, at least. He wanted to charge headlong into battle, but Grey steered him away from recklessness. There would be guards and traffic along the coastline. Better to head inland and approach from the far side.

Gunfire cracked through the air long before they saw anything. Grey felt reasonably sure who it would be—the Drovers. Geography said so. And Sal would be in the thick of it.

Choosing between abandoning her or heading straight for Jen was easy. Jen won hands down. Unless…

'What do we do?' Joey asked.

'Quiet!' Grey snapped. 'I'm thinking.'

Allies, he decided. If they helped the herders, some of their men might offer support at Upper Haven.

*

The Drovers had taken position inside a small crater, wagons placed around the outside for barriers. Their cattle were far away, probably taking flight when the firing started.

Thirty men, give or take, lay flat on the ground, trying to pick off anyone moving amongst the wagons. The Drovers were reciprocating.

Grey returned to a farmhouse nearby, where Joey waited with the horses. He had a plan—but it was risky.

Neither had ever rounded up cattle, so Grey gave the Rover his best advice. 'Make it up as you go along.'

Joey set off in a wide loop to avoid being seen by the soldiers—if that was what they were. Grey sneaked up to within fifty yards of the men all facing away, consumed with the fight.

Gunshots sounded in the distance, turning the soldiers' eyes in that direction, uncertain what to do. Their concern increased when clouds of dust came into view. They split into two groups: one to divert the herd, the other to focus on the Drovers, as Grey expected.

Joey rode behind the beasts, firing his gun in the air. He didn't have the know-how to keep them in one direction, but the ensuing chaos of panicked cattle only helped. None of the soldiers were aware of Grey aiming with his bow.

One man took an arrow in the buttock, a second through the shoulder. The angle was wrong for killing shots with the men lying on the ground, but two distractions were all the herdsmen needed to gain the upper hand.

Grey dived to the floor when a hail of bullets erupted from the wagons, followed by charging men. The soldiers firing at the cattle scattered as the stampede closed in. Those shooting at the wagons lost all sense of discipline when Drovers tore into them.

The Rage took over as Grey sprinted into the melee, handle ready. His ferocious blows sent bodies whirling and tumbling to the ground. When someone cut his arm with a knife, he spun and crashed the wood under the man's chin, lifting him off his feet.

Mayhem erupted all around. Knives flashed, make-shift batons broke skulls, and guns fired.

Two men faced Grey. One held a pistol the other a blade. Suddenly, they both lurched forwards, and Sal appeared. Her twisted face said she was hyped and pissed off.

Grey nodded a thank you and resumed his blistering attack. Sal stood her ground, firing with precision at anyone wearing a black armband. Slowly, the fighting subsided, leaving some Drovers dead, some doubled up with exhaustion and others finishing wounded soldiers with a shot to the head.

Sal ran over. She looked angry, but it was nothing like Grey's visage. The woman put a hand to her mouth in shock.

'Ignore it. I've got to go.'

'Where?'

Grey didn't answer. Instead, he ran to find Joey.

He spotted a body some distance away and shook his head. Sal followed and pointed at the prone figure.

'Who?'

'A brave man. That's all you need to know.'

Joey's pulse showed no sign of life from multiple gunshots.

Sal looked quizzically at Grey when he stood up. He knew why. All signs of the Rage had gone, leaving the man she'd spent time with.

When he turned away, she grabbed his arm.

'You're leaving?'

'To save a friend—if I'm not too late.'

'Upper Haven?'

He nodded.

'Need some help?'

Grey peered around to watch Drovers carrying the dead and wounded. Asking for their aid would be wrong. They had more important things to do.

After a glance at Sal and then at the coast, he said, 'Follow me.'

*

When fires haloed the dark sky, Grey considered whether to approach and check out the soldiers or give the camp a wide berth.

'Shall we take a closer look?' Sal asked.'

'No. There are six fires, say, ten men to each, not counting sentries. Too risky.'

'So, we circumnavigate?'

'Correct.'

THE ROCK

JEN was walking back to Upper Haven after a swim when a hail of fireballs began raining from the clifftop. She stood transfixed a moment, then ploughed through the sand, unsure where she was going.

Haven's residents ran about in confusion, trying to decide whether to search for cover or attempt to put out the lashing flames. Jen made for Ewan's cave, finding the door locked. Her small fist knocked on the wood. No response. Hammering with both hands, it still didn't open.

'You shits. Let me in.'

No one did.

Then it dawned. Jen could hide in the Captain's boat. If she could swim there without being seen.

She stopped in disbelief when bobbing objects appeared on the horizon. Boats were coming, which meant they would moor near The Violet.

'Think,' she said aloud, panic threatening to overwhelm her.

What would Grey do? He'd come unbidden into her mind, and in that second, she hated him even more for not being there.

'Screw you, Grey.'

Jen's head arced from side to side, searching for options. She looked up at the cliffs for a route to the top. Torches were coming down the steps. Climbing the cliffs meant certain death. But it gave her an idea. The monolithic rock facing Haven.

Jen struggled to maintain control when the current pulled her to the rock. Turbulence sucked her through an archway and then out again. There was no up or down in the maelstrom of seaweed and sand until her shoulder slammed into stone. Gasping, she grabbed a jagged ridge and vomited into the foam.

She heaved herself up, blood running from cut fingers that stung from salt. Slime made leverage difficult, almost sending her back into the water. Seagulls screeched, forced from their perch when she climbed. Wings flapped, and beaks lashed out at her hands.

'Keep going,' she urged herself. An indentation appeared above. It was only large enough to huddle inside, but it was safe—for now.

The shivering worsened from the wind whipping off the land and knifing through Jen's sodden clothes. She must make a move soon. Her only option to find a more secure hiding place was up to the top of the rock. At least there would be some warmth from the sun.

It proved more straightforward to climb than she expected, but the birds continued to create a commotion. Jen worried they would provide a beacon to anyone watching from shore.

The remains of a wood stairway appeared above—built before the strike to give visitors a view from the summit—but they looked precarious, lashed by the elements.

Jen knew she had to reach them regardless of the risk. Gritting her teeth, she made it to the bottom step. It wobbled, but the wood didn't fall away—until her fingers grasped the fifth rung. Everything below sheared off and crashed down the rock, leaving her hanging in the air.

Reaching up with her free hand, she grabbed the next step, feet scrambling for extra purchase. Finally, she reached the top and dropped onto the stone, scattering angry seagulls.

'Aww, fuck! Bird shit.'

Lying on her stomach, Jen watched the scene across the sand. Haven burned, flames clawing for the heavens. Bodies lay along the shore, stretching far down the beach.

A group of men stood around Ewan's cave, one towering above the others. Jen could just make out his bellowing voice when he strode to the partially open door.

Ewan and the Council came out, hands held high. One by one, a bullet exploded into their heads until only Haven's leader remained. The enormous man grabbed his collar and punched him in the stomach. Ewan fell, and the giant put a boot on his head.

Jen cupped her ears to block out the wailing until it became silent.

Arms hugging her body, she knew she couldn't stay put for long. Waiting until dark would be safest when, hopefully, the men who'd attacked Haven departed.

As the sun dropped, some invaders took to the boats whilst torches flickered up the steps.

Time to go.

Within a minute of the terrifying descent, Jen's fingers bled, the pain almost unbearable.

Suddenly, her feet slipped, leaving only her hands grasping the rock. Cycling her legs revealed nothing below. Gravity took hold and plummeted her into the sea.

The water hit like a sledgehammer, knocking the wind out of her. She had a second to breathe before the current bullied her through the archway. Mercifully, the flow carried her body to the beach.

Jen lay on the sand, not caring about the grit in her mouth. After a moment, she raised her head, spat, and peered around. One bonfire remained next to a burned-out cottage.

The smell of grilled fish drifted on the breeze. Six men drank from a flask, passing it around and talking loudly. Jen crept by in the shadows and headed toward the Captain's home to get something she needed. A weapon. Maybe one of his batons for killing fish and a knife. Afterwards, she could sneak to the steps and peep over the top to check if the men above had gone.

If not, Jen was out of ideas.

Tentatively, she peered through the broken door and froze when it creaked, hoping the noise hadn't carried. A cough came from inside the cottage.

'Captain, is that you?'

Another cough.

Jen found him lying next to roof timbers. The old man was conscious but one hand had sustained burns from warding off a piece of flaming wood.

'What the hell are you doing here, lass?' he croaked, trying to stifle another cough.

'Don't worry about that.'

She crouched by the Captain's side after pushing debris aside. 'We've got to get out.'

'Where to?'

'Away from here. Along the beach until we find somewhere to hide.'

The Captain struggled to walk, using Jen's shoulder for a prop. A voice came from the shadows.

'Oi, lads, we've got ourselves some unlucky stowaways.'

Two more men appeared. One held a gun, the other a knife.

'Don't fancy yours, mate, but I got the girl. Finders keepers, eh?'

It turned out to be his last words. A second later, an arrow took him clean through the chest. The man with the gun fired blindly when a figure lunged out of the gloom. A wood bar crashed into his head. An arrow from someone else lanced the other.

'Wait here,' Grey ordered.

A woman appeared alongside.

Jen was stunned, unable to make sense of the situation. *How the hell did he find me? Who is the woman?*

She turned to the Captain and threw her arms around him, sobbing into his chest.

'It's okay, Jen. Calm down.'

Emotions exploded. 'He left me, fucking left me, and now he's back.'

'Your father?'

'No, he's not. If I had a real father, he wouldn't have gone like that—that—piece of shit.'

Jen stormed to the back of the building.

The three remaining men ran from the bonfire towards the commotion, guns drawn. Two fell from arrows. Grey left one alive.

He eventually became talkative after some persuasion from the knife.

Grey's voice dripped with venom. 'Who did this?'

No answer, then a scream.

'I'll cut off your ear if you don't tell me.'

'The—the—Tzar.'

'And who the hell is that?'

No response. Grey grabbed his head and laid the blade across his ear. 'One last chance.'

He learned everything he needed to know about the Tzar and his so-called Troopers. The captive was left alive and bound to deliver a message.

'Tell the Tzar if he follows, he'll die. I'll make sure of it.'

'Where do we go now?' Sal asked.

'Can you sail the boat, Captain?'

A bout of raspy coughs delayed an answer.

'Tides in, which will help with the rowboat. Jen will show you which one to use.'

*

The Tzar returned to the beach the following day.

Troopers found the man tied to his comrades. A minute after he'd delivered Grey's message, his face had no recognisable features.

A bellow of fury came from the giant.

'You, Trooper. Bring those remaining skippers from Little Haven to me. I want a word. And tell that idiot lieutenant of mine to get his arse down here. Now! We've got hunting to do.'

THE VIOLET

SAL and Grey sat at the stern. Jen trimmed the sails whilst the Captain gave instructions and steered despite his bandaged hand.

When he spoke, his voice sounded like two pieces of rusty metal scraping together. 'We'll give Little Haven a wide berth and head north up the coast. Don't worry about the girl. She knows what she's doing.'

Jen glared at him. 'I've told you not to call me a girl, you old fart.'

The Captain tried to chuckle but burst into a hacking cough.

'Serves you right, dim'ead.'

'Why is the boat called The Violet?' Sal asked.

Before he could answer, Jen cut in. 'It's named after some woman who survived from a fucking ship that sank.'

'Titanic,' the Captain said. 'And give the language a break, will you? It's getting annoying.'

'You swear all the fu…time.'

'Shut it, Jen,' Grey said with more force than intended.

She eyed him, which was all she'd done since leaving Upper Haven.

He wasn't surprised. After all, he'd left her, and she'd nearly died because of it.

Grey gripped the gunwale and stared out to sea. He tried to convince himself it was only guilt that brought him here. Deep down, he knew it was more than that. He cared about Jen, and it scared him. And he regretted threatening the Tzar. It was driven by the Rage, with little thought. Because of it, Jen was in more danger.

The giant would try to hunt them down. He was a fanatic who couldn't let anything go, according to the Trooper on the beach. A monster who showed no mercy, killing without hesitation. Worse still, the man had substantial resources.

His army comprised around five hundred men who policed the north-east and fought for fresh territory. Behind everything was an efficient infrastructure. Strategy was cleverly conceived, operations coordinated, and tactics ruthless.

'Can you outrun any boats coming for us?' Grey asked the Captain.

'Aye. We'll see pinnacles soon reaching far out into the ocean. They're called The Teeth. Good name because the water's treacherous.' He chuckled. 'If the Tzar's boats get there, they'll bite off more than they can chew. Apart from me, there's one other skipper skilled enough to navigate them.

He's retired now. Too old to command a boat. If they come, their only option will be to head farther out. We'll be long gone by then. Good wind behind us, see.'

The Captain was right about The Teeth. He steered the boat towards a gap between two of the towering rocks. Sal gripped the gunwale, white in the face. Grey leaned against the cabin wall, holding onto a metal bar on the cockpit. Jen set the sails, then sat on a bench seat at the stern, looking unconcerned.

Swirling currents rocked The Violet when they entered the passage. The Captain scowled in concentration when he spun the wheel. Blood seeped into his bandages from the effort, but he carried on regardless.

The masts creaked, and sails billowed when the wind funnelled through the gap between rocks. Then they were out of the far side into a calmer sea.

Grey looked over his shoulder and nodded in satisfaction. The Teeth would hide them from any pursuers. He took the opportunity to speak to the Captain whilst Jen attended to the sails.

He asked him about his plans. The Captain explained there was a remote chain of islands far away from the mainland. Before the strike, he'd been there a few times to stay with a friend.

'A nice little community we can join. Be good for us all, eh?'

'And if the islands have been hit?' Grey asked.

'Oh, there are plenty more places farther up the coast. We'll find somewhere, for sure.'

'So Jen will be safe, and you and Sal will take care of her?'

'Aye. We will.' The Captain screwed his eyes when he realised the implications. 'You didn't include yourself.'

'I want you to put me ashore up the coast. You'll see the mountains long before we get there.'

'You'll break her heart again. You know that?'

'Yes.'

'You're an unfeeling bastard, that you are.'

'Safer this way. It's me the Tzar wants, not Jen. Once you've dropped me off, get away as fast as you can. And never come back this way. '

Grey sensed Jen watching from the stern. She turned her back to him when he glanced over. There was no point in trying to offer an explanation. It would only trigger an explosion of emotions and get nowhere. Besides, the more she hated him, the easier it would be for both of them.

*

Sal liked Jen. The girl was everything Grey had said—feisty, stubborn and rude on the outside, a wounded soul inside. Not exactly his words, but she could read between the lines.

Several times, she had to turn away and suppress a laugh at Jen's cursing. But she recognised the depth of vulnerability behind the anger. The girl was desperate for a place to belong and someone to care for her.

Grey had explained about Jen's life and her mother's demise. Despite his curt descriptions, Sal saw the sadness in his eyes. He worried about her, and it hurt. Why the man didn't acknowledge his feelings remained a mystery. Being together with Jen would make them both happy.

Sal sighed. She, too, needed a purpose, and maybe the girl was it. They had much in common, and both cared a lot about Grey.

The thought took her by surprise. Could she be—falling for him?

No. It was that stupid thing about people wanting what they couldn't have.

*

When mountains appeared in the distance, Grey pointed at a spit of land made up of boulders carried to the sea by a glacier. Knowing goodbyes would be difficult, he didn't want them to come ashore.

Sal put her arm over Jen's shoulders when Grey slung his bag, bow and quiver over his shoulders. He left his handle behind, knowing it would make swimming too difficult. No farewell was forthcoming, nor did he turn to look at them before diving into the ocean.

Jen shrugged off Sal's hand and made her way to the prow.

The Captain said. 'Leave her be. She needs time on her own.'

Neither of them noticed her jump into the water. They only registered her tiny form digging through the waves when it was too late to follow.

'No point trying to get her,' The Captain said. 'She'll only do it again.'

Sal reluctantly agreed, holding back tears.

MOUNTAINS

GREY grabbed a boulder, pulled himself out of the water and turned to watch The Violet. His face was a charade of unconcern, his mind the opposite. Twice now, he'd left Jen, and neither time had been easy.

Thinking of the island destination helped to justify his actions. Everything the Captain said sounded good. Safe for Jen and a better life than he could offer. He could live with that.

Lifting his bag and bow, Grey took one last look, shaking his head at the tiny figure thrashing the waves.

When Jen reached the rocks, he hauled her up by the collar. 'Stubborn, stupid idiot. Follow me, and don't say a word. You'll piss me off even more.'

By the time they reached a dry area beyond the rocks, their fingers and lips were blue from the cold.

'Sit there and wait whilst I get wood for a fire,' Grey said harshly.'

When he returned, Jen had her arms around her knees, shivering. The sight brought sympathy and calmed his anger.

It took a while with trembling hands to use his knife and strike sparks from a flint Sal had given him. When the dry grass curled smoke and caught light, they were both desperate for warmth. An hour later, their clothes steamed, and heat found its way into their bodies.

Out of the blue, Jen asked, 'Tell me something about yourself. You owe me that much. Just something—please. Promise I won't ask again.'

Grey wrestled with the decision. Would she believe him? Did it matter? Would it create a bond he didn't want? No, it wouldn't. The bond already existed.

'One question.'

'The tattoo?'

'I'm a traveller. Where I've come from and how I came here doesn't matter. Don't ask. Some of my people were not good, so I left. They are callous, and...'

'What's that bird shit word mean?'

'Cruel,' Grey answered impatiently, moving on before Jen asked why he didn't say that in the first place. 'They're divided into groups—specific marks show which they belong to.'

'The tattoo, right?'

'Blue marks represent high-born leaders, green for workers, and red for the soldiers. Mine is grey because I'm none of those things.'

Jen couldn't contain herself. 'Grey, like your name. That's where it comes from?'

'It's the name given to the few people like me—Greys.'

'How come you only use a bow and not a gun?

'That's three questions.'

'Two.'

'No, three. You asked me to explain a word.'

'Doesn't count, wasn't a proper question. Please?' She opened her eyes wide, in the best impersonation of a young child wanting more chocolate.

'That won't work with me.'

'What?'

'The look.'

'I didn't give you any look.'

Grey raised his eyebrows and sighed. 'I hate guns for what they represent.'

'What d'you mea...?'

'Four questions. Don't do the eye thing again.'

'Fuck, fuck, fuck, fuck, fuck—I'm not stopping swearing until you answer.'

Grey cursed. 'Okay, but no more questions. Got it? My father told me guns were for cowards—no principles. Just not right,' he added, realising Jen wouldn't understand the word.

'You swore.'

'Yup, but I'm an adult. Now be quiet.'

'But wh...?'

'Enough. Get some rest. We've got a long trek tomorrow.'

Grey couldn't sleep after the mention of his father. He wasn't sure if finding the man mattered anymore or if it was even possible. No sign of him had arisen over years of searching. Too many innocent people died along the way, as had much of him. Until now. Until Jen. He couldn't—wouldn't—be responsible for her death. It had to end.

The following day, he tapped Jen with his foot. 'Up. We're going.'

'Where?'

He pointed at the mountains. 'There.'

'I hate bird shit rocks, seen enough to last me a lifetime.'

'Come or stay, up to you.'

They made their way through a dark swathe of pine forest skirting the lower reaches.

Jen tripped over branches and stumbled on broken logs, whilst staring at the surroundings.

Grey noticed her pick up a cone, breathe in the smell, and throw it down, no doubt deciding it was a kid thing to keep.

They neared the treeline at the mountain's base. Grey halted when a cawing bird crashed through the undergrowth, holding up a hand for Jen to do the same. Listening for what spooked the bird revealed nothing.

'We need somewhere to stay the night. There must be a building somewhere.'

At the top of a slope, the remains of a stone cottage materialised. The roof had collapsed at one end, leaving a sheltered space at the other. Inside were the remains of two people—hikers, judging by the clothing they still wore.

'I'm not wearing that,' Jen protested when Grey threw her the mouldy waterproof coat. 'It's creepy, and it stinks.'

'Wear it or get wet, your choice.'

After an uncomfortable night, they clambered to the summit to check out the land ahead. At the top, Jen pretended to be disinterested in the lakes stretching into the distance and refused to admit the coat offered protection from the elements.

As Grey expected, strikes had hammered the far side, leaving shears of rock piled at the base. When Jen complained about the steep descent, he ignored her.

Towards evening, they reached an expanse of dull water. Piles of logs, branches and brown reeds lined the bank, dirty foam collecting around the edge. Threads of smoke drifted from chimney pots at a lakeside village.

A man emptying a rowboat watched them approach. He shouted to warn other residents. Grey raised his bow above his head.

'Far enough,' the stranger said. 'What do you want?'

'Somewhere for the night.'

Two men took his bow and knife and then searched them both.

'Keep your filthy hands to yourself!' Jen protested.

Grey threw her a sharp look. 'Quiet.'

*

Jen looked at the grilled fish on her plate and sighed. Why the hell did people eat this crap? It surprised her when it tasted okay—better than seafish.

'Trout,' A woman said. 'Lake's full of them these days— and perch. All but died out 'afore all this.'

The granite stone house was surprisingly cosy. A roaring log fire spread warmth around a room decorated with pictures on the wall. Grey and Jen sat in comfortable armchairs along with their hosts. Other residents filtered inside carrying their own seats. Hands cupped mugs filled with steaming herb tea whilst everyone waited for Grey to explain their presence.

He answered the expected questions about where they'd come from, where they were going, and what it was like everywhere else.

'Too many raiders farther south, so we're heading for relatives beyond the mountains,' Grey lied. 'Hopefully, they've survived. If not, we'll go on and look for a community to join.'

Jen looked at the floor and chuckled when someone asked if she was his daughter.

'No, she isn't,' Grey said emphatically.

Some residents raised an eyebrow.

'It's not what you're thinking. Ask her.'

Jen laughed, and several women smiled at her.

'Like to take a bath, m'dear?' One asked.

About to refuse, Jen glared when Grey nudged her with his elbow.

'Your coat stinks. So do you. I'll wash when you're finished.'

He looked at an elderly man who seemed to be the designated spokesman. 'Anyone else we'll come across?'

'Rangers, possibly. The lower lakes, especially the bigger ones, have settlements. Not always welcoming, though. They're not the nasty sort but don't like outsiders, nonetheless.

Grey asked about the Rangers.

Another man chuckled. 'They call themselves that on account of some of 'em being Park Rangers before the strike. Look after the area and those who appreciate having them around, like us. Good men and women, they are.'

A woman asked if Grey still wanted to stay the night.

'We'd appreciate that. Slept rough for a while.'

*

Before they departed, one of the men gave Grey a map. He decided they should head east to the lowlands, then cut north to avoid the rugged terrain.

At the largest lake, a settlement appeared. Five men waited on the road, blocking the way. One levelled a shotgun; the rest stood stiffly, a mixture of aggression and fear written across their faces.

'Don't want you here. Had men come looking for two people. Man and girl.'

Before Jen could respond to the 'girl' comment, Grey gave her a warning look.

An older man in a wax coat with a Labrador at his side spoke. 'Nasty lot they were and well-armed. Don't want any trouble, so leave us be.'

'How many?' Grey asked.

'Twenty, maybe. There's your answer, now go!'

The man with the gun jerked it.

Grey sensed eyes on them when they departed.

'Don't think the Tzar was with them,' Jen said.

'How so?'

'They'd have mentioned him. Being a big scary shit.'

'Good thinking.'

'How did Troopers know we were here?'

'How do you think?'

Jen went quiet and looked at the floor. 'They got them, didn't they? The Captain and Sal?'

'It's possible, but the Tzar may have sent Troopers overland just in case we landed.'

'I hope that's what he did.'

'Me too,' Grey said quietly.

'But why is he going to so much trouble to find us?'

'Because I killed his men. And I made a mistake by threatening to do the same to him. He's a psychopath—a madman—who can't let anything go.

*

The Violet had sailed ten miles up the coast when the Tzar's boats appeared in the distance.

'Damn it, he must have threatened the retired skipper I mentioned.' The Captain said. 'Taken them through The Teeth to be this close. All we can do is try to stay well ahead and hope they give up the chase.'

Soon after, the wind changed to a strong easterly, and the waves grew. If Sal had more experience, she could have handled the sails whilst he steered. As it was, a snapped line almost decapitated her. Consequently, The Violet struggled to maintain its course.

The Captain scratched his chin when the Tzar's boats headed out to sea. Cursing, he realised their plan.

'They're going to come at us from further out to cut off any attempt to escape.'

Sal cupped her hands over her eyes and squinted at the shore. 'Can we make that bay before the boats are on us? Maybe we can get ashore.'

'Get to the bay, yes. Get to the shore; unlikely if there are rocks blocking the way.'

'I think we should try.'

'Aye, lass. But I'm staying on the boat. You can swim if you want.'

'But..'

'No one takes The Violet whilst I'm still breathing.'

'Then we'll both fight,' Sal said with finality.

By midday, three boats anchored fifty yards from The Violet. Holding Grey's handle, the Captain yelled, 'C'mon, you turds!'

Sal raised her bow, trying to balance in the rolling waves. The few arrows she had fell short, dropping into the sea like a wounded bird. The Tzar's men didn't shoot back, waiting for her to run out.

'I've only got one arrow left.'

The Captain nodded at a gaff.

Wriggling across the deck, Sal pulled down six feet of sturdy pole with an evil-looking curved point.

'Let's give those bastards something to remember, eh?'

Sal hesitated. 'We could give ourselves up?'

'Not me. Like I said, The Violet's all I've got, and I'll protect her to the end.'

The Tzar's crafts had rowboats lashed to the cabin top. Four Troopers took their places in each and approached, circling like sharks.

'Surrender!' one man shouted. 'Stand up. Hands behind your head.'

'Piss off!' the Captain yelled in response.

When the first rowboat bumped against the gunwale, Sal sprang to her feet and brought the gaff in a vicious arc, sending a Trooper screaming backwards. His weight caused the craft to bob violently, giving her a second opportunity.

The point embedded in a Trooper's shoulder. When she tried to wrench it free from the writhing body, her grip loosened, and the weapon fell over the side. Once again, the rowboat took on the motion of a funfair ride, throwing a man into the sea.

Sal held a knife whilst the Captain raised the handle when the first Trooper boarded. He dodged a blow and punched the old man in the stomach, sending him gasping to the floor.

Another Trooper on the rowboat, pointed his gun at Sal when she took a step. Game over.

One sailboat took them back the way they'd come to a sandy beach where the Tzar waited.

Sal and the Captain tried not to show fear when they came face to face with the giant and failed. He walked around them, glowering.

'What do you want with us?' She asked, attempting to keep the quiver out of her voice.

'Shut your mouth. I ask the questions.'

She didn't.

'Screw you,' was as far as Sal got before an iron fist thumped into her mouth. The Tzar grabbed her throat and leaned in close. His stained teeth and acrid breath made her want to gag.

'Where d'you let them off the boat?'

Sal attempted to stare him out.

The Captain spoke up, trying to save her from more punishment. 'The spit. Edge of the mountains.'

The Tzar's eyes narrowed on Sal. 'I only need one of you, and I've always had a weak spot for a good-looking woman. Take the old man away,' he ordered a Trooper. 'You know what to do.'

Sal went wild, screaming, kicking and trying to get her fingernails in the Tzar's eyes. He hurled her into the air. When she crashed into the ground, he stomped over.

'Give me any more trouble, and you'll regret it.'

RUN OR HIDE?

BEYOND sight of the village, Grey turned away from the path they travelled.

'Where are we going?' Jen asked.

'Back into the mountains.'

'I thought we were heading inland?'

'The Troopers could return to the village. Find out where we went. Which would be good.'

'Why?'

'Because we'll be somewhere else.'

Grey had been considering their options—run or hide. The former was risky. He didn't know how many platoons were out there. Or their whereabouts. The latter depended on time and luck. How long would the Troopers stay before they decided he had given them the slip? Hiding was less of a gamble, though not by much.

He tapped his finger on the map. It showed an area marked as a slate quarry.

After an arduous hike, a yawning cave mouth appeared, hewn inside by miners to create a vast cavern. A tall stone column supported the top, with a pool of dark turquoise water to one side.

Grey threw a large rock into the middle, where it landed with a resounding splash, reverberating around the space.

Three tunnels at the far end spread out at angles, making no obvious route for Troopers to follow.

'Wait here,' he said to Jen.

He entered the left tunnel using his hands and feet to negotiate the passage. Several other openings presented themselves, each a curtain of blackness. Confusing for pursuers, potentially confusing for him and Jen, too. Farther on, the path ended in a wall of collapsed stone.

The centre tunnel reached a dead end with no second escape route.

'Third time lucky,' Grey muttered, shuffling into the last tunnel. A way inside, a faint light appeared, filtering from a crack high above.

Two more passages showed. The first led to another blockage. The second ended in a mound of stone through which a glimmer of daylight beckoned.

'We staying in the cave?' Jen asked when he returned.

'No.'

'Why?'

'Difficult to defend.'

'Tell me we're not hiding in a dark tunnel.'

'Yup.'

'Crap.'

Grey stood outside the cave entrance, looking at the apex.

'Follow me,' he said and set off to the top. 'We need to find the tunnel's exit.'

'Which direction does it go?'

'You work it out. Time you did some thinking rather than relying on me.'

Jen walked in a straight line, stopped, scratched her head and kicked the dirt. 'This way.'

'Seems right to me.'

With a spring, she set off through trees to find the exit. Grey didn't follow. Jen appeared ten minutes later, wearing a pissed-off frown.

'Shitty trees can't tell one direction from another. Got lost. And I didn't find the end.'

'So?' Grey waited until the gears clicked into place.

Jen sighed. 'We leave markers. Right?'

'How?'

'I don't know, scratch trees or something.'

'Easy for us to follow. Yes?'

'Yeah, of course.'

'And for others?'

'Bird shit.'

Grey showed Jen how to leave discrete markers with broken twigs, stones and foliage.

'Most of all,' he said, 'use this,' tapping his head, 'and these,' pointing to his eyes. 'Look for natural features and remember them. Daydreaming can get you killed.'

'And footprints? People follow them, right?'

'They can. We'll talk about that over the next few days. Just think about this in the meantime. It isn't always about hiding footprints; sometimes it's better to leave too many.'

'Fool the fishdicks,' Jen said with a gleam in her eye.

Grey pointed to the left, then right. The exit is somewhere between. How do I know? Because I estimated the angles when walking down the tunnels.'

They came to a deep quarry maybe two hundred yards wide and half that across. Chunks of discarded rock lay piled against the ragged slate wall. Below, a mound of displaced stone and slate slanted up to the exit.

'Wait here.'

'I'm fed up being told what to do.'

'Wait! And stay away from the edge.'

'I'm not a stupid kid.'

'No, you're not. But you are reckless. Like swimming across the open sea.'

Jen rolled her eyes.

Grey circumnavigated the quarry, searching for an escape route on the far side. Finding one that looked reasonably safe, he climbed down then back up, satisfied by the protruding features.

Fifty yards away from the quarry, a valley, overshadowed by vertical cliffs, materialised on the far side. Rockfall had accumulated on a slope underneath him, creating a jumble of ledges, boulders and scree—easy to hide, hard to get through without prior knowledge. A wide stream wound through an alleyway of stones in the valley's centre. In the distance, it disappeared. Beyond that were trees, and a shimmering lake.

Grey made his way down to the valley and used a slate to scratch a route on boulders. At the base, he followed the stream. It varied in depth, with unstable stones—not ideal for speed, but the larger rocks provided some cover.

Farther along, the flow funnelled through a gulley and tumbled over the edge into a pool. The water would be cold, but needs must if Troopers discovered them. Reaching the lake would provide more options.

Two hours later, he returned to the quarry. Jen tried to appear unconcerned, but he could see she was close to panic.

'Thought you'd gone and left me.'

'I wouldn't leave you alone in a place like this.'

'You would if it suited you.'

'We need to gather firewood and brush.' Grey said, ignoring her comment. Inside, he knew differently.

'What's brush?'

'Twigs, branches, dry leaves. Anything discarded by trees and such. Good for starting fires and making hiding places.'

Jen stayed close to Grey's back through the tunnel, cursing him. They made several trips, carrying the brush. Afterwards, he cleared an area and made beds twenty yards from the exit at the far end.

When he started a fire, Jen frowned.

'What about the smoke.'

'That's why we aren't right next to the way out. If I keep the flames small, it will disperse.'

'How do you know all this stuff.'

'Intelligence.'

'Yeah, right.'

'Tomorrow, we catch food and forage—look—for berries and nuts.'

They stared at the dancing fire, each following their thoughts.

Jen eventually blurted, 'Teach me to fight. Like you.'

'You can't.'

'I'll shut up and listen—promise.'

'Go to sleep.'

'Fishdick.'

Grey remained awake, thinking about her request.

He felt torn between equipping her with self-defence skills and controlling her impetuous nature. Jen would look for a fight, given the opportunity especially when temper took over. But he also knew he wouldn't always be around to protect her.

Turning to her curled-up form, he whispered, 'Okay. You won't let this drop, will you?'

He didn't think she'd heard.

Jen kicked him awake the following morning.

'Up, we're going,' she said, mimicking Grey's earlier comment.

He tried not to smile but couldn't help himself. 'Touché.'

'What?'

'Never mind. Where are we going?'

'To fight. And before you say anything. I'm not...'

'Going to stop asking. I know.'

She shot down the tunnel when Grey sat up, yawned and stretched.

They faced each other in the cavern, Jen holding his knife. When she lunged, he caught and twisted her wrist. Staying true to her promise, she said nothing, even when it hurt.

'Your arm's too short for that kind of move. You'll be down before you get anywhere near an adversary.'

'A whatwho?'

'Enemy.'

'Why don't you fu... Sorry. So, what should I do?'

'Run. Don't get into a fight you can't win.'

'What if they grab me? Like, where do I stab them?'

'In the groin.'

'Eh?'

'The balls. No one gets up from a knife in the balls.'

Jen seemed to like that idea, demonstrating thrusts to show her understanding.

'What if I attack them from behind?'

Grey pointed to a kidney. 'Stab them here, under the ribs. The blade goes in easier if you hold it like this.'

They spent the morning going through knife exercises and punches suitable for someone her size. Grey knew it would take more time than they had to make instinctive moves. But at least it provided something for Jen to focus on.

That evening, once she'd fallen asleep, he went outside and returned carrying long pieces of wood and shorter branches.

Jen jerked him awake again at daylight, beaming.

'You're making spears. Right?'

'Nope. A bow.'

'But you've got no string.'

'Twine.'

'Whatever. Still haven't got any, though.'

'Grey reached into his bag and pulled out a spare coil Sal had given him back at the Drovers.'

'Arrows. What about them?'

'That's what the thin wood and feathers are for.'

Oh, yeah. Dim'ead thinking.

Grey whittled sections, each with a flat side. Using pine resin, he smeared it down one length and then laminated them together. He tempered the bow in the fire, which also melted the resin. Twine wound around the centre made a hand grip.

Once complete, they went outside to practice.

Jen struggled to shoot beyond thirty feet. She threw the weapon down and shouted, 'Useless bow!'

'Patience. It takes time.'

Late in the afternoon, Grey checked the snares he'd set and brought back a rabbit.

Jen enjoyed pulling out the intestines. 'Be good to do this to the Tzar.'

'Don't intend to try.'

In the morning, he collected rocks to make obstacles and barriers in the tunnel whilst Jen practised shooting. She returned after a couple of hours, bursting with pride.

'What's that all about?'

She brought her hand from behind her back, holding a squirrel by the tail.

'Well, at least that's something.'

What he didn't know was Jen had left the killing arrow behind.

*

Grey was checking out the area when birds cawed. He reached Jen, firing at a tree, grabbed her arm and dragged her into the cavern.

'What? Crap. Troopers, isn't it?'

'Stay here until I get back. Listen for any sound coming down the tunnel. Do not. I repeat, do not hang about to shoot them. Push the stones out of the way, climb down and hide in the quarry. Got it?'

Tears rimmed Jen's eyes.

'You will come back. Promise.'

'Do what I say.'

His white face and the harsh way he spoke through a tight jaw said the Rage had come.

Grey watched two Troopers examining Jen's arrow. He needed to take them down. And fast.

One overweight man headed into the forest to alert others, smart enough to avoid shouting. The remaining Trooper arced a gun with each cautious step. Grey shot him, glad the man didn't fire when he went down.

Next came the fat messenger, easily discovered in the woods. After a few minutes of dodging between trunks, he stopped to catch his breath. A knife under the ribs finished him off.

Crouched behind a rocky outcrop, Grey watched Troopers combing the area.

Suddenly, the man he'd shot staggered out of the trees and fell to the ground. Grey sprinted for the cavern, cursing himself for not checking the body.

He stood behind the stone column, listening to the murmur of voices outside. A Trooper lifted his head over the rim of rocks, then eased upwards for a better view. An arrow through the chest sent him tumbling back. No one else appeared.

After several minutes, Grey threw rocks around the cavern, followed by a flat stone into the middle of the pool. He ran down the tunnel, leaving the Troopers undecided on how to proceed. Soon after, a storm of bullets splintered the walls.

Someone shouted, 'Clear!'

Men came inside and fired, testing each of the tunnels.

Grey kneeled behind the rocks he'd piled earlier, listening to boots heading down the passages. Just as he expected, the group had separated into three. A crunch of loose stones said some were coming his way. Two or three at most.

They crept along the tunnel, their shirts shushing against the walls. One stood on dry branches set for that purpose. An arrow speared towards the sound. A yell caused the remaining Troopers to fire randomly in the enclosed space.

Grey, now lying flat on the ground, pushed up to one knee when the shooting ceased. More arrows followed, eliciting a scream.

Jen waited at the end and almost shot him when he appeared. Her wide eyes betrayed her fear.

'It's okay. The Troopers are trying to pluck up the courage to move.'

Grey lifted stones away from the tunnel exit to make their way down into the quarry.

Grabbing Jen's hand, he pulled her up the route he'd chosen on the far side. A glance back showed no Troopers.

'Follow me down the slope to the stream. There are markers to lead the way. Keep low and stop when I do.'

The first rifle shot pinged off a rock to their right. Jen squealed, and Grey yanked her into a crevice.

'They're gonna kill us,' she said, panting.

'No, they won't.'

His pre-planned route took them around the largest boulders and slabs, making it difficult for sighting. Bullets ricocheted too far away to do damage until the firing ended.

Moments later, a Trooper shouted from another group across the valley.

Gunshots splinted stones and thudded into the ground when Grey and Jen sprinted alongside the stream. They reached the gully, where a waterfall dropped into the deep pool.

'Give me your bow.'

'No way. I'm not jumping down there.'

'Stay here and you die.'

Jen lost control when turbulent water somersaulted her body. Panic took hold from memories of Haven. A hand grabbed her collar, pulling her to the surface, then up onto the bank.

'Run!'

When they made it to the trees, Grey pulled Jen behind a large oak. Bullets thunked wood all around.

'Scream.'

'What?' She frowned at him, not understanding.

'Scream, make them think they've hit you.'

The ear-shredding performance paused the shooting long enough for them to disappear into the depths.

Grey looked around the lake. With steep mountains slicing into the water, it didn't present the choices he'd hoped for.

'Yes, I know.' Jen said before being told. With a deep breath, she waded into the shallows.

The bows had to be left behind. They would hamper a long and exhausting swim.

Beyond the windbreak of trees, waves grew, devouring energy. Grey swam with one hand and helped Jen with the other, heading for the closest cliff. Few shots sounded from the lakeside, none close enough for injury.

They had evaded the pursuers for now, but for how long? Would the Troopers abandon their chase or keep trying? Grey didn't know and didn't care. The cold was a more pressing enemy now.

Finally, the cliff dropped away, revealing a small bay.

Grey carried Jen and lowered her onto the ground.

When her eyes flickered closed, he said, 'Look at me. Look —at—me!'

A slap around the face brought no reaction.

He lifted her over a shoulder and lurched across the moorland, almost dropping her when he stumbled. His strength waned as her weight grew heavier with each passing minute.

Grey fought against the hypothermia closing in, knowing its icy fingers had already reached into Jen's body.

Shaking his head, he tried to re-focus on the way ahead and thought he saw ruins from a building wavering from his distorted vision like heat from tarmac.

'Yaaaaaaaaaaa,' he shouted to galvanise hollow muscles into one last surge.

After what seemed like an eternity, Jen's limp body lay on the cold stone.

'Wake up. Wake up,' Grey said, urgency in his voice. Her lids briefly opened, then fluttered closed. He tried again. No response. He shook her body. Still no response.

His own lids grew heavy. When his eyes misted, he knew he'd failed Jen.

REVELATIONS

GREY awoke on a comfortable bed. A woman lifted his head to take a sip of warm liquid and wiped residue from his chin.

'Where—am I?'

'You're safe.'

'Jen?'

'She's fine, still sleeping. Rest a while now. I'll come get you for the meeting later tonight.'

'Meeting?'

'The Rangers, of course,' she said, as if it was obvious. 'We'll all be getting together to talk about what's happened.'

Grey said nothing for a few moments, letting his head clear.

'Rangers. I've heard of you,' he croaked, thinking back to the conversation at the first village.

'All good, I hope?' Judging by her cheerful tone, she expected nothing different.

And it was. For now.

*

At least thirty people sat around a blazing fire, all talking at once. The atmosphere was convivial, like old friends chatting in a bar. When Grey slumped in a chair near the flames, someone handed him a dark, foamy beer.

Knuckles rapped on a table at the back of the room and everyone quietened.

A small, bearded man wearing a thick, home-spun wool cardigan sat next to Grey. He gave a friendly smile. 'I imagine it would be more comfortable for you if we did the talking first. We heard shots down by the lake. Out doing our regular checks. That's to say, we're Rangers, see. You know, like patrolling the area.'

'He knows who we are, Tommy,' came a raspy voice at the back. 'Just get on with it afore we all fall asleep.'

Chuckling circled the room.

'Okay then.' The man began once again.

A door creaked open, distracting him when Jen entered. She looked pale and cowed by the faces turned towards her.

Relief sent a warm glow up Grey's body.

Bodies shuffled, and hands guided her over. She sat beside him and rested her head on his shoulder.

The spokesman cleared his throat. 'Heard shots and went to investigate. We don't like t'hear guns round here. Saw men in the distance. They shot at us, we shot back, maybe hit a couple, don't know for sure. Scattered 'em soon after. We left 'em be. They headed for the forest. Too dangerous to follow.

Some of the lads will search around for look-see. We're good at keeping out of sight—just watching, y'know.'

'Seen men like that before?' Grey asked.

'Nope.'

'How did you find us?'

'We headed back by the sheep pen, lucky for you. Don't take that route often. You were at least thirty minutes from the lake. Impressive, given your state. Being wet in these conditions, like.'

Grey moved the topic on to the Rangers' general activities and how they lived. He made it seem harmless, thanking them several times for their kindness. Not the sort of conversation he'd normally waste time with.

When Jen leaned away from him, he knew why. She suspected he was sounding out the possibility of leaving her behind. And she was right.

Heads turned to the man at the rear when he cleared his throat. 'Tell us about you and where you are going.'

Grey repeated what he'd told the people who helped them earlier.

Chair legs squealed, and the man walked over and sat. Older than the others, he had a wiry frame and rheumy eyes. Questioning eyes. Not suspicious, just an unwavering stare.

'Names John. Leader of this lot for my sins.'

More chuckling.

'I think there's more to your story. A lot of well-armed men came after you. Too many for a minor altercation. Someone wants you bad, eh?'

Grey clasped his hands together and looked at the floor. The old man was no fool. He would likely see through a flimsy explanation.

With no other option, Grey told the Rangers about the Tzar. The more he said, the more the tension rose. No one said a word when he finished.

John addressed the room, rubbing the table as he spoke.

'Might need t' rethink a few things.'

Then he stood and brought the meeting to an abrupt close.

Conversation erupted. No longer convivial. Worried.

Feeling exhausted, Grey excused himself. Jen rose at the same time and walked silently to her room.

John's eyes tracking her didn't go unnoticed.

The next morning, she avoided Grey and had breakfast with a group of women. He left her to it and went outside for a walk.

Leaning against a gate to look across the valley, he sensed someone approaching.

'Lot more to you than you make out, eh?' John said. 'Bit like me. Listen, learn, give nothing away.'

Grey continued staring at the landscape, remaining silent.

'Took some doing, getting you and the girl this far. You're a man with means, that's for sure.'

'Two things. One, don't call her a girl to her face, and two, get to the point.'

John drummed the gate with his fingers. 'Where do you actually come from?'

'I've already told you.'

'You've told us what you wanted us to know. Where are you really going? Planning to take the girl with you all the way?'

'Meaning?'

'Meaning, I know what you are.'

'Which is?'

'I've seen that tattoo on a man once before. We were friends for a while.'

Grey's mind raced. Who the hell had he met? Unless—his father?

'Describe him.'

'Your size, lot older, white hair, only said what needed saying. Wary, too. Took some time before he trusted me enough to talk—bit like you, I guess.'

John raised an eyebrow. 'Know 'im?'

'Maybe.'

'That all you got to say?'

Grey didn't reply, trying to make sense of the revelation.

A rustle of fabric said John was taking something from a pocket. 'This change your mind?'

It was a leather flask.

'Called it Juice as a joke, like orange. Gave it to me. Tried it once. Made me feel ten years younger. Didn't like it, though. Aggressive effect. You want it?'

Grey reached out and took the flask, squeezing from the top down to work out how much liquid it contained. Two thirds full. Enough for what lay ahead.

'Let's walk,' he said, needing time to calm the whirlpool in his mind.

John led them along an overgrown path. They reached a small, abandoned cottage constructed of stone by calloused hands many decades past. Moss coated the uneven walls, and the roof bowed in the centre. Age-worn stone steps led to a crooked door.

The old man pushed against it, wood grating across the floor. Old sacking, rusty implements, and a stone-wheel knife sharpener carried more history than words could tell. John pointed at two wood chairs.

They remained quiet for some time. Grey stared at the ground, his hands clasped on his knees.

'Used to be his place, John said.

'He's my father.'

John nodded. 'Said you might pass by someday. Told me other people knew—those he trusted—in case you found your way there, too.'

'Do you know who they are?'

'Nope.'

'He must have stayed some time?'

'Arrived here before the strike, left a few months later. Said he was heading for the place. Can't tell you more than that.'

Both men contemplated what had been said for a few minutes until the old man narrowed his eyes. 'Jen know?'

'A little.'

'You gonna tell her?'

'What do you think?'

'Only way she'll understand when you leave her. Which we both know you will.'

'I've got to find her somewhere safe first.'

'Not here,' John said, anticipating Grey's request. 'Reckon we got some trouble coming. If that Tzar bastard catches her...' He left the sentence unfinished.

'What will you do—if they come?'

John tapped his nose. 'We'll have plenty of notice to make plans. No one knows the mountains like us.'

'Be careful.'

'Oh, we will, lad. We will.'

Grey nodded. I think it best we leave tomorrow.

'I'll see everything's readied tonight.'

'Jen will be worried I'll go without her. I'd better go and explain before she does something stupid. Like running away.'

When he told her, she glared at him suspiciously and asked, 'Both of us? You're not pretending?'

'Both of us.'

The concern on her face dropped like a sheet to the floor.

*

Grey awoke in the early hours, hearing the rider. He strode to Jen's room. 'Up. We're leaving.'

By the time she joined him, John waited, his forehead creased.

'About fifteen of 'em. Can't be sure, though. Well-armed. You've got a good start. Take them some time to get here. Not that they'll find anything.'

'Sure you'll be okay?'

'Like I said, we can take care of ourselves.'

He gave them supplies and a sturdy horse. Grey declined a gun but accepted a bow and axe handle.

'Seen that before,' John said, winking. 'Not the wood, though.'

A Ranger led them to the far edge of the mountains, then pointed out the intended direction and departed.

Grey said little whilst the horse plodded, his mind chewing over the news about his father.

Over the last few years, the search had felt as pointless as his own life. Now, the revelation stirred a small light of... What? Hope, closure? Were he and his father on the same path, led by a design Grey didn't understand? Was it fate if there was such a thing?

His thoughts turned to Jen, tightening his stomach.

How can I make her understand?

*

The Tzar set up headquarters in a country house close to the eastern edge of the mountains. The place was comfortable and maintained by a small commune. They had vacated the place—with a little persuasion.

His room was the largest in the house, dominated by a four-poster bed sagging in the middle. A large period table and six chairs sat in the centre. The giant tried one chair only because putting his fat arse on antique furniture amused him. It wobbled under the weight. Collapsing onto the floor would make him look like a dick, so he had a Trooper bring a solid item from somewhere else.

The Tzar knew it was a bad news day when three scared men came into the room. Inside, he felt the anger rising before they spoke a word. But to learn what had happened demanded control.

Raising an eyebrow, he growled, 'Tell me.'

He studied each man when they explained.

'That's—err—everything we know.' One Trooper stammered.

'Six dead, two wounded, who knows how many deserters, and you three still standing.'

The Tzar let the sentiment sink in, observing the idiots closely.

I wonder which one will piss himself first.

Huge hands thumped on the table. 'It's your lucky day. Know why?'

They all shook their heads, unsure what it meant.

'Because you were just following some dickhead's orders. And had the balls to come back and face the music. Now go.'

Leniency wasn't the Tzar's motive, it was practicality. He only had forty men with him, having sent the rest back east. Losing three more would be a pain in the arse. Fury came.

He bellowed obscenities and thrown furniture at the walls. When the door flew open, a Trooper was grabbed by the throat and told to fetch the Lieutenant.

Soon after, the officer stood by the Tzar's side. The two men looked at a map spread across the table, considering which route Grey might have taken.

'We know he's heading north. Fuck knows why?' The giant said, then pointed at the quarry and traced a finger along the river to the bay. Jabbing where the cliffs gave way to open ground, he growled, 'Only place they could have got out. The question is, will the shit follow the west coast or turn inland?

If Grey cut inland and headed north, he'd reach a spine of mountains and deep forests. However, if he continued west, the coastline passed a city and then became ragged with countless inlets and bays. A nightmare to search.

An area of coastline between the mountains and the city caught the Tzar's eye. He drummed his knuckles on the table and studied the map.

'River mouth, ships and docks. Bound to be a good-sized community there with resources. If I'm correct, they could prove useful. With the right incentive. Provided I get messengers there before the bastard and his girl.'

The Tzar retraced Grey's route and calculated timings. It would be close but possible, providing the slimy shit didn't head inland to the mountains first.

The Lieutenant jumped when a fist slammed into the table.

'What do you think? Well? Say something.'

'I—err—wonder if—err—we should—just stop searching. Head back to—err—Haven and fini...'

'STOP SEARCHING!' The Tzar yelled, spittle flying from his mouth. 'No one gets the better of me. That man killed my Troopers on the beach and issued a threat. He was also involved in the fight with the fucking cow herders we caught.'

The Lieutenant stepped back, white in the face. 'I was just —err—trying to be practical.'

'Practical, eh? The Tzar said in a quiet voice. A rumbling sigh followed. 'At least you're thinking about the bigger picture. However, understand this. Leniency in a leader leads to leniency in the men. Remember that if you want to keep your rank. Got it?'

'Y—yes.'

'Good. Now, let's get back to what happens next. I think he'll stick to the coast for now. Easier to hide than on open ground. At some point, he'll either keep going up or turn east. We need to get him before that happens. Now, I'll ask you the same question. What do you think? Try to placate me, and I'll rip your head off.'

The Tzar eyed the Lieutenant whilst the man thought.

'I—I—think we should despatch a smaller group of Troopers inland just in case. They could send back messengers if they find anything.' Touching the map, he added, 'If he's trying to move fast, he'll probably stay on the west side of the mountains.'

The Lieutenant risked a glance at the Tzar to check if it was okay to continue.

'Go on.'

'Well, there are only a few paths and one road going north. Nearest us, that is. Quickest way through the forest.'

The Tzar turned and glared at him, causing the Lieutenant to flinch and gulp.

'Good thinking.'

The giant stood and stalked the room, scratching his beard.

'Ten men to the mountains. Right now. Within the hour. Shoot any shit who moans. In case the stupid idiots can't work it out, only one of them reports back if they find anything.

Send scouts up the coast to those docks. Make contact with whoever's in charge. I'll give you a letter to set up a deal if it looks viable. Same as the others—one hour. Get the rest ready to leave tomorrow. We've got some catching up to do. Now fuck off and get on with it.'

Once the Lieutenant had left in a run, the Tzar stared out of a window.

'Who the hell are you, Grey? And why is the girl in tow? Mm, the girl. Achilles' heel?'

THE LOOP

WHEN the sun dropped, Jen and Grey sheltered in the lea of a hill and ate cold meat and bread John provided. He considered how much of his life to share.

Jen's patience ran out after a long period of silence between them.

'What's going on in your head?'

This is going to hurt—both of us. Grey knew.

'I learned some things, important things, back with the Rangers.

'Like what?'

'About what I need to do.'

'Which doesn't include me. Does it?'

Grey avoided looking at her.

'You almost died back there. Because of me.'

'That's bird shit. You saved my life twice.'

'I almost cost you your life. Twice.'

Jen crossed her arms in disagreement. 'Only once.'

'No. I could have let the Captain take us away from trouble. Find somewhere better for you. But I made him bring me to the mountains. For my reasons. Selfish reasons.'

'But I followed, you didn't ask me to.'

'What about Sal and the Captain? The Tzar might have caught them in the bay because of my decision. And he would have got you.'

Memories forced a break in conversation. Grey stared into the distance. Jen picked at her nails.

'So, what did you learn that's brought all this shitty stuff up?'

'My father. I found out John knew him.'

Jen frowned. 'You've been trying to find him all along, haven't you? That's why you're travelling north. To search for him.'

Grey moved when he thought she might reach out to him, relieved when she didn't.

'I was close to accepting he was dead. But yes, I am journeying north, just in case. Last chance, I suppose, before I —well—give up altogether.'

Jen's eyes opened wide. 'Give up? I mean, what kind of give up?'

'Doesn't matter. What I'm trying to say is, now it's even more important to travel north.'

'I can help, though.'

'No, you can't.' The words came out harsher than intended, causing her to flinch.

'Sorry. I didn't mean to say it like that.'

Grey could see she verged on another outburst. To stem the flood, he added, 'I'm going to tell you more about me. Maybe it will help. Look up at the stars.'

'I can hardly see any stars. It's not dark enough yet.'

He ignored the comment. 'Where are they?'

'In space, idiot.'

'Try to imagine more than one sky. Many, in fact. It's called alternate dimensions. Different places existing at the same time.'

'But it goes straight up there,' Jen protested, pointing upwards.

'No, it doesn't. There are other planets like yours.'

'Mine? What the hell are you talking about?'

'Think of them as copies. When I was young, my father told me that Greys—like my family—could travel between them.'

'I don't believe anything coming out of your stupid mouth. You're just trying to make excuses that make no sense. Even I know something about space from books.'

'There's no point telling you more if you refuse to listen. Is there?'

The way she tilted her head, fixing him with an intense stare, expressed her fight between interest and suspicion.

'There are a lot of other Earths. I've visited many of them. Most are like here, with similar landscapes, though not identical societies and histories. Everywhere I've been has problems and bad people. Some much worse than others. I've always hoped to find my father for two reasons: first and most obvious, he's all I have left. Second, to learn how to control where I go. If it's even possible. You see, my mother wasn't a Grey—she died when I was about your age. Which means I'm not pure.'

Jen frowned. What does control mean?

Grey fingered his hair before answering. 'My father said he could go where he chooses. I can't. Determining where I end up hasn't been possible. And, as I've said, nowhere on my travels have I found anywhere without conflict. I don't know why.'

Jen's narrowed eyes made it obvious she thought it was bullshit. Nonetheless, he continued.

'I always arrive in the same location in the south and leave at another in the north.'

'How. I mean, how do you go the different places, which sounds like bird shit to me.'

'There is one boulder in the south with a marking like my tattoo carved into the side. I arrive there. In the north there are a ring of stones. Depending upon which I touch at the right time of the month I make a crossing. For me it is a guess. For my father; a choice. Which means I'm trapped in a random loop of sorts. You're caught up in my journey—problems.'

'So, I'm a problem,' Jen shouted.

'Only because I can't take you with me—you would likely die in the crossing.'

'But... Why can't you just stay here?' The tremor in her voice sounded more like a plea than trying to understand.

Grey's head slumped. In a quiet voice, he said, 'Because people around me always get hurt.'

He paused, hoping the meaning would sink in.

Jen avoided his eyes. 'That's why you're angry all the time?'

'Yes. But also because I've also done—bad things.'

'What?'

'Bad things, leave it at that. You've seen the look. What I turn into with the Rage. Just accept that I'm not the person you think I am.'

She eyed him. 'Because you can do stuff other men can't. Like sensing danger and fighting.'

'Where I was born, Greys were different due to a genetic—body—aberration. The worst of my kind became soldiers; others lived far from populations. My family were among those. I was taught skills by my father because he believed in the end, we would be persecuted. He was right, and many were killed. To save me, he brought me to this Earth years before the strike. That's how I know I've been here before. Also, the Troopers wear black armbands with a symbol on them. Took me a while to make the connection to Nazis—evil people from the past.

'So, what happened to your father?'

Grey rubbed his chin, thinking about it.

'This Earth was a better place back then, though wars were still being fought. I was told to remain here whilst he went back to fight on my homeworld. When my father didn't return after a couple of years, I went looking for him. What I now know for certain is that he survived. He's most likely searching for me as I am for him. Another loop.'

Jen pulled a piece of soil from the ground and rolled it in her fingers. Grey said nothing, waiting to see what was going through her mind.

She narrowed her eyes on him. 'You said you couldn't take me with you—to another world. But your father took you here. How come?'

It took him a long moment to understand her question. 'You mean even though I have no control over where I go, he brought me where he wanted. That's because he held me in the crossing.'

'Thought it might be something like that,' Jen said. 'So, why can't you hold me and do the same—don't answer. It's because you don't WANT TO!'

Grey put a hand on her shoulder, but she jerked away.

'I have some of my father's genes. You don't. I'm sorry, Jen.'

'So, what about me?' She spat.

'I need to find somewhere better for you.'

Jen couldn't control herself. 'Like leaving me behind in this... this... place. Well, fuck you, Grey. I'm gonna follow if you try to leave, then you'll have done another bad thing.'

He winced as if she'd slapped him.

Jen pushed herself up and walked away. She stopped and turned to him. 'You're talking crap, making up stuff to get rid of me.'

Grey realised telling her had been a mistake. It was stupid to expect anyone to believe a story like this. And he'd only done it to make himself feel better, hurting her even more in the process.

He sat a while, looking vacantly around, trying to reason with himself. To find excuses that would justify his actions.

Never had he dealt with anything like this. To explain to anyone like Jen. But there wasn't anyone like Jen.

'No. Don't go there,' he said out loud. 'You've screwed her life up. She doesn't deserve that. Not from someone like you.'

Anger turned his voice to steel. 'Whatever it takes, you are going to find her somewhere safe.'

*

Over the following days, Jen only acknowledged Grey's presence by necessity. He couldn't see her sat behind but knew what she was going through—anger, sadness, disbelief and fear—round and around in circles. He had his own circles. Guilt, disdain for himself, confusion—the list seemed endless.

He tried to engage her in conversation about the landscape, horses, and any banal subject he could think of, but he didn't have the skills. Especially with someone so determined to hate him.

It was only when the outlines of a seaport materialised that Jen showed any interest in their surroundings.

Across a broad swathe of land, pipework twisted and turned in a maze. It wove in and out, thrusting into the air in giant hoops and connecting to tanks of various sizes. But it was only when the hulking carcass of a tanker revealed itself that Jen couldn't contain herself.

'What the hell is that? And them—them tall metal things with big beaks and ropes.'

'Ship for carrying oil, and the tall metal structures are cranes. For loading heavy stuff onto the tanker.'

'Why did they need all that oil before the strike?'

Grey explained what it was used for.'

'Didn't do them any good when all this crap happened.'

'That's for sure. If there's any left, it will be good for lighting lanterns and boilers for heat. That sort of thing'

Jen asked more questions, and he answered with as much enthusiasm as he could muster, trying to keep the conversation going. The atmosphere between them softened, making Grey feel a little better about the situation. Until everything changed. For the worst.

'Quiet!' he said, turning to scan the surrounding area. 'Hold tight, we're going to the ship. It's the only place to hide around here.'

The horse stuck to some self-imposed speed limit. Hooves thudded against dried mud, interspersed with patches of rainbow-streaked oil throwing globules out of dark puddles.

Riders appeared on each flank.

Grey ordered Jen off from the horse near a spiked railing of wrought iron. They ran for a pair of closed gates, the chain and padlock still in use. He threw his bag, bow and coat over the top, then lifted her up. She dropped to the floor, wide-eyed, when he didn't follow.

The men dismounted thirty yards away. Others appeared from behind a corrugated shed.

Grey picked up his handle and prepared.

'Hide,' he hissed to Jen over his shoulder.

'But.'

'Go!'

She ran to a pile of shredded iron and disappeared behind.

Two burly men, each taller than Grey, walked towards him. Both carried a length of steel scaffolding, sporting knuckles and bolts at one end.

'Go on, lads, give it to him!' someone in the surrounding crowd shouted. Others cheered, excited by the beating about to be handed out.

Releasing the Rage wasn't an option. Grey needed to keep the fight going. Otherwise, the men would go down in seconds. A prolonged contest was better, giving Jen time to hide and plan an escape.

He parried and dodged blows, landing his weapon to goad them on. Enough to hurt, not enough to kill. When the crowd tired of the uninspiring fight, he sensed several men step behind, ready to join the fray.

Time to finish it.

He swept the handle across the ankles of one man, cartwheeling him backwards. The other tried to bring his weapon down on Grey's back, only to feel the detonation of recoil from the floor. His legs whipped into the air from a kick, landing him in oily sludge. Moments later, Grey dropped his handle to await the beating, shutting his mind off to as much pain as possible.

Three men held him by the arms. One of the downed opponents, his face streaked with oil and dirt, pounded a fist into his stomach. Grey sagged, and the men allowed him to fall to his knees. A boot thudded into his back, sending him face-first to the ground. After a few kicks to the ribs, they hauled him upright to face a man with one milky eye.

*

Jen stayed where she was, willing Grey on. When he dropped his weapon, her heart sank. She winced at the stomach punch and almost yelled when a boot thumped into him.

She couldn't stand it anymore and ran, trying to control the sobs, fearing they would kill him.

'Cool head, cool head, that's what he always said. Focus on the task at hand.' Jen muttered.

With a deep breath, she wove through discarded machinery, ignoring the black grease and oil underfoot. Grey's bow snagged on protrusions, and dislodged metal fell to the floor. Small footprints betrayed her path, feet slipping in the black puddles.

Jen ran between two mountains of scrap metal, sloping down to a concrete concourse. On the far side, a wall of horizontal pipes provided cover. After crawling inside, she paused, listening for footsteps. No one followed.

THE DOCKS

GREY took deep breaths to calm himself whilst fighting off nausea from the gut punch. The man with one eye, stood before him, asking questions he refused to answer.

'Won't do any good, not answering. Broke tougher men than you, that's for sure.' To his men, he snapped, 'Put him in the hold. He can have a talk with the rats till tomorrow.'

They took Grey across the tanker's deck to an open circular hatch.

One man gestured with scaffolding. 'Down there dickhead. Into the oil tank.'

Metal steps dropped deep below. The hatch's clunk resonated around the vast hold.

Clothed bones of bodies lay against the far wall. Rancid oil and decay permeated the air. Grey focused on a partially eaten corpse several yards away. The man lay on his back, staring blankly at the light filtering through a grill high above.

A black armband labelled him a Trooper.

There would be bodies everywhere if the Tzar had already paid a visit. Which meant the giant only suspected where they were. But he would know for sure if his Trooper had failed to return or another was heading back. Sending scouts meant the monster was a distance from the docks; otherwise, all hell would have broken loose. Maybe two or three days away.

When the sun dipped, the hold darkened, leaving only watery moonlight inside. The first rodents skittered across the floor, staying close to the walls.

Grey dislocated a femur from one skeleton to use as a weapon and headed to a corner.

When the hatch opened, someone hawked above. Something bounced off the ladder on its way down—a mucus sandwich. Rats ran for the stale bread. Grey left them to it.

Scuttling feet and chittering said there weren't as many rodents as he expected—rats were food, too—but enough to brave an attack. Sleeping was out of the question.

Shouting began from behind the far wall, turning to high-pitched yelling. Grey's heart pounded when he thought it was Jen, then realised it was a man. Though he sounded young, judging by the octaves.

The approaching rats scattered whenever the bone scythed. Broken bodies flew in the air to provide diversionary food for the rest. Grey felt confident he could see the night through if the numbers didn't increase. At least the horde would divide between him and his neighbour.

When dawn crept through the grill, the rats dispersed, leaving eaten carcasses strewn across the floor. Grey leaned against a wall, exhausted.

His head cleared enough to focus on Jen, reassuring himself she would be okay for now. Surviving at the Station and the skills he'd taught were a valuable education. She was smarter than these thugs, for sure. Except for the milky-eyed man, a shrewd-looking son of a bitch.

*

Lenny rubbed at his good eye, reading for the fourth time the written message delivered by idiots. One courier was terminated for being cocky. The other, a boy, had provided information about Trooper numbers before being thrown into the second hold. This Tzar—stupid name—might still come, but he'd crap his pants when faced the dockers.

The man had offered to barter for arms, horses, whatever Lenny wanted. He would hear him out if he turned up. Most likely, though, he'd set his men on the Troopers—another stupid name—and accept the one-sided deal.

Lenny had been a union leader back in the day. And bloody good, too; antagonistic towards management and a hard negotiator. The men revered him. After the strike—he loved the irony in that word—no one opposed his leadership.

Brawny men to defend the place, fish in the sea, and women to cook made life bearable. The occasional female 'visitor' entertained the men. That type of thing passed Lenny by these days, but it kept the lads happy. Not that the Comrades, as he called them, went without. There were enough volunteers among the resident women.

The community had few kids, though not healthy ones, due to inbreeding. It didn't concern Lenny because he would be six feet under before it became a big problem. Humanity was screwed anyway.

Fighting tournaments were the big thing amongst the Comrades. As long as there were plenty of bouts n' blood, it kept aggression at bay.

Men captured outside the docks had been slim in the last few months. So, tonight would be special because Grey—as the letter named him—could handle himself.

Lenny's thoughts turned to the girl who'd escaped. Once they caught her, she'd be looked after before joining the conveyor belt. There would be no underage stuff under his watch. Lenny had principles.

*

Two men armed with large spanners brought Grey to the office mid-afternoon. The man with one eye introduced himself as Lenny. During the interrogation—if you could call it that, given the lack of violence—the man only received silence.

Lenny looked more like a walking corpse than a leader. Deathly pale and missing four front teeth. His filthy fingers and yellowed nails periodically raked across greasy grey hair.

But the weasel had a cunningness about him. His so-called Comrades, once muscled from hard physical work, now rolled in fat, betrayed little in the way of intelligence.

He fixed Grey with his good eye, the other appearing to turn in unison. 'Seems someone wants you and the girl. Willing to pay for the privilege. Want to tell me why? No? Thought not.'

Grey now understood the greedy little turd's leniency. But there was more to it.

'Consider yourself a hard man, don't you? Well, I've got a surprise for you. We'll be having some fun tonight. Entertainment for us at least—not for you.' He chuckled.

'You want me to fight,' Grey stated and shrugged.

Lenny tried to bait him. 'Got the girl. Easy to find a frightened child, eh?'

Grey smiled inwardly. Jen was free. Scared, but definitely not easy to find.

His smile turned to a gut wrench. She wouldn't try to escape. She'd attempt a rescue.

Lenny chuckled when his face dropped.

*

Jen lay underneath a vertical cylinder, surrounded by worming pipes. The only drawback was the black stuff leaking from the rim. Avoiding the drips wasn't hard, but a sticky residue pooled on the ground. She had to lie at an uncomfortable angle on the floor, thinking about what to do next. And it was bloody cold, even wrapped in Grey's coat.

Why had he given it to her in the first place? Was it to say he wouldn't need it again or keep it until he came?' Either way, she would make sure he did wear it again.

A more secure hiding place and gathering information was essential. Jen considered what Grey had said about footprints. The men would follow her tracks and come soon, which was good. They'd stay in this area for some time because she would be somewhere else.

Shadows from the falling sun made it easier to sneak alongside machinery. To confuse the men, she walked in one direction, climbed on pipes for a way, then doubled back and started again.

Eventually, a large horizontal cylinder standing one foot off the ground appeared. Jen could slide underneath an adult couldn't because criss-cross pipes and valves created a tangle on each end.

On the far side of the cylinder, a dark space allowed her to sit and think. Until men started banging on pipes, the reverberation travelling like deep voices in a tunnel.

'Fishdicks, thinking you can scare me out,' she muttered. 'I'm not about to run like a dim'ead rabbit out of a hole.'

The men were filthy, like Scabs, a suitable name for them. Ten touching heads together couldn't make one brain. Jen knew she could outsmart them. Grey's words came to mind. 'You can't devise a plan if you don't look for one.'

When the moon showed, the Scabs gave up banging. Jen waited a while, then rolled out of the temporary Dig after pulling at the sticky coat.

Only the cry of seagulls and the occasional clang from pipes disturbed the air. She decided that making for the tanker seemed a good option because the Scabs might live there.

Dilapidated rectangular buildings materialised beyond the machinery. Most of the roofs had caved in or lay twisted on the ground. Useless to live inside.

A square tank provided cover to check out the tanker at the far end of the concrete concourse.

Groups of men climbed a long wood gangway to an entrance below the deck. Two guards, blowing into their hands, remained silhouetted by what looked like lamps, using oil for the flame. It seemed dangerous to Jen but worth some consideration—any information was good information.

The top deck was lit up with a string of lamps ending at a massive cabin near the stern, which remained in darkness—more intel.

Periodically, the guards disappeared behind the entrance and smoke from totes sneaked outside. Which seemed odd. Surely, they wouldn't have tobacco. One of them appeared to wobble when he came outside. Strange.

With nothing more to see, Jen returned to the makeshift Dig, where her mind worked overtime. What Grey told her about himself made no sense at the time. Thinking more, she'd never met two people in the same person. One with the Rage, the other, not exactly talkative, but controlled. Except that changed whenever he explained something. To her, at least. And there was the strange stuff he called Juice with its effect. Nothing Jen had ever heard of did that.

Maybe he was telling the truth after all? Which meant he was leaving and she couldn't go with him. Losing Grey and being alone yet again would be horrible. Better to kill herself first. That thought scared her even more. Tears turned into uncontrollable sobs spasming her body.

When she calmed down, she got angry—muscle-stiffening, shaking hands, angry. Not at Grey. At those stinking Scabs who had him.

The next day was the longest Jen could remember. She lay under the tank, sleeping on and off between voices and footsteps moving around the pipes. It didn't concern her. The place was enormous, and impossible for the men to search everywhere.

Someone shouted close by. Jen wriggled through the pipes to see what happened. A Scab pointed out tracks to four other men. They zigzagged back and forth for ages. She chuckled when their frustration turned to bickering, name-calling, and a big argument.

In the end, the Scabs gave up.

*

Grey paced around, impatient to get on with whatever Lenny had planned.

Bread and a few cold potatoes were tossed into the hold, the drop smashing the vegetable into pieces. Disgusting as it was, he ate some because food brought energy.

Footsteps echoing across the deck said many people were gathering for the spectacle. He stretched his muscles, releasing knots and filing away aches and bruises.

When the hatchway opened, he was ready.

Men and women worked themselves into a frenzy of chattering whilst Grey stood silently near the towering cabin. How should he play this—end it fast or draw it out to inflict more pain? Pain, he decided, until it was over for him.

He took two steps towards the centre of a human ring.

'Hold your horses, there,' Lenny said. 'We got a warm-up act first.'

Two men with scaffolding pipes stepped before Grey to hold him back.

Someone pushed a young, trembling Trooper into the middle. The lad's wide eyes settled on Lenny, begging for mercy.

'Gonna give you a bit of an advantage,' the weasel said, throwing a stumpy chair leg. 'Pick it up. I said—pick—it—up!'

The Trooper's shoulders dropped, knowing he had no choice. Retrieving the weapon, he stared at it like a foreign object until one man beckoned him closer. The lad ran at him with the club held aloft. His adversary side-stepped and delivered a vicious punch, sending the Trooper to the deck.

After he stood and spat blood, the lad surged forwards in desperation and threw a haymaker. Another hard punch sent him to the deck.

The Comrade locked an arm around his neck, biceps bulging as they tightened. Red-faced, the Trooper tried in vain to pull the arm away. A minute later, his body sagged and crumpled.

Jeers and shouts erupted from the crowd until Lenny held up his hands for silence and turned to Grey.

'Hope you do better n'that.' he sneered and winked his good eye.

Grey had maintained control over the Rage, wanting a protracted fight to make whoever he fought suffer. Now, it was different—they had killed a boy no more than four years older than Jen.

Spectators shouted 'Gord' when a fat man in a stained white vest walked into the arena. He swayed whilst punching a fist into a palm. When the Comrade lurched, Grey lashed a foot into his knee, the impact sending Gord to the deck, where his head cracked onto the wood, knocking him out.

Suddenly, the onlookers chanted, 'Beast, Beast, Beast.' A thick-set man with broad shoulders, enormous flabby arms and a tattooed bald head bearing his nickname strode into the ring. His stance and calloused fists told of a seasoned fighter.

Beast's eyes narrowed then he slapped his bare barrel chest covered in coarse black hair. Grey feigned a step to the left and launched a jaw punch, rocking his opponent. When a fist in the cheek returned the compliment, he staggered, righted himself and delivered an uppercut. Both men took steps away and glared at each other.

The Comrade roared and charged, only to be met by a boot in the ribs. He slipped to the side, stood straight and slapped his hairy chest again to psyche himself up. Neither gave ground as the ferocity increased. Beast threw punches; Grey parried, kicked and lashed out, but the onslaught forced him back to the baying crowd. The Rage wasn't enough to tame the man.

A shove from the audience sent him straight at his adversary, whose thick arms locked him in a bear hug from behind.

Grey smashed his head back into the Comrade's face, loosening the grip enough to break free.

Beast forced a sludge of snot and blood out of his nose, then charged. Grey dropped and scissored the thick legs, sending his opponent crashing to the deck.

A wheeze behind said Gord had regained his feet. Spinning around, Grey rammed his shoulder into the Comrade's gut, sending them both tumbling. Meanwhile, Beast levered upright.

There was only a second to act. His heel connected with Gord's temple before he dived, rolled and swayed on leaden legs. Spectators hushed.

Beast lurched, arms held wide, and took Grey in another bear hug. This time, the two men faced each other eyeball to eyeball.

With a protracted grunt of effort, Beast tightened the constriction. Spears of pain circled Grey's midriff when a rib cracked. The Comrade turned his head away to avoid another head butt.

Unable to take in air, Grey knew it was game over—unless...

He brought his hands together across his captor's breastbone. Beast bellowed when handfuls of hair ripped from his chest, anchored to ragged slices of skin.

The Comrade rocked and threw his head back in agony. A thundering punch to his windpipe sent him gasping to the floor.

Grey dropped to his knees, unable to finish his adversary, torment coursing through his body. A bony hand pulled his head back, and something cold and sharp pressed into his throat.

*

Jen headed for a row of collapsed sheds running parallel to the ship. The remaining brickwork, strewn with beams and roofing, made a shadowy obstacle course—her kind of place.

She studied the tanker, searching for a way to get aboard. Only heavy ropes reached from cleats to the ship.

Farther along, a wood shack stood close to the quayside, fishing nets and lobster pots against the sides. Jen sprinted and stood flat to the wall. Voices came from way down the quay.

She slid inside, waiting for her eyes to acclimatise. Suddenly, arms circled her from behind.

'Gottya!' a man snarled.

Jen tried to rake a foot down his shins, not wanting to shout out in case the sound brought others. He held her tight until her struggle abated.

'Please, don't hurt me,' she said, playing scared.

The Scab turned her around. 'Bet you're a pretty girl.'

His eyes bulged when the blade plunged into his groin.

'Girls don't carry knives,' Jen hissed.

She hesitated, closed her eyes and pushed the knife under his chin.

Retching, Jen realised no pleasure came from killing, even with an animal like this.

Worried others may have heard, she peeped nervously outside. Distance, chattering and laughter said no one had.

Thinking about the steps leading up to the ship sparked an idea.

A collapsed roof, lying at an angle from a partial brick wall provided good cover to watch the procession.

Men walked in groups, and women carried baskets of fish.

Jen listened to their gaggling and caught mention of the forthcoming tournament. Relief and fear hit her with equal force. Grey was still alive, but he would fight later in the evening.

She followed the procession until they climbed the gangplank, then headed back along the quayside to prepare. A while later, she returned to her hideout.

Her plan was to wait until the sentries went inside for a tote, then climb up to the ship without being seen. Once in bow range, she would call out, sight the men and force them both to surrender.

Grey would have said it was a stupid idea. It depended upon both men complying without shouting for help. But if it didn't work, they'd probably take her prisoner, and Jen could try to stab them.

'That's dim'ead thinking,' she muttered to herself.

'Patience,' Grey always said. 'Don't rush things. Wait for the right opportunity.'

Which Jen did. Now she needed energy—Juice. It tasted disgusting. When the rush came, her luck changed and she felt ready.

The sentries disappeared when cheering erupted and didn't return.

*

Lenny gave Grey a lopsided grin.

'You did well there. Better than expected, that's for sure. Crowd enjoyed it, too. But now I have a dilemma. Took out our champion, you did. No other contenders now. So, should I keep you for more entertainment or slit your throat?'

Grey didn't answer, nor did he show fear. His only thoughts were for Jen. He didn't care about himself.

Bitter regret forced a wince. Lenny chuckled. Then his good eye opened wide when the swish of an arrow sounded.

*

Standing in the bridge's shadow, Jen shot the scrawny man in the thigh.

'Any of you fishdicks move, and I'll put one in his neck.' she yelled.

Grey staggered to the voice, leaving Lenny yelling and writhing on the floor.

'Take this!' Jen hissed, handing his bow across, then disappeared up a short flight of steps to a gantry.

Seconds later, oil lamps began arching to the deck. People shouted, screamed and backed away as the flames snaked along the deck.

Grey managed a few poor shots, unaware if any found a mark. But at least they helped to keep the Comrades back.

Jen handed him the flask. 'Here, drink some of this.'

He took a quick gulp. 'It'll take a few moments to work.'

'Know that. Already tried it. Couldn't have shot your bow properly otherwise, dim'ead.'

'It was stupid coming after me.'

'Save your complaining for later, we've got to go before they get organised.'

At the gangplank, four burning lamps stood in a line at the top.

Jen said, 'There's a rowboat farther along down some steps. Don't fall over the side. I'll see you there. Got things to do first.'

'What?'

Throw those lamps, dim'ead, then get your belongings.

'Leave them.'

'No way. I promised myself you would wear your coat again.'

She pushed his shoulder. 'Go!'

Soon after, burning oil fanned across the entrance.

Grey ran like a drunkard until the Juice kicked in. Then he halted and looked back, annoyed with himself for letting Jen go alone. He sighed with relief when a dark form appeared, dragging his coat along the ground.

Despite her protests, Grey took the oars. He followed instructions to head for pilings supporting the quayside, then used rusted support struts to haul them to a barnacle-encrusted wall.

'The men will search the pipes for ages,' Jen said. 'I left tracks all over the place, like you told me. Good thinking, eh?'

Grey mumbled, then closed his eyes.

Jen shook him awake sometime later. For a moment, he struggled to remember where they were until the fog gave way to searing pain.

A cough from the first mouthful of Juice caused agonising spasms. The second attempt allowed the precious liquid to find its way down.

Grey's gravelly voice asked, 'What's the plan?'

'Out to sea, idiot.'

'I meant, after that.'

Jen raised her arms in a confused gesture. 'No idea.'

'Mm.'

'What's that mean, dim'ead?'

'No idea,' he replied, mimicking her.

'Shit for brains. Did good though, didn't I?'

Grey shrugged, 'You did okay.' Before she hit him with curses, he added, 'You did brilliantly. Let me think a moment.'

'I want to think, too. Proved I can.'

'True, but I know where we are.'

'On the fucking docks!'

He ignored the comment.

'Okay,' he said. 'We stick to the coast for now—there's likely to be places to hide if necessary.'

'Why?'

'The Tzar's coming. There were a couple of Trooper messengers on the tanker. Getting away from here is a big problem, though. The Comrades—don't ask—will follow in fishing boats.'

'Nope.'

'Why?'

Pride in her voice, Jen said, 'Cut some ropes and slashed the sails.'

They pulled the rowboat along the pilings until the hull of a small open boat with a single sail appeared.

'Left this one untouched,' Jen said.

After reaching the end of a short pier, angry voices came from the quayside. A cacophony of 'fucks' sounded like paddling ducks.

*

The Tzar's men arrived two days later.

Lenny's confidence evaporated when he saw the giant riding what looked like a carthorse. Troopers stood in an orderly line holding rifles, sending Comrades scattering to take cover behind scrap metal and pipes.

A Trooper walked confidently to the gates.

'The Tzar wants to negotiate.'

Lenny at least had a hand to play. He knew the area and offered to help track down Grey.

When the gates opened, Troopers marched through, guns lowered.

'Bring your men out as a sign of good faith.' The messenger said. 'Ambush won't help any of us.'

Comrades holding handguns and scaffolding edged out of hiding to Lenny's side.

The Troopers dropped their rifles to the floor. After a barked order from Lenny, his men dropped their weapons.

The Tzar gave a lopsided grin. Lenny gave a toothless grin. Then he didn't.

Clicks sounded behind from Troopers who had cut through the fence farther down the refinery.

Comrades were forced into a line. Some looked at their feet, others at each other in fear.

The Tzar dismounted with a grunt, rubbed the old injury on his leg, and pointed at a large man with a bloody chest and broken nose.

'What's your name?'

'Beast.'

The Tzar laughed. 'Looks like you've had a tussle with Grey.' He nodded at a Trooper who yanked Lenny to one side. No Comrades survived the hail of bullets.

Blocking out the sun, the goliath loomed over the cowering old man.

'First, you kill my messengers. Then you let Grey and his bitch escape. Not good negotiation, eh?'

When the Troopers departed, Lenny didn't watch. He cradled his remaining eye, wailing into the darkness.

DECISIONS

JEN handled the small fishing boat with ease. Grey struggled with the tiller, screwing his face whenever a sharp turn came. She urged him to take more Juice, but he declined. The remainder would be needed later.

They passed a city on the first night, where pockets of light flickered. There were no tall structures, only sizeable gaps between the silhouettes of dwellings. The strike had been severe.

Grey nodded at the fires. 'It'll slow the Tzar down if he goes there for information.'

'You don't think he'll come after us by sea?' Jen asked. 'Those boats I damaged can be fixed, and any of those Comrades left alive can sail.'

'Too slow, and we've got a good head start. Better to come along the coast on horseback and try to cut us off.'

On the second day, Grey said, 'We need to go inland soon before we both dehydrate—die of thirst.'

Hours later, Jen pointed to a wide inlet between escarpments.

She pushed the tiller; Grey screwed his eyes and pulled to make a ninety-degree turn. He couldn't have done it without the tailwind and calm sea.

They sailed into a bleak landscape with rocks and hillocks on each side. Patches of purple heather and yellow gorse dotted the slopes, the odd sheep grazing in between.

Grey's mood improved. This was an environment suited to his skills.

A dark stone building with a single turret on a promontory appeared.

'Good vantage point and shelter,' he said. 'And there's a stream for fresh water.'

It spooked Jen when they walked inside the stark interior. Large blocks of stone had tumbled from walls where grass fought for light, and moss thrived in the damp decay.

A winding stone stairway next to the wall led up to the turret. Grey found the going hard whenever a broken stair required a handhold to cross over. Jen provided the best support she could manage.

At the top, a stone platform circled the turret, with a hatchway leading to the summit. Ladders had once provided the means to climb up, but they lay broken on the ground.

Jen tried to sweep away layers of dust from the floor, resulting in a bout of coughing from Grey.

'We need food,' he croaked.

'Where from? I'm not going fishing. If you say that, I'll kick you in the ribs.'

Grey attempted a small smile. 'I saw sheep on the hill.'

She looked at him incredulously. 'How am I supposed to catch one of those? They'll run like rabbits—uphill!'

'Imagine it's Lenny you're shooting.'

Jen returned exhausted and pissed off, dragging a leg up the steps. 'Don't laugh, or I'll hit you with it. Bet you've never had to get a lumpy bone apart?'

Grey raised an eyebrow to say he had.

'You can do it next time or starve. Suppose I've got to use the flint thing Sal gave you and make a fire?'

'Yup.'

The more Jen struck the flint without success, the angrier she became. Each time smoke wisped, the dry heather didn't catch. Grey was told to fuck off when he made suggestions. Eventually, he had to suffer agony from his ribs to do it. Jen refused to help build the fire with the broken ladder.'

'So, you going to get the wool off?' She asked.

'Nope.'

'How the hell do I do it?'

'Work it out. I need some sleep.'

Soon after, Grey shot up, pain cutting his side made worse by coughing from smoke.

Jen had given up trying to get the wool off and thrown the leg onto the fire. 'Don't say a word. It's dying down now.'

'So am I.'

'Stay awake and watch the meat, lazy arse, while I go for drinking water. Have to use the piss bucket on the boat, though. Think about that when you take a slurp.'

The half-cooked meat took some chewing but tasted delicious. Grey's throat hurt, so he ate slowly. Jen tore at the blackened muscle, swallowing lumps large enough to choke anyone else.

'Wipe the grease from your mouth,' he said.
'How about you mind your fucking own?'
'Can you stop speaking like that?'
'What?'
Grey tilted his head.
'Okay, I'll try.'
It didn't last long.
'Fuck—spiders in my hair,' Jen complained once they settled.
'They're attracted to talking.'
'What?'
'Go to sleep.'

This time, Jen jerked awake when she heard barking in the night. Forgetting about Grey's ribs, she nudged him.
'What the...?'
'Shush. Wolves.'
'Dogs.'
'What's the difference? They can still follow blood.'
Grey sighed. 'Yes, they could, but they're unlikely to cross the broken steps. Besides they'll come up one at a time and you can shoot them.'
'What if there are loads, though? I'll run out of arrows.'
'Better make the shots count then. Now shut up. My ribs are hurting like hell. Don't do it again.'
Jen smirked.

Morning brought a drop in temperature. Dark clouds in the distance threatened snow. Grey stretched, testing his injury. Better than yesterday, but he'd still have to take care.
'We staying here or moving on?' Jen asked.
'Moving on. Cut some meat for us and chuck the bones outside. It will look like dogs have eaten a kill.'

'Cinders?'

'We'll throw larger pieces in the water and scatter the rest. Best we can do. It's the boat I'm concerned about. Hiding it farther down will be difficult.'

'You said the Tzar wouldn't follow by sea.'

'No, he won't. But it might be visible from land.'

'Not if there's trees or high rocks.'

'Maybe.'

Jen licked her finger and put a hand between the broken glass in the window. 'Moderate onshore wind. Easy sailing.'

'Aye aye, Capt'n.'

The water ended in a bay. Rocks on either side sloped down to a curving beach covered in stones. A deep cleft offered a place to secure the boat.'

'Not ideal cover, but at least it can't be seen from a distance.' Grey said. 'Now we need warmer clothing and a ride.'

'But there's only sheep. Even a big one couldn't take your fat arse.'

'Very funny.'

Early evening, a settlement came into view. Hidden behind a rocky outcrop, they studied the buildings. Five small, terraced cottages and a larger farmhouse sat alongside a dirt road. Smoke curled from several chimneys, and people milled around the grounds. A large barn stood to one side, suggesting livestock and perhaps a stable.

'Are we gonna ask them for what we need?'

'No. We'll wait until lights go out and take what we need.'

'You're not going to kill anyone, though. I'd rather starve than that.'

'Still thinking about the man in the shed?'

'Yes. It felt horrible. And no one here deserves the same.'

Grey ruffled Jen's hair.

'What's that for?'

'Because you're a good person. Better than me. Don't change. You'll be happier for it.'

They targeted the farmhouse to avoid what looked like kennels adjacent to the end cottage. Jen waited in the shadows, holding Grey's bow whilst he went inside.

The interior was sparse but functional, with the remains of supper still lingering in the air.

At the top of a stairway, the soft vibration of a light snore drifted from one door down a corridor. Three others were ajar.

A quick check confirmed small humps under blankets in two rooms, the third empty. The adult's door stood open an inch. Thankfully, the hinges didn't squeal.

Grey edged inside, taking slow steps to the largest mound on the bed. A hand over the mouth sent a flush of air through his fingers. He pointed his knife against the man's throat. It took a second for eyes to spring open, one more to register the blade.

'Wake your wife,' Grey ordered.

The woman rubbed her face, then started.

'Quiet.' His sharp voice brooked no other option.

She nodded once.

'Here's what's going to happen.'

The woman carried jumpers, thick socks and waterproof leggings downstairs. Her husband followed with his hands on his head.

Grey moved to the front door, beckoning Jen inside and winked at her to say no one had died.

The couple were bound, gagged and told any noise would have consequences.

Jen took a brown waterproof coat hanging on a brass peg to replace the one taken from the corpses in the forest. Hiking boots caught her eye. Grey nodded in approval.

They found four horses tethered in the barn with tack hung over a wood rail. Jen put everything over her existing clothes. Grey rolled his eyes when she tutted about overlong sleeves and trousers.

'I look fat in these.'

'Yup. But you'll be warm.'

Once they'd mounted and set off, Jen said, 'That was great. Best scavenge I ever did. And you didn't kill anyone. You're learning, Grey, you're learning.'

*

They entered a pine forest along a vast mountain's edge. Snow, a foot deep, had accumulated. Flakes falling through the canopy said more was on the way.

Abruptly, Grey pulled on the reigns.

'Wait with the horse.'

'It's okay to kill Troopers,' She whispered. 'So that you know.'

'Thanks for permission.'

He crept through the trees, stopping to look and listen behind trunks. Two figures—men, not boys—sat inside the treeline, looking bored. Both wore black armbands.

Taking a different route was an option. However, reducing numbers in the event of a fight with any more men ahead would be better.

An arrow could finish one, but the other might run and start shooting. His handle would have been better, but Lenny had taken it. So, it had to be the knife which demanded stealth —unless the men came to him.

A crunch of twigs got the Trooper's attention, spinning them around. One pointed to the left and right, indicating they'd go in different directions.

Grey approached from behind and swung a thick branch at the first target, unconcerned about noise. As anticipated, the other Trooper came over at a crouch, gun drawn. He didn't expect a sweeping thump to the ankles from underneath a bush.

Once he hit the floor, Grey leapt from cover and delivered an arcing blow. The effort caused him to grunt in pain when taught muscles pulled at his ribs. He rested on one knee until the spasms diminished.

'You okay?' Jen asked, concern on her face.

'I'm fine.'

'Liar.'

He told her what happened.

'So, the Tzar knows we would come this way?'

'Not for sure. He's working all the angles. Those Troopers were scouts gathering information. Probably sent a while ago.'

Jen led the horse whilst Grey scouted ahead.

It was some time before he returned.

'Smoke farther on.'

'You rest, I'll go take a closer look,' Jen said. 'I'm a great sneaker. Done lots of it.'

'No.'

'But.'

'No.'

Seven Troopers sat around a fire. More than Grey expected. Too many to risk an attack. No sentries meant they were either complacent or confident he and Jen weren't in the area.

Nine men, including the two corpses, was an odd number. Ten made more sense, so one must have gone to report findings. He might stop at the farmhouse for information, and the Tzar would come.

Jen and Grey travelled in a large arc around the camp. Late afternoon, he spotted another trail of smoke, deciding it would unlikely be more Troopers, but it needed checking out. After twenty minutes or so, he came back.

'Cabin and family,' he told Jen.

She said they should warn them. Grey refused.

'Remember when I followed you from The Violet? At the place we rested, you told me to come or stay, when I complained. Same thing now.'

He reluctantly agreed, knowing she wouldn't accept anything less.

They tethered the horse in the forest and crept to the tree line. Two children played outside a log cabin. Grey and Jen walked into the clearing and waited, bows held high.

A woman stood by the door. 'Greg!' she shouted in alarm, then called the children indoors.

Holding a shotgun a tall man appeared from behind the building.

He narrowed his eyes on the newcomers. 'What do you want?'

'We want nothing,' Grey shouted. 'Just letting you know there could be men heading this way. They're not friendly.'

'Leave the bow and come nearer until I tell you to stop.' They halted when he said, 'Coats, packs, weapons on the floor, then take ten paces towards me.'

'Emma.' A girl not much older than Jen peeped through the door. 'Get their things and bring them here. You two sit, hands on your head.' Greg waved the shotgun and focused his gaze on Grey. 'The girl's your daughter? He asked.'

'Shut it, Jen,' Grey said before she could protest the use of 'girl.' 'No, she's not my daughter.'

'He's a friend,' Jen cut in. 'Done nothing wrong—you know, that kind of thing.'

'Good.' Greg sounded like he didn't care.

She told him about the men they'd seen. When she called them Troopers, no recognition dawned on his face.

'There may be bigger trouble coming,' Grey added.

The man raised his eyebrow. 'And why are you telling me this?'

Grey gave a short explanation about the Tzar.

'Is he chasing you?'

'Yes.'

Greg's face reddened. 'And you've led this Tzar here. Right to my door!' His knuckles turned white on the gunstock.

'Greg!' his wife said from the doorway. 'That's enough. I'll have no violence here. Remember the children.'

The woman tied them to a post on the veranda whilst her husband levelled the shotgun. Grey felt confident the man wouldn't kill them without provocation. His only concern was the Troopers back down the trail. They'd come searching when they discovered the bodies.

He sighed.

'You angry at me?' Jen whispered.

'At myself for listening.'

Inside the cabin, an argument started. Within minutes, the door flew open, and Greg stormed out. He leaned into Grey. 'If you make one move out of place, I'll blow your brains out.' The shotgun barrel twitched to reinforce the threat.

He led them inside.

The woman bound them to another post supporting the roof. She asked their names and introduced herself as Mary.

The children, ushered to bed, looked over their shoulders at the captives.

Grey and Jen, grateful for the fire's warmth, remained silent when Greg relayed the whole story to Mary. She looked across at Jen a few times, frowning as if she struggled to believe a young girl's involvement. Her hard eyes condemned Grey for allowing it to happen.

Greg stood over them, waving his gun as a final threat, then followed his wife upstairs.

Mary had tied the ropes under her husband's armed supervision. She wasn't good with knots. Jen was.

When a bow in a corner caught Grey's eyes he gave it to her then retrieved his own. The door closed silently, and they headed for the trees.

The following day, raised voices came from the cabin. Soon after, shutters closed, and scraping wood said barricades were being put in place. Greg came outside carrying a hunting rifle. He put his mouth close to the door and said something. Grey assumed it was to bar the entrance.

Mary poked the shotgun out of a partially open window. Her husband disappeared behind the cabin and then emerged on the roof.

Soon after, five Troopers walked into the clearing and spread out in a line: two held handguns, the other two carried rifles. The last one had a revolver tucked into his belt.

'That's far enough!' Greg shouted.

Raising his arms, the man not holding a gun, said, 'Just want to talk.'

'Nothing to talk about.'

'Seen any strangers, a man and a girl?'

'Not our business, so move on.'

One Trooper took a step. 'We'll make it your business.'

Greg's rifle made an audible click. 'There are others in the house with weapons watching your every move.'

'Wife, maybe. Place is too small for more. Except kids, eh?'

At the obvious threat, Greg sighted then fired a warning shot near the man's leg.

Three Troopers ran for cover behind barrels. The other two stood their ground and shot at the cabin. When wood splintered near Greg's head, he fired back, wounded a man, then ducked down.

More bullets peppered the cabin's roof. Mary's shotgun boomed and hit nothing. The last Trooper in the open sprinted for an old water tank, firing as he went.

'Cease fire!' He commanded before addressing Greg. 'Wasting ammo. You'll run out before we do.'

He started when a Trooper behind the barrels yelled in pain.

'Arrows are never wasted,' Grey called out. 'Dead men give them back.'

The two still behind the barrels shot blindly at the voice in the trees. Greg fired at them, his bullets cracking into the wood. The leader at the water tank called for his men to stop. Cordite and an eerie silence filled the air.

'More of us than you,' the man yelled in a cocky voice.

Grey shouted from a new position. 'Only if you include your friends in the woods.'

'All dead,' Jen added from the opposite side of the clearing.

One Trooper behind a barrel aimed in Jen's direction. Oblivious to Grey crouched nearby, he received an arrow through the chest. The other ran to an open shed and only just made it inside when Jen's arrow flew by.

Greg took the distraction and shot at the water tank.

'Okay, okay, I give up,' the leader called. Hands up, he moved out from cover. The man in the shed followed.

When Grey and Jen emerged, Greg thanked them. His tone conveyed no depth of gratitude.

'Go inside with your family until I call you.' Grey said firmly. 'Jen, go with him.'

'But...'

'Go—with—him.'

Greg followed her into the house, slamming the door behind.

Grey herded the leader and wounded Troopers into the forest. He returned after a while to drag the dead away.

Only a trail of blood staining the snow showed a fight had taken place.

*

Mary spoke in a friendly tone to keep the children calm. Periodically, her eyes wandered about the room.

She explained Greg had spent time in the Navy before working on the Rigs as a diver, and she'd grown up on a lowland farm. After the strike, they moved to the cabin for safety.

'Yeah, right.' Her husband mumbled.

Trying to bring humour to the table, Mary said children were inevitable, rolling her eyes at Greg.

'Mum!' Emma, the oldest, said.

Jen smirked.

The conversation gravitated to her. She was candid about her background, only letting slip the occasional expletive, and avoiding the worst word. Mary was still shocked whilst Emma looked to the floor, trying not to laugh. Sarah, the middle daughter, giggled a few times, receiving a withering glare from her mother. Charlie, the young boy, was more interested in a hand-carved toy.

Greg said little. He sat back, eyeing the pair, scratching his red beard.

When Grey suggested his family should leave the area for a time, he gripped the table.

Mary said, 'Greg.'

He stood and strode outside.

Grey approached soon after, making solid footsteps so as not to startle him. The air was as cold as the atmosphere between them.

'You don't trust or like me, and I don't blame you.'

'Revelation, that is.'

'The Tzar's coming this way. Fact.'

'You know that how? By using a knife to prize it out of one of those sons of bitches?'

'I did what was necessary,' Grey replied coolly.

'How long have we got?

'A messenger was sent to the Tzar. He will have likely discovered we came this way. Depending on distance, the psychopath could arrive within a week, maybe sooner.'

'So, you're saying we must be away within a few days.'

Grey was emphatic. 'Tomorrow. And hope for more time.'

Greg thought for a while. 'How many men will he have?'

'Too many.'

'And if we stay?'

'There's a high chance he'll kill all of you. The man is a monster.'

'Like you.' Greg's hard voice matched his unwavering stare.

There was no point in answering.

That night, Grey and Jen lay on the floor downstairs. They heard Mary sobbing and the reassuring tones of Greg's deep voice.

'Think they'll leave?'

'Stupid not to.'

'And if they don't, what do we do?'

Grey sighed. 'We leave them to it.'

'But...'

'We go! Nothing more we can do.'

They both spent a restless night. Jen turned and mumbled in her sleep. Grey lay back on his arms, thinking. Before her, this situation wouldn't have happened. Now, she was his conscience. But there was a time when caring became dangerous, a lesson she had yet to learn.

The husband and wife came down early. She had been a woman with an air of confidence the day before. Now, her pale face and uncombed brown hair gave her a worn appearance.

Greg's jaw clenched when he saw Grey. His fist opened and closed, knuckles white with the pressure.

It was apparent they had decided to leave.

'Can we help?' Grey asked.

'You can piss off outside is what you can do. Leave a decent family to pack.'

Jen's and Grey's mount took much of the load whilst the younger children rode Greg's only horse.

'Where do you intend to go?'

'North. Town on the coast.'

'We'll stay with you in case there's trouble.'

'Trouble! If it weren't for you, there'd be no trouble.

'Not true. Regardless of whether we came here, the Tzar won't believe it. Those Troopers threatened your children. Their leader wouldn't think twice. I've seen the evidence.

When the family left, Jen and Grey waited in the clearing.

'We'll follow at a distance. They need space.'

Towards midday, snow fell. By dark, a full-scale blizzard arrived.

Greg led them to a deserted cottage. It was dry inside and soon warmed with an open fire.

Later, Grey heard Jen get up. She crept to the room where Emma sobbed and stayed with her.

The next morning the snow was knee-deep. Both men went outside to talk.

'I have no choice but to accept your help,' Greg said. 'I'm a proud man, and it's tearing me apart to ask, but my family won't survive this without it. Like you said, I don't like you, but now I must trust you. Can I trust you?'

'Yes. You can.'

The day saw more snow. Not a blizzard, but enough to keep adding inches to the white carpet.

Greg waded fifty yards ahead. Jen, Emma, and Mary led the horses. Charlie and Sarah rode. Grey stayed at the rear, halting periodically to look behind. The Tzar was too far away to surprise them; however, relying on assumptions was dangerous.

They entered a large ravine. Steep-sided cliffs sloped down to the valley floor and closed the path to a width of five yards. Snow had sculpted cornices along the top. Greg and Grey cleared a passage for the horses, steering them around boulders thrown from the cliffs over time.

The younger children shouted to create echoes until their mother chastised them when snow puffed from the ridgeline.

It took an hour of hard going to reach a cave Greg knew. Grey started a fire, and they huddled close to eat a watery broth made from leftover meat and vegetables.

By morning, the children cried with the cold whilst Mary offered soft words. Emma trudged beside Jen, grabbing her arm for reassurance every so often.

By midday, the blizzard attacked again with blinding snow and a blustery wind. Grey made his way to Greg. The man's brow creased when he tried to look ahead.

'Smallholding in a few miles,' he shouted, the wind whipping at his voice. 'Stay here while I go for help.'

'I'll take them into the trees and leave a marker on the path.'

Mary glanced at Greg, concern in her eyes. Cupping his hand around her ear, he leaned in close to explain. Reluctantly, she accepted there was no alternative.

Grey led them down a slight incline into dense pines for protection. Dragging broken branches, he arranged them across the path and placed rocks on top. Back with the family, he held the children wrapped under his coat and a blanket. Mary and Jen hunched on either side of Emma.

The light had faded when Greg arrived with two men carrying extra blankets. After a gruelling trek, they arrived at the homestead exhausted.

Two women cuddled the children next to a roaring fire. Emma and Jen held their hands out to the flame. The adults stood behind to let the young ones thaw first.

Grey sat deep in thought at the back of the room. He considered taking some Juice for his ribs but discarded the idea. There were perilous times ahead if his plan came to fruition.

He asked Greg to join him in a barn for a talk. The sticking point came from the weaponry Grey needed. In the end, he got his way.

'Still despise you for what you've done to my family,' Greg said, 'Could have killed you without remorse.'

'Understandable.'

'But. At least you're trying to make amends. I'll do what you ask—for the girl's sake. I don't give a toss which way it goes for you.'

'All I can ask.'

Jen raised an eyebrow when they returned, but Grey shrugged a 'don't ask' gesture.

*

There was no sign of him the following morning. Jen gave Greg a quizzical look when he handed over a note.

"I'm going back for the Tzar. Stay with the family. They're good people. Don't follow. I must do this alone.
I'm sorry, Jen.
Grey"

Mary held her when she cried.

*

Despite his reluctance to use such a weapon, Grey carried Greg's shotgun and all the cartridges the man had. He retraced the journey through thickening snow from the blizzard, stopping at the cave for the night.

Sleep wouldn't come. Thoughts of Jen had plagued his mind on the journey and continued through the night. He believed he'd made the right decision leaving her behind, and in time, she would adjust to life with the family. But knowing he would never see her again felt bittersweet. He already missed her spirit, determination and even the obscenities. That feeling would stay with him for as long as he lived—which might not be long.

Dried meat provided fuel to continue the tiring plough through the snow to Greg's cabin. Once there, Grey began preparations. He hid his bow in the trees, heaped snow on top and readied arrows, placing them point down in the quiver to keep them dry. Then, he set about getting everything else ready.

After a few hours inside the family's old home, a modicum of life returned to his weary limbs. Soon after, he headed for the ravine.

Climbing up the rock face was impossible, even without snow. A long, arduous walk up the adjoining slope was the only option. Several times, compacted patches sent him sliding downwards, exacerbating his aching muscles and throbbing ribs. Reluctantly, he stopped for a sip of Juice to lessen the pain.

When he reached the top he dropped to the floor. Exhausted though he was, shelter was imperative.

After what felt like hours, a domed snow cave offered protection from the elements.

He stood outside briefly, listening to the wind whistling around the side. Snowflakes twisted and turned in the turbulence until they disappeared seemingly towards the abandoned cabin. And the Tzar.

Inside the refuge, Grey took kindling for a fire from a backpack. Extra clothing and food filled the remaining space. As the interior warmed, he watched water drip from the roof and went over his plan yet again.

There was one major concern. If the Tzar didn't arrive soon, he'd have to keep returning to the cabin and back again to survive the cold. Each trip would deplete his strength and the chance of being spotted increase.

Luck was on his side a day later.

GOLIATH

A Trooper ran into the cabin where the Tzar waited. 'Dead men in the woods—laid out in a line,' he panted.

'So, that shit Grey's left me a message.'

He stomped outside in fury, circled the camp, and threatened anyone who irked him.

'Fucking snow,' he kept repeating.

The next day, orders to move out were given.

He scowled when Troopers looked at each other, concerned about the weather.

'Anyone got something to say?' He bellowed.

No one uttered a word.

The Tzar brought up the rear once they entered the ravine, preferring men at the front to take any risks. After thirty minutes of slow going, shotgun blasts sounded ahead, followed by a rumble. The noise came closer. A Trooper yelled, pointing to the ridgeline directly above. Overhangs broke away and fell to the slope below. Soon after, snow thundered down the ravine, bringing rocks along for the ride.

*

Grey moved along the ridge, firing blast after blast, dislodging the cornice as he went. The ravine was soon engulfed in a white cloud. How many would survive the onslaught was impossible to predict. But some would die, for sure, and others suffer serious injuries. Those who made it then had to fight through deep snow to get back to the cabin. Which was the only way they could go. Grey had fired enough shots ahead to block the way.

Satisfied he'd done as much damage as possible, he headed back to the cabin, hoping to arrive before the Tzar—if the man had survived.

Grey breathed a sigh of relief when he got there first. Now, it was a waiting game.

Wrapped in a black fur coat, snow over the shoulders, the giant and his surviving bone-weary men led the remaining horses into the clearing.

For the first time, Grey saw the Tzar limp across the clearing. He was enormous, larger than any man he had ever seen. A prickle of fear tingled up his spine. 'Stop it. The bastard must die for Jen's sake,' he said to himself. 'Get on with it.'

Troopers set about sorting the camp. Any who didn't make an acceptable effort received a bellowed warning. There was no anger or challenge in their posture, just compliance from fear. Except for one person who appeared to berate a Trooper.

They were shoved to the Tzar, who doled out a backhand, sending the defiant man to the floor. Except it wasn't a man, Grey realised. It was Sal.

She stood and glared at the giant. When the man's fist clenched, it looked like he was going to deliver a hell of a punch. Instead, he grabbed Sal's hair and pulled her to the cabin.

Her presence complicated Grey's plan. He faced a choice —her or Jen. Unless he could pull off a rescue and still kill the Tzar; otherwise, it was Jen all the way.

Either Sal made a break for freedom when the action started or stayed to face the consequences.

Late evening, four lookouts took up positions whilst the other Troopers slept in tents pitched side by side. The Tzar, Sal and three men stayed in the cabin. Lieutenant and two Sergeants Grey assumed—the favoured few.

Two sentries took their places in the gloom a distance away from each other. The fools were seated—easier to approach, difficult to fight back. Both died from the same tactics. Hand over mouth, knife to the throat.

The other two were more challenging to sneak up on. Each man leaned against a tree on opposite sides of the clearing. The closest made the mistake of standing inside the forest, invisible from his sidekick. Fortunately, Grey had discovered a large axe behind the cabin and removed its head. He'd got used to a handle and liked the ergonomics.

The takeout required a single hit. Anything more, and the Trooper might yell.

Grey crept towards him. One light footstep. Stop. Another footstep. Stop. A leopard stalking its prey through the jungle.

He came from the side and swung the weapon with all his strength into the man's chest. A head blow would risk crashing the handle into the tree.

Only a dull thud made it into the clearing, masked by the crackling fire.

One sentry remained. Grey circled the man's throat with his handle and pulled back. None of the other Troopers heard a thing. Tired men slept soundly.

Grey retraced his steps into the trees and used his flint to spark a small fire into life. With a burning branch, he went to a pile of logs stored in a lean-to next to the cabin and lit the kindling he'd left.

Back in the forest, a row of arrows wrapped in cloth were set alight. Satisfied the flame was intense enough, Grey aimed at two tents in the centre of the others. It was a tricky shooting because the arrows had to land at the bottom of the fabric. He needed time before it caught and the alarm was raised. Seconds would make all the difference. Fortunately, his aim was true.

Moments later, two burning arrows pierced cabin shutters. Soon after, shouts began.

The bottom of the door flamed when the first Trooper ran out. He fell across the entrance, an arrow through his thigh. A second man tried to bolt and stumbled over the body, taking a hit on the way.

A voice roared from inside, followed by snapping wood. Two sections of a tabletop landed over the fallen men. The Tzar thumped across the platform into the clearing, dragging Sal behind.

The giant pulled her to his chest before Grey could line up a shot. He hesitated, trying to avoid hitting Sal and aimed for the giant's neck. Pull, breathe, fire. The arrow only skewered a shoulder.

Grey reached for another, hoping for a second chance. He was too late.

The Tzar yelled and stomped away. Sal broke free and staggered for the treeline to where the shots came from. Reaching the forest, she threw herself to the floor and snaked in Grey's direction.

'Here,' he called, reaching out to haul her to safety. 'Follow me.'

Sal stumbled over a tree root. Grey yanked her up.

'Keep moving, or I'll leave you behind,' he hissed.

The trees ended at the top of a steep rise, below which his backpack marker had been placed.

'I've cleared as much snow as I could. It's still going to be bad. No choice.'

Holding the bow and handle in each hand, Grey slid over the edge. Sal followed close behind. His boots dug into the snow, finding enough purchase to control the slide. Hers were loose, and one came off halfway down, tumbling like a thrown dice.

Grey knew he could outrun the Tzar's men, but Sal wasn't in good shape. They made it through knee-deep snow to a crevice between two rocks.

'Stay here whilst I get your boot.'

Back at the rock, Grey yanked out spare clothing.

'Put on everything you can,' he said, pulling oversized socks onto her feet, then tying the boot laces.

Sal leaned against the rock, panting hard. Her tear-rimmed eyes landed on Grey. 'Thank you.'

Uncomfortable with the emotion, he turned away. Only Jen mattered now. Reluctantly, Grey took a sip of Juice and handed the flask to Sal, who grimaced at the bitter taste.

'What is it?'

'Wait to feel the effect.'

'Whoa. What now?'

*

The Tzar snapped the arrow and pulled it out himself. The only sign of pain came from an eye twitch and a grunt. After a Trooper bandaged his shoulder, he swung his arm and walked away, focused on Grey and Sal.

She had made for the trees in his direction, judging by the line of fire. They would run together, and she would slow him down in the thick snow.

The question was, did Grey have a horse hidden somewhere for an escape? Doubtful. Leaving the animal tethered in this weather would be a problem. They were most likely on foot, and his men had horses sheltered in the shed. By morning, they'd be good to go.

The giant spent an uncomfortable night inside a low storage barn, open to the elements on one side. His men cleared out the gardening and maintenance tools before squeezing into the remaining space. No one wanted to be next to their leader. Last in got the pleasure.

In the morning, whilst the Troopers prepared to depart, the Tzar strode into the forest, spread his arms and roared to the sky. A calm head was impossible until he released the fury within. After a deep, rumbling sigh, he dropped onto a wet log and studied the map.

There were two routes around the ravine. The west side, which Grey and Sal had taken, and the east, over exposed terrain above the ridge. They would stay close to the treeline for cover, expecting pursuit. Once past the ravine, they'd likely continue north. The girl had to be somewhere farther on. No way would Grey risk bringing her here.

If the Tzar took the eastern side of the ravine, there would still be two options—wait for Grey or go for the girl, which wouldn't be too difficult, given the number of dwellings along the route. Someone would be happy to point him in the right direction.

He decided on four Troopers to follow his prey.

'Wound either of them, fine. But do not kill them. That will be my pleasure. Got that?'

Four nods.

'They'll be on foot, so you'll have no trouble catching up. Herd them to here,' he said, stabbing at open land. 'I'll send ten men there to cut Grey off.'

The map hit one of the Troopers.

'Study this. When you have digested the info, presuming at least one of you can read a map, bring it back to me. I want to see leave within thirty minutes.'

*

Sal and Grey made their way along the treeline, stopping occasionally to check for signs of pursuit. No one came after them, but they would when dawn broke. Time enough to rest and explore options.

He started a small fire twenty paces into the forest, knowing smoke wouldn't be visible this far from the cabin. Their spirits lifted when flames danced around and warmed tired limbs.

Grey stared into the fire, considering everything that had taken place.

'What was it like—being with him?' He asked Sal.

'Not what you think.'

'I'm not thinking anything. Just want to know more about the Tzar.'

She frowned. 'Strange. He was violent when something pissed him off, but not enough to cause serious damage. I think he needed me around as a sort of token.'

Grey raised an eyebrow.

'He never forced me to have sex. I don't think he could. Didn't want the men to know and made filthy comments about what he'd done to me. I was close to telling them otherwise, to humiliating the beast, but the consequences were terrifying. Can we not talk about this anymore?'

'Okay,' Grey said, though his sympathy evaporated when her revelation about the Tzar hit home. Leaning back on his hands, he watched the canopy sway in the breeze, lost in thought. Something valuable had arisen—a weakness in the giant's armour.

An owl hooted in the distance, and another answered close by. Grey remained distant. Sal jumped.

'What are you thinking?' She asked.

He sighed, tapping the map Greg gave him. 'Two ways around the ravine. The Tzar has three options. Hunt us down on the west, take the east and wait farther along where the land opens or go for Jen. What do you think?'

'He'll take all three. The man's obsessed with finding you and won't take any chances.'

Grey poked the fire with a stick. 'So how many will come after us here?'

'Depends on the Troopers he has left. Best guess, around twenty able men, excluding the wounded.'

'Three or four, then. Enough to push us towards an ambush, not enough to dent his capability.'

Sal changed the subject. 'Where will Jen be?' she asked in a gentle voice.

Grey pointed at the map. 'There or there.'

When she realised he indicated a coastal settlement and the ocean, Sal frowned in confusion.

'She's with a family in the village. If the Tzar comes, she'll hide on an oil rig.'

'Oil rig?'

'That's what I said.' Impatience coated his tone.

'You're not sure she will be safe. You expected to kill the Tzar—or be killed by him. And he'd leave her be if you died.'

Grey snapped the stick, threw it onto the fire and walked into the trees, angry with himself. Sal had caused him to falter, and now Jen was in peril. This would have been over if the woman hadn't been there. He could have taken the monster down.

Jen's vulnerability ate at him. Pictures of the Tzar holding a knife to her throat flashed through his mind. Emotions followed each image. Fear, failure and guilt brought boiling anger. Which was what he needed to turn the turmoil into one vision—his knife pressing into the Tzar's throat.

He returned once he had more control.

'First, we kill whoever's following. Then I'll take out the Troopers waiting on open land.' Grey's eyes were as cold as mountain granite when he added, 'Then I'm going to tear the Tzar apart.'

'You said 'I' not 'we?'

'We both need a horse,' he said harshly. 'Then you leave.'

'But...'

'You leave! I do this alone.'

*

Grey figured any pursuers wouldn't close the distance significantly over the next day. The snow was too deep for riding at speed. Every mile or so, he and Sal detoured into the forest to delay Troopers following their tracks. But the ruse would end once the trees gave way to open ground. Now was the time to act.

When an inward curve around a rocky outcrop appeared, he decided to set an ambush.

'Eat, rest, get ready.' he told Sal, then explained her role.

He lit a fire to signal their presence, sending smoke girating into the air. Without another word, he disappeared into the trees, heading back along their previous route.

The land sloped up to a rise where he left footprints and hid behind a trunk.

Four Troopers came soon after, following the smoke.

They all stiffened at the top of the incline when the flickering fire materialised. Two men dismounted and found tracks in the trees. They looked at each other, then the leader still mounted. He flicked a hand at the forest.

The Troopers stayed close together, their twitching guns conveying nervousness, as Grey hoped. He breathed out, holding back the Rage. Stealth was needed, not extreme violence—yet.

Avoiding noise to alert those on mounts meant luring the two men a distance away, so he left prints beyond where he waited for a rear assault.

A fierce blow to one Trooper's shoulder knocked him into the second, who received a killing strike. The first man down got a clump on his temple to render him unconscious.

'See you soon.' Grey whispered.

Barely registering the handle arcing from below, the closest rider toppled from his horse, dead before hitting the snow.

The leader panicked and spurred his mount down the slope. Grey watched with his hands on his hips, unconcerned. Sal would take care of the rest. He had other work to do.

After a kick, the Trooper in the forest rolled to his back and scrabbled backwards, seeing the apparition above. 'Time to talk, Grey said.'

Once he'd gleaned enough information, he left the corpse and led a horse down the incline. The leader's body lay flat in the snow, an arrow through his chest.

Sal sat against a trunk, still holding his bow.

'Good shot.'

She nodded.

Grey helped her onto one horse and mounted the other.

As they rode in silence, he thought about what the Trooper said. The Tzar wasn't with the men waiting ahead. He had gone to find Jen like Sal said.

Bile rose in his throat, and his hands tightened on the reins.

When he spoke, Sal listened without interruption. After the clipped explanation, he said firmly, 'We find somewhere to rest for the night, then separate. Up to you where you go.'

By midday, the forest thinned in the distance. Grey halted and studied the map. Troopers waited somewhere beyond.

There were too many for a direct fight. It was better to leave obvious tracks and lead them to a place of his choosing.

One of their number would leave to report back to the Tzar whilst the rest followed him. After that, the giant would go for Jen. Not to kill her. She'd be bait to lure Grey in the event he escaped. If the Tzar could track her down.

A small town on the map caught Grey's attention. He circled it with a finger, then jabbed at the centre.

*

Sal sat on her mount, watching him. There was no doubt in her mind that she loved the man. Was he abandoning her for her own safety? No. He'd decided she would get in the way just like she'd done with the Tzar.

With a heavy heart and wet eyes, Sal left, knowing Grey was too fixated on his plan to even wave goodbye.

NOTHING LASTS FOREVER

JEN sat alone, facing the sea like she'd done every evening since arriving at the village. She tried to imagine Grey killing the Tzar, but the opposite scenario invaded her mind.

Tears came as they always did, along with the emptiness inside.

After a deep sigh, she wiped her wet cheeks, then trudged back to the cottage Greg had secured.

Emma became irritating, following Jen around and talking meaningless girl crap. Mary fussed, trying to be her mother. Sara didn't shut up with her high-pitched chatter. Charlie was okay because he played with toys and said very little. Worst of all, Jen resented Greg for helping Grey leave. And his shitty rules.

Rocking her head, she mimicked him—cut the swearing—tidy up—don't chew with your mouth open—you will go to school. What the...?

Jen went to the 'lovely' school with a fishdick teacher who gave boring lessons. Three days later, she'd had enough and considered running away to find Grey.

Then everything changed.

Greg crashed through the door early afternoon. Mary ran over, wide-eyed, concern written on her face. Emma and Sara stopped eating. Charlie carried on. Jen's heart sank. The Tzar was on his way.

After gulping down a mouthful of potato, she smiled. It meant Grey was still alive. Otherwise, the giant wouldn't be coming for her.

Before that happened, she needed to get away.

Mary came out of a bedroom, dabbing her cheeks. Greg followed, his face flushed. He looked Jen in the eye, then inclined his head to her room.

'The Tzar's on his way here,' he said once they were alone. 'A wounded rider from a settlement came into the village an hour ago.'

Jen remained calm, thinking about what to do.

She jumped when Greg said firmly, 'Get your things. You're leaving.'

'Where?'

'Somewhere the Tzar will never find you.'

'What about you and the family?'

'Mary will get everything ready, then head farther along the coast. I'll join her once I've shown you where to go. We've already made plans for this situation.'

There was little time for goodbyes. Mary and Emma cried whilst hugging Jen, who couldn't find it in her to respond in kind. Mother and daughter stood at the door watching her go, but she didn't look back.

Greg followed a trail along the coast. His eyes remained fixed on the horizon, clearly worried about his family. Jen thought about where she was going—an oil rig. Whatever that was. But if Grey had devised the plan as a backup, it must be good.

Soon after, Greg halted and pointed into the distance. 'See that headland, there's a cottage on the beach a few miles beyond. It won't take more than a couple of hours to walk. Jim, a friend of mine, will be there. He already knows about the plan, and he'll take you to the rig. I've got to go back to my family now. I don't know how far away the Tzar is from the village, but when he gets there, it won't take long before someone tells him a man and a girl set off in this direction.'

Jen didn't react to the word girl. She had more important things to focus on.

Greg looked solemnly at her. 'Maybe we'll meet again someday. I really hope so. For now, though, you must follow Grey's instructions to the letter. The Tzar will never find you.'

Jen wasn't convinced but said nothing. Instead, she took Greg's outstretched hand, dropped from his horse and turned away, not wanting to watch him go.'

When she arrived at the cottage, a wiry old man wearing an ancient roll-neck jumper opened the cottage door and ushered her inside.

'It happened, then?' he asked.

'It happened.'

'We'll be away soon. Got a small sailboat down on the beach.'

Jen met Jim's grey eyes. 'You must not come back here for a week or two. The Tzar will find out I've come this way.'

The old man stroked his white beard. 'I'll think on it.'

When she jabbed his chest with a finger, Jim took a step back.

'You will stay away from here. Got it!'

'Now, lass, no need to get worked up, I'm a wily old dev...'

'The Tzar isn't stupid, you dim'ead. He'll kill you.'

Jim held up both palms, 'Okay, okay, I'll do as you say. Got some family inland I've been meaning to visit for some time. That satisfy you?'

Jen skewered him with her eyes. 'You better. For your own good.'

The man clapped his hands to end the conversation and pointed to two chairs by a stone hearth.

'Me an' Greg go back a time,' he explained. We worked together on the rigs. Expect he's already told you that. Been on the water before? Likely to be rough, maybe make you throw up.'

Jen rolled her eyes. 'I've worked as a deckhand.'

Jim raised his brows. 'Hard work, that is. Well, judging by your—err—determination, I guess you held your own.'

'I don't want to talk about it,' she said, thinking about the Captain.

'Fair enough. Let's see if the tides in far enough to push the boat out. Probably used to that, eh?'

Jen didn't answer the question. Instead, she asked, 'Who's on the rig?'

Jim chuckled. 'Only Oscar. He's a good man, if a little crazy.'

*

The Tzar rode stiffly into the village. There were no women or children about, just six men awaiting his arrival.

A small man with a puffed-out chest took two steps, determined not to show fear. 'What do you want?' he snapped.

The Tzar shot him.

All of the others backed away, horrified at the sight of blood leaking from their friend's head.

'Stop where you are!' the giant boomed. Leaning in the saddle, he hissed, 'Where is the girl and whoever brought her here?'

'Not sure,' one man said, his voice quivering. 'Greg—the family—she came with have gone.' Speaking fast, he added, 'Honestly, we don't know where. Just—err—upped and went.'

'Direction?'

The terrified villager looked side to side, his eyes pleading for someone else to explain. Heads turned away.

'Direction?' the Tzar bellowed.

'I—only saw them from a distance. Don't think the girl was with them, though.'

'So where the hell did she go?' He was losing patience.

'Err...'

Another man plucked up the courage to speak. 'West along the coast.'

The Tzar pointed his gun. 'Anyone up that way might know?'

Wringing his hands, the villager mumbled, 'Jim, he—he—lives alone on the beach.'

Stroking his chin, the Tzar smiled then said to himself, 'Well, Jim, whoever you are, you will enjoy our brief chat.'

THE RIG

JEN thought the oil rig looked like a giant spider from a distance. She wondered how four legs could withstand a fierce storm. Jim noticed her frown, 'Don't worry, it's fixed to the seabed. Solid as a rock.'

While he lashed the craft to a leg, Jen craned her neck to see the top, unconvinced by his reassurance.

The ladder attached to the side was slick with green slime, causing her first step to slip. Memories of falling from the monolith at Haven brought panic. A drop into the choppy ocean out here meant certain death as far as Jen was concerned.

Jim grabbed her ankle and squeezed.

'Take it steady, lass, and don't look down.'

A head appeared over a gantry and shouted, 'Don't worry, Jim's at the bottom, and I'm at the top to help.'

Jen yelled, 'But you're not in the middle, fishdick, are you?'

Anger came to the rescue, forcing her up the ladder, determined not to behave like a stupid girl.

At the top, a chubby hand grabbed her wrist. Moments later, a bedraggled and pissed-off Jen threw herself onto the gantry floor.

A short, portly man with thick hairy forearms and balloon cheeks grinned down.

'I'm Oscar,' he said, holding a hand out to shake.

Jen gave her name and glowered a warning, 'Never even think about calling me a girl.'

The man chuckled and raised his arms like a hostage. 'Better say goodbye to Jim.'

'See you soon, Jimmy Boy.' Oscar bellowed over the rail.

'Bye,' Jen said, making no effort to be heard.

They watched the boat for a moment, and then Oscar led the way up a flight of steps onto the main deck and inside the quarters.

Jen hoped Jim would heed her warning to stay away from the cottage for a while. Something told her he might not. A shudder down her spine followed.

Once in her room, Jen splashed water over her face to wash away the salt, only to discover it contained more salt. She thumped onto a metal-framed bunk bed and slumped her shoulders in resignation.

'I'm stuck with a grinning idiot in the middle of the sea on a giant spider covered in bird shit. What the hell am I doing here? I should be...'

A knock and Oscar's voice disturbed the gloomy mood. 'Food's ready.'

'I hate fish if that's what you mean.'

He chuckled. 'All we got.' His footsteps rang on the metal floor when he walked away.

Groaning, Jen stood and followed. She could only ignore a grumbling stomach for so long.

The squat man chattered away while she forced down the fish in silence.

'Want to see around the rig before it gets dark?'

Jen gave way to his enthusiasm. 'Okay,'

Oscar talked about drilling mechanics to a bemused—trying not to be interested—Jen. He pointed at the derrick only to be told, 'I'm not blind, dim'ead.'

Water, he explained apologetically, was pumped from the ocean, but the desalinator no longer worked. What that meant, Jen didn't know but got the gist.

'Now,' he went on, 'here's the fortunate bit. Just before the strike, a gadget was installed below the waves. The flow turns fins to produce electricity. Can't process the oil for energy on here. One day, it will break down, I suppose. Until then, we at least have some power. Need to use it sparingly, though. Understand?'

Jen didn't but humoured Oscar with nods.

The drill at the end of a thick rod caught her interest, imagining it grinding into the seabed. Enormous machines with chunky rubber pipes, buttons and levers were also intriguing. They looked complicated and clever.

Grey stressed the importance of gathering information. Nothing so far seemed useful. Jen looked to the sky as if answers were written in the clouds.

Over the next few days, her attitude to Oscar warmed. Sure, his constant chatter was annoying, but at least he tried to make her feel welcome. She also suspected he was lonely.

He didn't seem to mind Jen's cursing and sulks, though he never swore in front of her. And he never called her a girl. The fish was a pain, but the vegetables Jim brought once a month were okay. The last delivery included meat, but Oscar had eaten it all.

Throughout the day, his cheerfulness helped to take the edge off Jen's concerns about Grey. However, at night, they came rushing back. Desperate to know he was okay, she longed to see him one more time.

The truth was, though, it would never be enough.

Sometimes, her thoughts created a hollow feeling inside, sometimes a flood of tears, and often, pillow-punching anger.

She tried not to think about the Tzar but couldn't dismiss the fear that he would come.

One evening, Jen and Oscar discussed her life at the Station, the Tzar and Haven. The man's expression flitted between horror and concern.

He explained how he'd lost a wife and daughter in the strike. It was the only time his bearing changed, moistening his eyes.

'I know about that stuff,' Jen said, thinking about her mother, Irvine, the Captain, Sal—and Grey.

The Rigger blew out his cheeks and rubbed her arm. 'Too many memories, eh? Too many memories.'

Five days after Jen arrived, she awoke to cracking thunder and rushed outside. Oscar was at the rail looking across the ocean. They watched in silence as the storm gathered its might.

Dark clouds tumbled like dense smoke across the horizon, punctuated by thunder rumbling a challenge. Every time sheets of lightning illuminated the clouds, Jen flinched.

Oscar noticed her fear when her hands clasped the rails, feet anchored to the deck, and legs braced against the wind.

'It's okay,' he shouted. 'Nothing the rig can't handle. Seen much worse.'

It wasn't just the approaching storm. It was as if the Tzar rode behind, gathering his fury in an unstoppable charge.

When Oscar pulled her towards the cabin, she turned back, imagining the giant's shaking fist rising out of the sea.

'Get dried off. I'll make a hot tea.'

Jen stayed at the entrance, watching Oscar force his way through the onslaught to the rain tank. Leaning over the side, he scooped a pan of salt-free water. She saw him look up at the derrick, deciding he knew it wouldn't last forever.

Oscar dunked his rationed tea bag between mugs, chuckling. 'Bet no one else in the country has tasted this stuff for a long time.'

He explained the rig had been home to many men, requiring large stores of essentials—many usable for years. By conserving stocks, he still had some luxuries. And the tea was that to him. Even if a little stale.

Jen held the mug in cupped hands, blowing at the steam. Oscar's insistence that it should be drunk hot had burnt her lips before.

'What are you thinking?' he asked when she looked absently at rain battering the windows.

'He'll come.'

'Now, what's brought you to that gloomy conclusion? The storm?'

'Kind of. But I just know it.'

'No one will find you here. Greg would have gone when the Tzar arrived.'

'Jim knew.'

'Naw. Old Jimmy Boy's much too smart.'

'You don't know the Tzar.'

Jen sensed the man was trying to hide his concern.

'Tell you what. Once this storm blows past, we'll make some plans if it makes you feel better. No one'll get past old Oscar's tricks. Fought off pirates before now, I have.'

'Liar,' she said with a smile.

The storm raged for three days, waves smashing into the rig legs and firing cascades of water onto the deck.

Jen braved the onslaught several times daily, looking towards an invisible shore. She knew a boat couldn't survive the violence but felt compelled to check.

When the sea calmed, anxiety took hold. Oscar changed, too. He chuckled less and sometimes appeared distracted.

Preparations began soon after. The Rigger occupied himself with a piece of machinery, using spanners, screwdrivers and curses he hadn't uttered before. Now and then, his grease-smeared face popped out from behind dismantled generator parts to wink at Jen. He told her to wait and see each time she asked what he was doing.

Jen was a hive of activity, stopping occasionally to scratch her chin, searching for ideas.

Oscar nodded when he saw her carrying heavy objects and placing them around the rails for projectiles.

As they sat together for a break, he watched her test the bow, check arrowheads and smooth out flights.

When he frowned, she knew her capacity for violence unnerved him.

Jen took knives from the kitchen, along with a heavy meat cleaver she took a fancy to. Trying out a few double-handed skull chops brought a wicked smile.

Oscar stepped back in surprise when asked to lash knives onto broom handles for spears. Rubbing his head, he came up with a new idea—coating the ladder with grease.

He volunteered to hang one-handed off the ladder and smear the top few rungs with a sweeping brush. Jen held onto his stained dungarees, trying not to laugh in case she let go.

After that, they blocked off the stairwells from the gantry below. Metal sheeting found its way over the apertures with weighty objects placed on top.

One day, a hum vibrated through the deck whilst Jen peeled potatoes for supper. Oscar appeared covered in oil, wearing a big grin.

'Still got the magic touch,' he said, winking. 'Electricity powering the generator won't last long but at least it will give us an advantage.

*

When two white triangles appeared in the distance, Jen knew Jim had stayed in his cottage and paid the price. Oscar handed her an old telescope, explaining how to use it.

As soon as the sailboats neared, men took to two wood dinghies.

Oscar carried a long hose to the rails, a wicked grin creasing his face.

'Secret weapon,' he said.

One boat drifted fifty yards out, the other made for a leg, rowed by two men. Jen lined up a chunk of iron and dropped it. The projectile landed on a Trooper's hand gripping the oar. She hoped for a body strike, but the yelling and rocking boat sufficed.

Grey's explanation about controlled aggression kicked in.

'Focus on your target and imagine what's going to happen, then don't hesitate.'

The boat thumped against the leg with the men trying to regain control. Jen hefted an engine part, grunting at the strain and rolled it under the rail. It smashed into the gunwale, the momentum pushing the boat under the rig.

'Bird shit!' she shouted, losing the initiative. Still, the other ladders had long since broken away.

Meanwhile, the second craft lurched with each oar stroke.

'Showtime,' Oscar said. He hauled the thick hose to the rail, his hands vibrating to the hum across the deck. Jen watched in awe when a gout of water powered to the boat.

'Fishdicks.' she yelled at the top of her voice. 'Didn't expect that, did you?'

The boat rocked violently, throwing a Trooper holding a rifle overboard. Jen fired two arrows, missing with both.

Oscar hammered the craft until it capsized. Moments later, the two oarsmen and a third Trooper swam towards the rig. Jen whooped when the water jet battered one man's body and forced his head below the sea. Whenever he came up for air, Oscar blasted again until a body floated to the surface. Suddenly, the pump ground to a halt when the power ran out.

They peered down at a Trooper climbing the ladder. The sight of him trying to grasp greasy rungs would have been funny if the situation hadn't been so deadly. Hands wheeling, feet trying to find purchase, the man fell backwards into the sea.

A second Trooper followed. Jen gave a malicious grin. In one hand, she held a chuck of metal. The other grasped the chopper, causing the man's eyes to widen.

'Which d'you want? Can't make your mind up? Okay, chopper it is.' She had to turn away, listening instead to fading screams and a splash.

A shot hit Oscar in the shoulder, throwing him back onto the deck. Jen wheeled to see a Trooper leaning over the circular rail surrounding the drill. She sprinted for the cabin and dived behind a stack of iron crates, realising they'd forgotten to secure the drill area.

'He'll die!' the Trooper shouted, pointing his gun at Oscar.

Jen rose from behind the crates, bow curved, arrow primed, and fired. The Trooper's brows shot up in surprise. He hesitated a moment too long. Jen's arrow speared his hip, sending him to the side.

The man's feet left the deck when Oscar surged upright, grasped him around the waist and staggered to the drill head. Seconds later, the Trooper's body crashed into the railing, eliciting a yell of pain.

But the man refused to be beaten. He rained blows onto Oscar's head with the gun, forcing him to the ground.

The Trooper tried to locate the trigger, then froze. A twelve-inch filleting knife attached to a pole, attached to a very pissed-off girl, wavered close to his neck.

'Don't. I won't... urgh.'

'Too late,' Jen hissed.

A click sounded behind. She spun to see another Trooper twenty feet away, aiming a handgun. He waved the barrel towards the floor. Jen hesitated, looked at her friend, then the gunman, and sat.

Blood ran down Oscar's cheek and into one eye. He still managed a wink.

The Trooper pressed the cold muzzle on Jen's forehead.

'Give me one excu... '

Oscar grabbed the ankles and heaved them towards him. Jen moved before the man hit the floor. She kicked the Trooper's face several times, then helped her friend up.

'We've got to go. Now!'

They stumbled to the quarters. Jen tried to turn the door handle with trembling hands, but it slipped from her grasp. She tried again, gripping it tighter. A single shot reverberated around the deck. Oscar's body slammed into the wall.

'Sorry,' he rasped, then slid to the floor.

Jen dropped beside him.

'Oscar, Oscar, please!' Her words fell on deaf ears.

Rough hands hoisted Jen off the floor. She screamed and kicked in fury when the Trooper backed away from her dead friend.

A fist turned out the lights.

*

Hands on his hips, the Tzar watched Jen exit a rowboat. He laughed when she marched up the sand and said, 'Fuck you, you piece of shit.'

His face turned red with anger when she added, 'Grey's gonna slice you to pieces.'

'Take the bitch into the cottage before I rip her head off,' he shouted to a Trooper.

*

Once Jen's blind fury abated, her body convulsed from an explosion of sobs. 'Ossccaarrr!' she shouted as if the words alone would bring him back. The walls received drumming slaps from open palms.

'Shut it!' a Trooper behind the door warned. 'I'll put a gag over your mouth if you don't.'

She kept going with high-pitched curses.

Minutes later, a gag soaked up the flood of tears.

The unmistakable thump of the Tzar's heavy boots entered an adjoining room, followed by a chair scraping across the floor.

Jen's heart thudded when the deep voice cut through the walls. Anger and fear fought when the door banged open.

Grey's words took over. 'Deep and slow breaths until calm returns.'

The Tzar's immense arms rested on the table whilst he glared with dark eyes. His purple cheeks, pock-marked skin and a frown like tree bark made him look every inch the monster he was.

She jumped at the booming voice. The Trooper behind dug his fingers into her shoulders, causing a wince and groan. Her head dropped in defeat.

'Look at me,' the Tzar growled. 'Look—at—me.'

Unable to resist, Jen complied. A shudder ran up her spine.

'I'll tell you this once. And once only. Give me any trouble or try to escape, and I'll kill you. With this.' He pointed at his boot. 'Got it?'

Jen dropped her head.

The Tzar leaned forwards, spittle in the corner of his mouth.

'And as for Grey. I will make you watch when I grind his head into the dirt.'

For the first time, Jen hoped Grey didn't come. The giant would make good on his promise. Even the Rage couldn't defeat this beast.

'Take the bitch back to her room.'

*

A map lay spread across the table. Squinting, the Tzar searched for the ideal place to await Grey. Flat ground and no buildings to play cat and mouse would be best. Whether his men brought the bastard in or he somehow took them out, the giant knew he would come.

Tracing the coastline, he tapped a point where a wall of rocks created a half circle of land overlooking the sea.

'Amphitheatre. Perfect.'

RESOLVE

GREY studied the village from a rise. Snow-clad roofs suggested renovation and upkeep. He searched chimneys for signs of smoke. Strangely, nothing showed, yet the sun had dipped, bringing an icy chill.

A small church with a square-topped belfry dominated the settlement, providing a good vantage point. Before checking it out, though, Grey needed to rest, which was fine because the Troopers were at least a day behind.

Back near the forest, after ordering a tearful Sal to leave, he'd studied them from some distance away, then arced away towards a thin green line of pine trees to the west. When night fell, he lit a fire against a trunk and placed stripped branches on top. Adding more wood eventually created a bonfire.

He knew the Troopers would come to investigate, but it would take time to search the trees, especially with the threat of arrows in the dark. After that, waiting until daylight would be the only way to follow his bewildering tracks.

Since then, he had ridden in circles, turned back and headed west to delay the Troopers more. When the time was right, he'd left a trail straight to this place.

Set away from the village, stone peeked out of a white blanket. Grey pulled on the exhausted horse's reigns and made for the cottage.

It took a while to clear snow from the door and kick free the wood. Inside was murky, the windows blocked by ice. Plates covered in dry mouse droppings lay on an oak table. The residents had left in a hurry, probably to escape raiders.

Grey's first task required clearing a space large enough for the horse.

It was reluctant to bow under the door frame when he pulled on the reins. After a hard yank, his mount gave a loud snort, billowed clouds of breath and relented.

Soon, a fire crackled, warming the room. Melted ice splashed onto a stone floor in one corner where the ceiling sagged. Grey tested it with his palm, deciding to sleep at the far end.

A floor-to-ceiling cupboard in the kitchen revealed an assortment of dried herbs hanging from nails. Whether the horse would eat them, he didn't know.

The animal looked over after several mouthfuls as if to say he was mean.

Jars on a shelf contained preserved vegetables to supplement his own declining supplies.

Eating at the table, he wondered if Jen was complaining about a fish diet on the rig. He dropped his head. If that was where she was, the Tzar had discovered the settlement.

The dusty bed felt spiky from a straw mattress, but at least the horse would eat in the morning. With his body clock primed, sleep came quickly—until something disturbed it.

Howling sounded in the distance, soon followed by snuffles at the door.

What had to be a big brute scratched high on the wood. These feral hounds were likely one reason the residents fled if ammo was in short supply.

Grey considered the situation. The dogs would attack before the horse made it outside, so running was the only option. First, though, he needed another exit. Even then, fighting off the whole pack wasn't possible. But he had to try.

The sagging ceiling in the corner gave way after firm pushes, sending damp plaster to the floor. Rafters snapped with little resistance. Once a space opened large enough, Grey positioned a chair and climbed onto the roof.

Below, eyes glowed in the moonlight; fifteen sets, at least. Maybe more waiting in ambush farther out.

Two dogs fell to arrows, their yelping drowned by cannibalistic savagery. Grey slid down the back of the roof and made for the village centre.

When the first building neared, his spine sent a warning tingle. Bow raised, he turned and faced three black shapes, moonlight streaking silver across raised hackles. One took an arrow in the chest before he discarded the bow and wielded his handle.

When a second leapt, the wood knocked it out. The last dog crashed into his side, sending him to the snow. Within a second, it loomed over him drooling saliva from bared teeth. A knee in the ribcage, threw the brute sideways.

Grey fumbled at his belt for his knife. When the dog lurched, a well-timed thrust under the chin finished the attack.

Grabbing the handle and bow, he sprinted, hearing the pack getting closer. The church seemed a good option. If they were open, heavy vestibule doors would provide a solid barrier. If not, there should be a drainpipe up to the roof. Failing those, he'd have to find refuge in another building.

The church doors stood slightly ajar. With a shoulder push, Grey gained a couple of inches. He sensed movement behind. A smaller dog, faster than the rest, careened around the corner straight into a solid kick.

Heaving the doors with his back, he made it inside.

Moonlight came through broken stained-glass windows above the altar, casting a tinted glow. Ten pews caught his eye, an idea taking shape.

At the top of the tower steps, Grey cut down two bellringing ropes. Thick, fibrous tentacles snaked to the floor, throwing up dust clouds when they landed. The ropes were knotted together, and one end tied to a round wrought iron door handle at the entrance. Two pews at the bottom formed a barrier.

Grey made an incision across his arm, sending drops of blood to the stone. Back at the steps, the remaining pews created a barricade. With the rope threaded through a gap, he heaved it until the door squealed open enough for bodies to get inside.

Dogs started shoving through. They ran to the barricade, throwing themselves at the pews. Soon there was a large pack of frantic hounds. Grey walked up the stairwell, squeezing blood onto the steps, leaving the dogs fighting to follow the scent trail.

Climbing back to the bell ropes, he pulled two up, cut them and knotted them together. Attaching one end to a railing on the roof, he dropped the rope over the tower and abseiled down.

At the vestibule doors, he sneaked a look inside. The dogs remained at the barricade, snarling at each other, still trying to get through.

Silently, he reached around the door and cut the rope. Once apart, he pulled a length through the gap, trapping it between the doors. The dogs were imprisoned after Grey slid his handle through the wrought iron rings outside.

Farther down the street, a cottage offered somewhere to wait out the day. Inside, he found what he was looking for on a hook. The beds upstairs still had pillows; they, too, had a purpose.

Three men sneaked into the village late evening to recce the buildings. Tendrils of smoke drifted into the air from the cottage where Grey had been. They edged to a boarded window and peered through a gap. Inside, the silhouette of a man sat in front of a fire.

Grey watched from across the street, smiling. A stuffed coat was all it took to fool the idiots. Three more Troopers arrived from a different direction and joined the others in a whispered discussion. They split up, one group heading to the rear of the cottage, the second remaining in place, ready to enter the door.

A Trooper opened the entrance and edged inside. The other two waited outside, guns drawn. One of them screamed when an arrow lanced through his back; the second dived to the floor, firing randomly. Bullets from all the men soon peppered dwellings in the vain hope of finding a target. They petered out soon after.

Grey left the Troopers trying to decide what to do next and sneaked to the church.

Listening between the entrance doors, he heard padding feet, sniffs and growls. Slowly, his handle slid out of the rings. The aperture grated open, alerting the dogs.

He sprinted to the church tower and watched from the shadows, ready to grab the rope and haul himself up if any brutes sensed him. They didn't. Instead, the pack hurtled to the dead Trooper.

Growls and yelps erupted from the first dogs to the corpse. The rest of the crazed pack ran at full pelt towards the men down the street.

When gunshots and yelling started, Grey made for the rope. He pulled himself up the tower to wait out the carnage. At the top edge, he stopped dead when a cold barrel touched his temple.

'Sloppy work leaving a dangling rope, eh?' A man said.

*

Two Troopers stood over Grey, lying on the floor inside the church, his wrists bound. One waved the handle close to his face.

'Nice. Would love to try it on your head. Can't, though, unless you give me trouble. Tzar wouldn't like it. Shame.'

The other man slid Grey's bow through a gap between stones in the wall. Red in the face, he heaved, cursed when it wouldn't break and heaved again. The sound of splintering wood reverberated around the church.

He walked over to the backpack thrown on the floor, a self-satisfied grin on his face. Tipping the contents out, he picked up the Juice flask and popped the stopper.

'Smells strange, but could be a celebratory drink for later, I reckon.'

'Dogs still lurking outside?' his sidekick asked.

'Yup. Best wait till morning to move on.'

At daylight, one Trooper went outside to look around. When he returned, a hand drawn across his throat said there were no survivors.

The two men led Grey to where their mounts were tethered.

'What about my horse?'

Neither saw fit to free it, shrugging off the animal's impending death.

They headed east to find the Tzar.

Several hours later, Grey sensed someone following, too concealed for his captors to notice.

For once, he was pleased his orders had been disobeyed.

When the sun dropped, the Troopers decided to take shelter in a deserted cottage. They sat around a fire, talking. Grey, forced into a corner away from warmth, sat on a mound of rubble for maximum discomfort.

One man took out the Juice, tested it on his lips, then spat. 'What the hell?' he said, replacing the stopper and dropping the flask to the floor.

Grey knew Sal would wait for the magic hour, three in the morning—deep sleep time. For one Trooper, at least. The other kept watch over the prisoner.

When loose masonry tumbled outside, the lookout dived for the entrance and called his sidekick. Door slightly ajar, they listened, guns ready.

'We know you're out there. Come for the prisoner, eh? Not much good if he's dead.'

'They won't do it, Sal. Too scared of the Tzar,' Grey shouted.

A Trooper came over, aiming his gun. When he touched the barrel to his captive's neck, a boot thumped into his knee. Yelling, he fell to the ground. Legs around the man's neck, Grey bellowed, 'Now, Sal.'

Bullets splintered the door, sending the lookout ducking inside. The panting man stood back against the wall, glaring at the captive wrestling his sidekick. His finger trembled on the trigger, fighting the urge to shoot. Instead, he plucked up the courage to open the door a few inches and fire blindly through a gap.

More bullets hit the door, keeping him occupied whilst Grey locked his adversary's neck between his knees. He rolled from side to side, trying to snap the writhing man's spine.

A hail of gunshots resounded from Sal. The Trooper on the ground raked with his hands and pushed with his feet whilst the lookout kept glancing across between firing out of the door.

Grey kept up the pressure, feeling the Trooper weakening.

'Fuck it,' the other said, ceased firing outside and aimed at Grey. He was prepared to shoot through his sidekick just as Chance had done.

The Trooper's eyes narrowed, ready to press the trigger when Sal burst through the door. Wood slammed into the gunman, knocking him to the floor.

Grey's thighs trembled at the strain, trying to finish his opponent. Suddenly, the Trooper found the strength to arch his back. It took every ounce of the Rage to keep him trapped.

When the man's thrashing subsided for a moment, Grey risked a look at Sal.

She aimed at the Trooper, now stood, and pulled the trigger. There was a click, then silence. No bullets remained in the gun. Her adversary slammed into her, throwing them both to the ground.

Grey knew Sal could die if he didn't get there quickly. With a mighty heave, he twisted his body over to snap his opponent's neck. Vertebrae clicked, and the body slumped.

Meanwhile, Sal grappled with her adversary, trying to rake his eyes. Time was running out fast. Grey attempted to stand and slipped. He tried again and made it to his knees.

Just as he closed the gap, a gunshot filled the air. His boot cracked into the Trooper's jaw.

Sal wasn't moving, blood soaking her shirt from a wound in the chest. She looked up, tried to say something and closed her eyes.

'Yaaaaah!' Grey hollered, trying to gather the strength to snap the rope binding his wrists. It wasn't enough. He sank to his floor, unable to do anything, and watched her chest slow until the last long exhale.

A groan came from the Trooper across her body. Lurching to his feet Grey heeled him off her body. The Rage reached a crescendo, pistoning his leg like a car on full revs until the man died.

Images of people who had lost their lives because of him flashed through his mind until he could take no more.

Turning away from Sal, he rubbed the bindings on a sharp rock until they snapped and dropped his head, spent.

Once he'd recovered some strength, he carried the woman's body outside to bury her under a mound of stones.

No tears came. They never did. Instead, Grey whispered, 'Bye, Sal. I'm so sorry.'

*

The ocean pounded rocks below the cliffs. Gulls wheeled above, their screeching like a warning of impending doom. Grey glanced west towards the departure point. Would he make it there when this was over? Did he care if it wasn't to be? No. All that mattered was saving Jen first.

'I'm coming, you fucking monster. And I'm going to rip out your heart with my bare hands.'

Grey turned in the direction of the rig, his eyes as cold as the lashing sea.

ONE WAY OR THE OTHER

GREY spotted a cloud of billowing smoke farther along the coastline. When he neared, a single Trooper approached hands in the air. He pointed behind without speaking. The Tzar was waiting somewhere ahead.

A gulp of bitter Juice brought hot blood and a surge of energy when Grey neared a ring of boulders.

Two more Troopers tracked his progress, their guns lowered.

He climbed the rocks to the summit and looked down to where the snow had been raked from the killing floor.

It wasn't the giant who caught his attention. Jen was sitting against a rock, her hands around her knees. A gag had been tied around a vivid bruise on her jaw. She tried to stand, but another Trooper by her side pushed her back. Her eyes begged Grey to go. Leave her. Run from the goliath.

He considered offering his life for hers—a small price to pay. But it wouldn't work. The Tzar would stop at nothing less than humiliating him before grinding his head into the dirt.

Wearing only a vest and stained jeans too tight for his overhanging gut, the giant sneered.

'Piss off back to the village and wait for me there,' he bellowed at the Troopers.

Grey's jaw muscles tightened when he stomped to Jen, grabbed her hair and ripped off the gag. She screamed and tried to wrestle free of the iron grip. Thick fingers tightened more.

'Please,' she cried out between sobs. 'Please don't kill him.'

The Tzar laughed. 'Please,' he mimicked.

Taking hard steps down the rocks, Grey restrained his fury. He needed to wear the man down to beat him.

Arms like tree trunks came up. 'Hold your horses. Drop the stupid stick and the knife.'

Grey threw them to one side, along with his bag and the flask. He'd vowed to kill the man with bare hands, and he would.

'Here's the deal,' the Tzar growled. 'You win, the girl goes free—obvious, right? I win, which we both know I will, and she gets to know me better. How's that for an incentive, eh?'

'I don't need incentives.' Grey's voice was pure venom.

'Sure of that?'

Jen yelled and kicked out when she was dragged to the rocks. When she bit into the Tzar's hand, he said, 'bitch,' and threw her body into the air. She hit the frozen ground and lay still.

Grey's nails bit into his palms, drawing blood. He made to move, but the Tzar wagged a finger. 'One stamp on her pretty head is all it'll take to finish the job.'

It took every ounce of discipline for Grey to stay put. He breathed deeply to lower the Rage and maintain control. Peering across at Jen, he saw her chest rise and fall. At least she was alive.

The Tzar strode into the centre of the arena and stopped. Arms by his side, feet planted apart, he ramped up the tension.

'Nice tattoo. Think I'll have it mounted.'

Grey remained silent for a few seconds, remembering what he'd been told. 'You know what they say. Big mouth, limp dick—according to Sal.'

The Tzar bellowed in fury and charged.

Grey moved to one side and walked calmly away.

The giant swung around, his arms ramrod straight, fists clenched into hammers. He panted deep and fast. Not from exertion. It was bestiality unleashed.

Thundering towards Grey, he threw a sledgehammer punch and met thin air. This time, he held himself in check and glowered, only an eye twitch signalling pent-up anger.

When the Tzar feigned an attack, his adversary didn't move. He pretended twice more before surging. Grey side-stepped and punched the back of the giant's shoulder, aiming for the arrow wound. Only a grunt escaped the man's mouth.

Moving in and out of range, he taunted the Tzar, whose punches weakened with each wayward strike. Or so Grey thought.

He took one step, then two. When a lurch caught him off guard, knuckles glanced off his head. Stumbling to one side, he avoided an arcing blow, then backed off to clear the fog in his mind.

The Tzar sneered. 'Just a tap. Just a tap.'

With lightning speed, Grey ran and dropped his shoulder, intending to barge into the giant's weaker leg. He slipped on a patch of snow, delivering a poor strike.

A thump in his back sent him to the floor, rolling just in time to escape the enormous foot coming down.

*

Jen surfaced from the darkness. A rumbling voice echoed down a long tunnel. She knew that voice. Memories flooded back—the Tzar and Grey were fighting.

Her eyes sprang open, revealing only blurred silhouettes. Shards of light cut through her vision until the scene came into focus.

Grey lay on the floor beneath the Tzar's boot. Jen tried to shout, but her words were too weak to register. When Grey rolled away, she tried to push herself up on shaking arms and fell back, her heart thumping in terror.

*

The Tzar noticed his opponent glance to one side, took the opportunity, and charged. A force like no other he'd experienced slammed into Grey's chest, spinning him around to land on his back. Again, the Tzar stomped, missing his target.

Grey crabbed backwards, only just avoiding a second stamp, then a third until the enormous boot landed on two of his fingers. Bone snapped.

His heel thudded into the tender spot on the Tzar's thigh, causing a roar.

Pain from his hand lanced up Grey's arm, and his chest felt on fire. He was in trouble and knew it.

The monster lunged when he risked another glance at Jen. A vice-like hand lifted and threw him across the arena.

His shoulder crashed into the floor, momentum turning him twice. Disorientated, he attempted to push up, but a sweeping foot kicked his arm away.

Grey twisted to one side when the black boot loomed and bit hard into the ham-sized calf.

The Tzar yelled, swayed, and fell on top of him. Air ejected with the force of a blacksmith's bellows, leaving Grey unable to inhale. A huge hand circled his neck, pinning him to the floor.

Grabbing the arm, he attempted to push it away but couldn't match the power. When the Tzar dropped his fist, levered upright, and placed a boot on his victim's chest, he leered in satisfaction.

Then he shook his head and tutted in disdain, Grey knew what was coming. His insides knotted like thick twine, and terror clawed at his heart. For Jen's life. Not his.

Words wouldn't form when he tried to plead with the Tzar to let her go. His bloodshot eyes darted for a last glimpse of Jen to convey his sorrow at failing her, but the gigantic legs blocked his view.

The Tzar raised his foot and smiled.

*

Jen forced herself to her feet, swayed, and staggered to Grey's weapons. She gave a high-pitched primal scream and ran.

With all her strength, she plunged the blade into the Tzar's waist. A hand larger than her face sent her spinning, still clutching the knife.

Jen pushed upright and yelled, 'C'mon, you pile of shit,' trying to draw the giant away from Grey, who struggled to rise.

She slashed with the knife, trying to stay clear of the snarling beast, his spittle flailing in the air. Her legs buckled, dropping her to the floor.

The Tzar hoisted her by the hair, grabbed her hand and pushed the knife to her side.

'Bitch,' he growled, then slid the cold steel under her ribs and threw her to the floor.

Jen opened her mouth to speak, but nothing came. She pressed her hand to the wound, feeling the spread of blood, just before dizziness took hold. Her eyes flickered, and the lights went out.

*

Grey watched Jen slashing at the Tzar, knowing he only had one chance to save her. Closing his mind to agony, he crawled desperately to the handle and Juice. Fumbling with the flask stopper, he pulled it out and gulped.

When the monster stabbed Jen, he yelled, 'No!'

A surge of energy forced him to his feet as the Juice began to take effect.

The Tzar looked over his shoulder. Swivelling around, he laughed at the soon-to-be-dead man holding his weapon and rocking from side to side.

The Rage built beyond anything Grey had ever felt previously, extinguishing the agony in his fingers. When the Tzar limped closer, he dropped to one knee, feigning exhaustion, then cannoned the handle into the goliath's knee with every ounce of strength he owned.

Bellowing in pain, the Tzar took two ungainly steps.

Grey smashed the handle into his face, blood and teeth exploding into the air. The giant's head pivoted from the unrelenting ferocity of blows.

With each strike, he stumbled. When the attack ceased, he glared at his nemesis through swollen eyes and spat blood.

A crack echoed around the arena when the handle swung down on the Tzar's collarbone.

The wood pounded his chest, pushing him back until his boot grated against loose rock. His arms cycled like an immense bird trying to take off.

It only took a prod to send the giant over the cliff edge.

'Fuuuuck you!' the Tzar yelled on the way down until a wet thump ended his reign of terror.

*

Jen lay cradled in Grey's arms while he stroked her hair. She opened her eyes and looked into his, whispering, 'You did it, didn't you?'

'We did it.'

'Mmm,' she mumbled, then closed her lids.

Grey lowered his head to touch hers, tears running down his cheeks. 'I'm so sorry.'

Dressing Jen's wound with a strip of his shirt, he watched her face for a reaction—anything indicating a connection to what was happening. Nothing came. Jen's breathing remained shallow, her body temperature slowly dropping.

The jagged cut was deep and angry, with bruising already circling the wound. Assessing internal damage was beyond Grey, but the gash was close to vital organs.

His injuries hurt like hell, but they were irrelevant. Only Jen mattered.

He blocked out the emotions battling for release. Her life depended upon his decisions.

Taking her back to the village, at least a week's ride away, wasn't an option. Nor did Grey know if anyone there had the surgical know-how. Only one choice remained. Stay here and give what comfort he could until she took her last breath... unless? Could Jen survive the crossing? If so, might the transition heal her wound as it did his?

His father had said Greys alone had the ability. But what if he carried her? Would Jen be a part of him? Should he even try?

EPILOGUE

GREY ran his hand over the boulder he'd chosen for a crossing. His fingers touched the spiral indentation carved into the surface, mirroring the tattoo on his neck.

The full moon cast a silvery light across the rock. Only an hour remained until the void between Earths opened.

Jen's chest rose and fell rhythmically after the last of the Juice.

He kneeled beside the small body, took her hand and said, 'Hi,' when her eyes opened a fraction.

After a cough, she mumbled, 'Where are we?'

'At the crossing.'

Jen frowned, trying to understand what he'd said, then smiled when realisation dawned.

'You brought me?'

'Yes. You were...'

'Dying,' she said, finishing his sentence. 'I know.'

Grey waited patiently. He knew what her next question would be. It didn't take long.

'We're going to another Earth?'

'Nothing much else to do. After all, leaving a *girl* behind wouldn't be right. Would it?'

'Fishdick,' Jen retorted.

•••••••••••••••••

Printed in Great Britain
by Amazon